Parnell Hall is a licensed private detective in New
York City.

DETECTIVE

A NOVEL BY
PARNELL HALL

AN ONYX BOOK

NEW AMERICAN LIBRARY

NAL BOOKS ARE AVAILABLE AT QUANTITY DISCOUNTS WHEN USED TO PROMOTE PRODUCTS OR SERVICES. FOR INFORMA-TION PLEASE WRITE TO PREMIUM MARKETING DIVISION, NEW AMERICAN LIBRARY, 1633 BROADWAY, NEW YORK, NEW YORK 10019.

This is an authorized reprint of a hardcover edition published by Donald I. Fine, Inc. The hardcover edition was published in Canada by General Publishing Company Limited.

 Onyx is a trademark of New American Library.

SIGNET, SIGNET CLASSIC, MENTOR, ONYX, PLUME, MERIDIAN and NAL BOOKS are published by NAL PENGUIN INC., 1633 Broadway, New York, New York 10019

First Onyx Printing, July, 1988

1 2 3 4 5 6 7 8 9

PRINTED IN THE UNITED STATES OF AMERICA

For Jim and Franny

1

"I WANT TO KILL SOMEONE."

"Who doesn't."

"No. I mean it. I really want to kill someone."

"Everyone wants to kill someone. It's no big deal. I, myself, have a long list, usually headed by my wife."

"You don't understand. I'm going to do it."

For the first time, I gave him my full attention. I looked him over and tried to recall his name. I'm terrible with names. He was a short, plump man, somewhere in his mid-forties, with a bald head ringed with black, greasy curls, and a pudgy face moist with perspiration, which didn't necessarily indicate nervousness on his part since it was mid-July and I have no air-conditioning in the office. I was perspiring freely too, and I wasn't a bit nervous, at least not until I realized this unattractive man really was contemplating murder.

"That," I said, "is different."

He leaned in eagerly. "Then you'll help me?"

"No."

"I'll pay you."

"No."

"I'll pay you well."

"No."

He opened his mouth to say something, then closed it again. He didn't seem to know what to say next. He fished in his jacket pocket for a handkerchief and mopped his brow. The handkerchief was soaked already, and the result was negligible. It didn't matter. He was just buying time. I waited.

"Look," he said. "I think I got off on the wrong foot here. I'm a little upset, as you can see. I'm in terrible trouble. I need your help. I'll give you $10,000."

"No."

He stared at me. Just a trace of annoyance crept into his voice. "How much do you want?"

"That's not the point. You want me to help you kill someone. I'm not going to do it. It doesn't matter how much money you offer."

His head was shaking back and forth rhythmically. "No. No. You don't understand. I don't want you to kill him. I'm going to kill him. I don't need you for that."

"Well, that's a relief."

"But I still need your help." He leaned in ingratiatingly, and his name almost came to me. Morris. Morris something. Something Jewish.

I held up my hand. "All right. Hold it. You're telling me you're going to commit a crime. Whether you want me to do it or not, you're getting me in a lot of trouble. I'm not a lawyer, I'm a private detective. Anything you tell me is not a confidential communication. What you are doing is making me an accessory before the fact to a crime, in fact a capital crime, to wit, Murder One, a cold-blooded, premeditated killing."

"No. I'm not."

"Yes you are. You—"

"But you haven't heard my story—"

"I don't want to hear your story. I don't want to know anything about this."

"But you don't understand. I'm going crazy. I have to talk to someone."

"Why me?"

"I was going by. I saw your sign."

I groaned. My sign. I had listed myself as a private detective on the call board in the lobby because I needed to get mail. It never occurred to me someone would walk in off the street.

I hesitated, thinking about the sign, and he pounced. "Please. At least just listen to me. I've got to talk to someone."

I sighed. All right, if I took the job, I had to accept the responsibilities. "O.K.," I said. "But no names."

"What?"

"Just give me the general picture. No names, no addresses. I don't want to know the names of anyone involved."

As I said that, the name Alberg rang a bell. Morris Alberg. "Can you do that, Mr. Alberg?"

"Albrect," he corrected. I began to doubt the "Morris." "Yeah, yeah, sure."

"O.K.," I said, "*why* do you want to kill this guy?"

I didn't care. Nothing he had to say would change my mind. Maybe I'm from the old school, but, as far as I'm concerned, killing people is a no-no. I am not a violent person by nature. I do not like violent people. I do not like violence. By and large, I don't like the detective business very much, and I don't like most of the people I come in contact with in the course of my work. I didn't like Morris Alberg, or Albrect, or whatever, and I could think of no conceivable reason why I should be concerned in the least with his reason for wanting to kill someone. I had asked the question simply as a matter of form, or politeness, if you will, but I knew that there was nothing he could say that would make me the least bit interested in his case.

I was wrong. There was one right answer, and Albrect had it.

"Because he's trying to kill me first."

2

I GOT UP, went and sat behind my desk, and took out a pad of paper and a pencil. I had no real intention of taking notes. This was just my way of buying time. I composed myself, resigned myself to the situation, and raised my eyes to meet those of my potential client.

I sighed. "All right," I said, "tell me all about it."

Now that he had my attention, Albrect didn't seem to know how to begin. He fidgeted. "I'm in trouble," he said.

"So you said."

He lowered his eyes. "I, uh, you gotta understand. I did some things."

He hesitated and looked at me for encouragement. I wasn't about to give him any.

"It's hard to talk about," he said.

"So don't," I told him.

"What?" he asked, startled.

"I didn't ask you to come here. I didn't ask you to tell your story. You forced it on me. If you don't want to tell it, that's fine with me. I'm not going to drag it out of you. You want to talk, talk—otherwise get the hell out of here. I've got work to do."

His face purpled and for a moment I thought he was going to punch me in the nose. Then he exhaled and collapsed like a paper bag.

"O.K.," he said. "O.K., you're right, let me tell you. It all started when I met—"

I held up my hand. "No names."

"How the hell am I going to tell it if I don't mention any names?"

"Just leave out the names. Don't tell me you met so-and-so, just tell me you met a guy."

"That's going to be confusing."

"Why?"

"Because there's a lot of different guys."

"O.K., so give him a name."

"What do you mean?"

"Give him a name. Call him something. Just so long as it's not his real name."

"Call him something?"

"Yeah."

"What'll I call him?"

"Anything you want."

"O.K., I'll call him—" He broke off. "This isn't going to work."

"Why not?"

"I'm not going to remember who is who."

"Sure you are. This is the first guy you're talking about. Just give him a name you'll remember."

"I don't understand. What do you mean?"

"Just call him something you can't forget."

"Like what?"

"Dumbo."

"What?"

"Dumbo. You know. Walt Disney. The flying elephant."

"What are you doing, kidding around?"

"No, I'm not kidding around. I'm trying to get your story out of you and it doesn't look like it's going to be easy. I said call the guy 'Dumbo' because you have to refer to him and I know it's a name you won't forget. You gonna forget the name 'Dumbo'? That gonna give you any problems?"

"No."

"Good. Now tell me what Dumbo did."

He looked at me as if trying to decide if I were serious. He must have decided I was.

"O.K. It all started when I met this guy, uh, Dumbo."

He hesitated over the name as if trying it. It must have been O.K., because he plunged right ahead. "He works at the company I work for. I didn't know him very well—that is, I knew who he was, but I didn't know him socially, just as a co-worker, you know? But one day he mentioned that he was going to this poker game, and I have a weakness for poker, so I told him I was interested, and one thing led to another, and he invited me to go along. It was a friendly neighborhood game, low stakes, dollar-two, high-low game, you know what I mean."

"Only too well," I told him, remembering what my wife had said not a week before when I'd come home from a friendly high-low, dollar-two game a hundred and forty-five bucks in the hole.

"Well, this guy, Dumbo, was a regular at the game, and I started playing there pretty regular too, so I got to know him pretty well and we got to talking and he told me this game was O.K., but if I really wanted some action there was this place he knew about that was 'the place to be,' as he called it."

"A casino?"

"Yeah."

"Here in the city?"

"Yeah. I mean, I know it's illegal, but, hell, the lottery's legal, there's OTB. If you go to Atlantic City gambling's legal, but who's got the time to go—"

I stopped him. "Hey, I'm not your mother. I'm not shocked out of my mind that you've been gambling illegally in New York City. Stop trying to justify yourself and tell me what happened."

"Oh. Well, I went to this place. It's a little place down in SoHo called—"

"Hold it." I held up my hand.

"O.K. Right. You don't want to know. So I went down to—" He broke off. "What should I call it?"

"Are there more than one?"

"No."

"Then why not call it the gambling joint?"

"Right. Anyway, I went to the gambling joint, and you know how it is."

"I don't. Why don't you tell me?"

"Well, the first few times I won. Not big, but I won. Maybe fifty, or a hundred. Once over three hundred."

"And then?"

"Then I started to lose. The more I bet, the more I lost, and the more I lost, the more I bet."

"What were you playing?"

"Roulette."

"You think the wheel was rigged?"

"Sure it was."

"Then why'd you keep playing?"

"Because—I didn't—I mean, I did, but—it's really hard to explain. You wouldn't understand."

"Yeah. I would. So what happened?"

"Well, I got in over my head. See, some nights, when I got cleaned out, since I was sort of a regular there, Mr.—" He broke off. "The guy who ran the place," he explained.

"Bambi," I said.

"Right," he said. "Anyway, since I was a regular there, Bambi would give me credit. You know, he took my marker."

"Yeah."

"And, of course, having a credit line made it easier to bet higher. I mean, if I dropped five or six hundred in the course of an evening, I could always put my marker down and go double-or-nothing on red or black."

"There was no limit?"

"Technically, there was a house limit of one grand on any single bet."

"You say technically?"

"Yeah. In a special case, you could go over that."

"You have any special cases?"

"A few."

"Ever win one?"

"No."

"Go on."

"Anyway, as I said, I got in way over my head and then Mr., uh, Bambi called in the marker."

"For how much?"

Despite the fact that I had assured him I was not his mother, he could not quite bring himself to meet my eyes.

"Fifty-six grand."

I didn't tell him he was a bad boy or threaten to cut off his allowance. "So what did you do?"

"What could I do?" he said, looking at me ingratiatingly. "I don't have that kind of money, and I didn't know where to get it."

"What do you do for a living?" I asked him.

"O.K. to mention names?" he said, hopefully.

"Unless it's involved in the case."

"Oh."

"Is it?"

"Only indirectly," he said. "So what shall I call it?"

"How about 'the firm I work for'?" I suggested with just a trace of irony. "All right," I went on. "You ran up some gambling debts. You embezzled money from the firm you work for to cover them. Then you got faced with an audit. You were afraid your embezzlement would be discovered. You needed money fast. Then what?"

He stared at me. "How do you know all of that?"

"What else?" I told him. "So what did you do?"

"Well, I told, uh, Dumbo, and he happened to know a loan shark who was willing to cover the whole amount."

"At a modest interest, no doubt."

"Yeah. It was backbreaking, but what could I do? It bought me time. I covered the shortage, and then I started to work on paying off the loan."

"Which you couldn't do?"

"No, I was handling it."

"Then what went wrong?"

"Well, one day I went to pay off this guy and he tells me I don't owe him any more."

"What?"

"Yeah. He says some guy bought out my loan."

"You're kidding."

"No. He says he owed the guy money, so the guy took my marker."

"What guy?"

"Bambi."

"Oh. I see."

"Yeah. See, it turns out this loan shark was pretty good friends with Bambi."

"What a surprise."

"What? Oh," he smiled sheepishly and nodded. "Yeah. Well, anyway, Bambi told me he was sorry about the whole thing. It was just a coincidence. The guy owed him money and, since he couldn't pay, he gave him my marker."

"And you believed him?"

"No. Particularly when he told me something else. He said he knew I was in trouble and was going to have a hard time paying off the loan, but maybe he could help me."

"How?"

"Well, it turns out he knew this other guy—" he looked at me.

"Pluto," I told him.

"Who?"

"Mickey Mouse's dog."

"Right. Pluto. It turned out Pluto had some work he needed done and it would pay well and it was my chance to get out of the hole."

"What was the work?"

"I'm coming to that."

"Today, I hope."

"O.K., O.K. Well, you see, one of the things about my job is that I have to travel a lot. And I hate to fly. I'm afraid of flying, to tell you the truth. So I do a lot of driving. At least on the East coast. California, I have to fly, but I hate it. Anywhere else, I drive. Chicago, Detroit, Atlanta, I drive it."

"So?"

"Well, it happens that one of the largest accounts I handle is the Whitney Corporation in Miami."

"I think I get the picture."

"Yeah. Well, it turns out Pluto had some business in Miami. He needed something delivered and something picked up."

"No kidding."

"So they made me this proposition."

"Who?"

"Bambi and Pluto."

"Both of them together?"

"Yeah. Well, first just Bambi. Then he took me to meet Pluto."

"Why?"

"What do you mean, 'why'?"

"If Bambi was the go-between and Pluto was the big cheese, why would he want to meet you personally? Why would he want you to know who he was?"

He shrugged. "I don't know. Maybe he wanted to approve me personally before he was willing to let me go. Or maybe he wanted to give it to me himself, so if anything went wrong I'd be the only one to blame. At any rate, he was the one who gave it to me."

"Gave what to you?"

"The suitcase."

"Suitcase?"

"Yeah. The one I was to take to Miami."

'I see. And what were you supposed to do with it?"

"I was supposed to take it this address in Miami and give it to someone."

"Floridian #1."

"Huh?"

"The guy you gave it to. Floridian #1."

"O.K. You keeping track of all this?"

It *was* getting a little complicated. I wrote, "Dumbo," "Bambi," "Pluto," and "Floridian #1" on the pad of paper. After "Dumbo," I wrote, "gambling contact from firm." After "Bambi," I wrote "casino owner." After "Pluto," I wrote "N.Y. drug connection." After "Floridian #1," I wrote "Miami drug connection."

"Go on," I said.

"Well, I took the suitcase out there like they told me and met Floridian—Jesus, what a word—Floridian #1."

"And gave him the suitcase."

"No. He wouldn't take the suitcase. He made me hold onto it all the time. He drove me to a private house somewhere out of town. He took me inside and left me alone in a room. After a little while another guy came in."

"Floridian #2."

"Uh huh, and you don't have to worry about my telling you his name, because I never knew it."

"So what happened?"

"He took the suitcase, told me to wait there, and left the room. About five minutes later he came back with the suitcase and gave it back to me and told me to return it."

"And then?"

"Then he left me alone again. About five minutes later the first guy, uh, Floridian #1, came back, drove me back to where he picked me up, and let me off."

"So?"

"I drove back to New York and delivered the suitcase."

"To whom?"

"I don't remember."

"You don't remember who you gave the suitcase to?"

"No, I don't remember which damn Disney name you gave him. I told you I wouldn't be able to keep them straight."

"You gave the suitcase back to the guy who gave it to you in the first place?"

"No. To the other guy."

"You gave the suitcase to the casino owner, the one we designated as Bambi."

"That's right."

"And then what happened?"

"He paid me $10,000."

"In cash?"

"No. It was a squidge. He just knocked it off my debt."

"So you reduced your debt by ten grand. That still left you forty-six grand in the hole."

"Right. So I did it again."

"How many times?"

"Six in all."

"So that must have wiped out your debt."

"Well, yes and no."

"Which is it. Yes or no?"

"Well, no, see, because in the meantime I was still gambling."

I sighed. "All right, so you got involved in an illegal operation. But so far, I can't see any reason why anyone would want to kill you, with the possible exception of me."

"I'm coming to that. I'm coming to that."

"Great. Come to it."

"Well, as I said, I made several trips for these guys and I still hadn't paid off my gambling debt. And it was getting to me, you know. I mean it seemed like there was no way out. So I had to do something."

"I should hope so."

"What?"

"Go on."

"Well, I never knew what was in the suitcase. It was always locked. Of course, I suspected, but I never knew for sure. Anyway, the last time I got the suitcase back from the guy—Floridian #2, I think you called him—I decided to find out. I still had one more day in Miami. So I hunted up a locksmith and told him I'd lost the key to my suitcase."

"Did he believe you?"

"I don't know. I think he did at first, but then when he got the lock open I didn't want to open the suitcase while he was still in the room, and when he saw I wasn't going to open the suitcase, he charged me a bigger fee than he'd quoted me originally."

"Great. Then what?"

"Well, after I got rid of him I opened the suitcase and guess what was in it?"

"Ten kilos of cocaine?"

"Twenty."

"You knew it was coke?"

"I figured it was. To tell the truth, I do a little coke now and then. You know, it's helpful with the ladies."

I tried to envision Albrect as a sly dog entertaining the ladies. I couldn't do it. "Go on."

"Well, I tried a little, and sure enough, it was coke. And good shit, too."

"So what did you do?"

"Well, I figured this was my chance. As I said, I know a little bit about coke, so I knew what to do. The stuff was about a fifty-fifty mixture of rocks and powder, so I knew I could cut it. So I got a lot of milk sugar and I cut myself some coke."

"How much?"

"I took four ounces out of each kilo."

"Jesus Christ!"

"Yeah. So there I was with five pounds of really dynamite coke. I locked up the suitcase and made my delivery as usual to what's-his-face, to Bambi. I was scared to death. I waited to see if they'd find out, if anybody would notice that anything was wrong. But they didn't. I went to the casino, same as always. I saw the guys there, and no one acted like anything was wrong. In fact, Bambi asked me when was the next time I was scheduled to go to Miami."

"He didn't notice you were stoned out of your mind?"

"What? Oh, yeah, I did a little coke, but he wouldn't notice that. I always did a little coke when I gambled. In fact what's-his-name, Dumbo, used to supply it for me."

"So what went wrong?"

"Well, I had to move the stuff. I mean, where the hell are you going to get rid of five pounds of coke? I sure couldn't approach anyone remotely connected with any of these guys. So I started looking for a buyer. Now, there was a friend of mine, not from the office, that did a little coke, so I talked to him, sold him a few grams. Told him I had a new connection, asked him how he liked the stuff. I sold it to him real cheap, made him happy, got him talking about his connection and how much he usually paid, and the long and the short of it was that I found out who his connection was, and I went to him and showed him a sample of the stuff."

"The guy like it?"

"He liked it fine, and he liked the price I quoted to him. The only problem was he wasn't big time. I mean, he couldn't handle any real quantity. He was just a guy who sold a few grams to a few friends."

"So what did you do?"

"Well, I sounded him out and made him a proposition. Tried to see if he would be willing to turn his business around, and instead of buying, start selling to *his* connection, undercutting whoever was selling to him."

"Did that work?"

"No, because he said he thought his connection wasn't really big time either, just another guy who moved a little coke because he liked to have some around to snort. So I made him another proposition."

"What was that?"

"I gave him an ounce of coke to introduce me to his connection."

"And he did it?"

"Yeah."

"And he didn't get paranoid that maybe you were a narc?"

"If he did, he didn't let on. I mean, you gotta understand the psychology of the coke-head. It's pretty hard to turn down a free ounce of really high-grade shit."

On the yellow pad I had written "coke friend," and "C. Friend's Connection." I now added, "C.F. Connection's Connection."

"So what happened when you met the next guy?"

"That was different. This guy was dealing ounces,

which meant he was buying pounds, which meant the guy he was buying from was dealing pounds. Which meant we had a market. This guy and I agreed to try to sell pounds back to his source. It wasn't that hard to set up a deal, because this guy was paying a fair amount for his pounds, and all I had to do was undercut that enough to assure that the guy made a grand or two on his sale, and that the price would fall under his connection's buying price. I could do that, no problem, since I hadn't paid anything for the coke and I didn't have to worry about profit margin. Anything I made was pure gravy. So I gave this guy a pound to sell."

"Did you know who he was selling it to?"

"I knew the guy's name and address, I made him give me that. But I never met the guy himself. I didn't want to. He was some Hispanic guy from the lower East side, and he was obviously into some very heavy shit. I knew who he was, just to protect myself, but I didn't want him to know who I was."

"So what happened?"

"The guy came back, gave me the amount I'd asked for, and said he could move some more."

"Which he did?"

"Sure. We moved a total of seven pounds in five weeks."

"I thought you only had five pounds."

"Yeah, but in between I made another Miami run."

"I see."

"Yeah. So I made enough profit to pay off the debt and get out from under."

"What'd you tell your friends at the casino?"

"About where the money came from?"

"Yeah."

"I told 'em I made a killing at Atlantic City."

"They buy it?"

"They seemed to. See, I was very careful. I really did go to Atlantic City. I even asked my friend from work to go with me, knowing he couldn't come. So I think I pulled it off."

"What about the other guy?"

"The casino owner? Uh, what the hell did we call him?"

"It doesn't matter. I just gave you the bullshit names because you didn't seem to be able to tell your story without 'em. You seem to be having no problem now."

He thought about it. "Yeah, I guess so. What were we talking about? Oh yeah, the casino owner. Well, there didn't seem to be any problem with him either. In fact, he told me the other guy who'd been giving me the suitcases wanted to know when I was making another trip."

"So what went wrong?"

"I don't know. That is, I don't know for sure, but somewhere, somehow, the trails of the guy who was giving me the suitcases and the guy who was buying our pounds must have crossed."

"How do you know?"

"Because when the guy who was selling for me went to deliver the last pound, the guy who was buying from him was dead."

"What!"

"Yeah. And it wasn't pretty, either. He'd been shot in the head, execution style. And his cock had been cut off and shoved in his mouth."

"When did this happen?"

"Two days ago."

"What are the police doing about it?"

"Nothing. They don't know about it."

"Why not?"

"My man wasn't about to go to the police, you know. I mean he was scared. Not just about the drug rap, about the murder. I mean, if you're dealing with a drug trafficker, and he gets bumped off, who's the first suspect."

"So what did he do?"

"He got rid of the body."

"How?"

"Dumped it in the East River."

"Tied to some concrete?"

DETECTIVE 23

"Yeah."

"You guys watch a lot of late movies?"

"What?"

"You making this up?"

"So help me."

The phone rang. I picked it up. It was one of the secretaries for the lawyer I work for. She said he had a new case in Brooklyn he wanted me to go sign up. I wrote down the info, told her I'd handle it, and hung up.

"I'm sorry," I said. "Go on."

"That's it."

"What's it?"

"That's the story."

"No it isn't. How does this involve you? The killing, I mean."

"I told you. Somehow their paths must have crossed. The guy who got killed and the guy I ripped the shit off from. They found out the guy was selling their own shit, so they killed him."

"That doesn't make any sense. How would they know it was their own stuff?"

"Only one way. They must have traced its source back to me."

A light went on. "So that's what you're worried about."

"Of course."

"And that's why you think they want to kill you."

"Of course."

"Is this just paranoia on your part—forgive the word. Are you just deducing this from what happened, or has there been an actual attempt on your life?"

"No. Nothing like that. See, I haven't been near the casino, I mean, since the murder. So I haven't seen any of the guys. But I have been to work. So, if they're checking on me, they know I haven't been around since the murder, but they know I'm not sick because I've been going to work. And then this morning I got the phone call."

"What phone call?"

"Well, you gotta understand. I have a private office. My secretary works outside. Then there's the main switchboard for the company. This call came in through the switchboard. The operator rang my secretary's number. She answered. It was a man asking for me. She'd never heard his voice before. She asked his name. He gave her his name and the name of a company we do business with. She put him on hold and rang me. I recognized the name of the company, but not the name of the man. I told her I'd take it. I pushed the button for the line and said, 'Hello.' The line immediately went dead."

"Maybe the call got disconnected while he was on hold."

"No. You can tell the difference. The line was open when I picked it up. I said 'Hello' and it went dead."

"Yeah, but—"

"Wait a minute. I called the company he said he worked for. They'd never heard of him."

"When was this?"

"This morning. Just now. I figured it was them. They were just checking to see if I was at work. That's why I got out of there. I was afraid they were coming for me. Or if not, they'd be waiting for me to get off work. So I left. I didn't know where I was going, I just wanted to get out of there. I guess I panicked. Anyway, I got out of there fast. I didn't know what to do. I didn't know where I was going. I was just going. Then I saw your sign."

I sighed. Shit. That goddamn sign. The ball was in my court now, and this guy was about to discover I didn't have a backhand.

"So?"

"So that's the story."

"No it isn't. You said you wanted to kill someone."

"Yeah."

"Who?"

"Whoever's trying to kill me."

"And who do you think that is?"

"I don't know."

I gave him a look.

"All right, all right," he said. "I do know. It's Bambi and Pluto, for Christ's sake! But it's not them I have to watch out for. They'll send somebody. Somebody who kills people. Jesus, what have I gotten myself into?"

I took a deep breath. "Look," I said, "I know you're upset. I'm trying to make allowances. But you're not making very much sense. Just what are you going to do?"

He tugged out his handkerchief and mopped his face again. "All right," he said. "I don't think anyone followed me here. I think I'm safe now. So I'm going to stay out all day. I won't go back to the office and I won't go to my apartment. Then tonight I'm gonna drop by the casino, place a couple of bets and leave. I won't stay long enough to get involved in any conversations. I'll just pop in and out."

"And?"

"I'll see who follows me."

"How?"

"That's where you come in."

"I see. You want me to stake out the casino and get a line on anyone who tries to follow you when you leave."

"That's right."

"And then you're going to kill that person."

This time he didn't bother with the handkerchief, he just mopped his brow with his hand. "Ah, shit, I really don't want to kill anybody. I mean, when I said that I was upset. Besides, it wouldn't do me any good. Obviously the guy's not doing it for himself, he's doing it for the other guys. What I really want to do is head the guy off, buy some time, try to figure some way to get these people off my back. I don't want to wind up with my dick in my mouth."

"I understand the sentiment."

"That's also where you come in. I may not be able to spot the guy who's following me. I probably won't. Now, he may just tail me. In that case, all I need is for you to get a line on him, tell me who he is. But he may try to take me out right then and there. In that case, I need protection. Now, I understand your not wanting to get involved in a murder, but I take it you would have no scruples about defending a private citizen from assault."

It was time to end the game.

"Look, Mr. Albrect, I have to tell you something. What you really want is a bodyguard, and I'm not it."

He looked betrayed. "You're a detective. You've heard my story. Forget what I said about killing someone. I'm not asking you to do anything illegal."

"I know. You just picked the wrong guy."

"But—"

"Look, I'm not going to argue with you. Just let me tell you who I am. Then you decide if you want me."

I paused, groping for the right words. None came, so I plunged right in. "I'm not really a detective."

He opened his mouth to protest.

"Well, I am, but I'm not," I said. "I chase ambulances."

"What?"

"I'm an ambulance chaser. Look, you know all the lawyers that advertise on TV for accident cases? Well, I work for one of them. He handles insurance claims. People fall down and break their legs, they see his ad on TV, they call him up. He calls me. I go interview the people, take down the information about the accident, try to get 'em to sign a retainer. Then I go take pictures of the scene of the accident. Sometimes I interview a witness. Sometimes I serve a subpoena or summons. I don't do surveillance. I'm basically non-aggressive. I don't carry a gun. I couldn't fight my way out of a paper bag. The most dangerous thing I do is go into some pretty undesirable neighborhoods to interview prospective clients. I don't like it. I always feel as if I have a sign saying "mug me" on my back. Actually, I've never had a problem. People who see me going into slums and housing projects figure I'm either a cop or I'm out of my mind, and they leave me alone. That's what I do. And that's all I do. You're the first person who's ever asked me to do anything else."

I stopped talking. He looked at me. He'd been looking at me the whole time I was talking, and his expression didn't change when I stopped. He just kept looking at me. It was hard to read his expression. He looked a little like a steer must when it's just been hit over the head with a sledgehammer at the slaughterhouse. Incredulous. Disbelieving. But something else, too. He blinked his eyes. His lips moved, but nothing came out. Then he said, almost in awe, "You're useless." He shook his head. "Jesus Christ, you're absolutely useless, aren't you."

He got to his feet as if in a daze and started for the door, still shaking his head. "Useless," he muttered. He opened the door and went out. The door closed behind him.

I sat there as his steps faded away down the corridor.

3

I LIVE IN A TWO-BEDROOM APARTMENT ON THE UPPER
WEST SIDE OF NEW YORK—five and one-half rooms for
750 a month. People always tell me that's really cheap.
Of course, they aren't paying it. I have to scrabble for
the rent, and at ten bucks an hour and thirty cents a
mile, it isn't easy. See, I don't get paid for an eight-
hour day; I only get paid when I'm on a case, and
some days are slow. That's why a nice sign-up in
Brooklyn is a break, because I can turn it in as three
or four hours on the clock, and a good thirty or forty
miles round trip. Whereas a sign-up in Harlem is four
miles, and a lot less time. The actual sign-up interview
never takes me more than twenty to thirty minutes,
tops. The travel time is where the bucks are. Give me
three cases spread out in Brooklyn and Queens and I
can charge for an eight- or nine-hour day and anywhere from fifty to a hundred miles. But give me a
slow day and I won't make squat.

Today, I hadn't made squat. The sign-up in Brooklyn was all there was. It was on Flatbush Avenue right
over the Manhattan bridge, which made it nothing in
mileage, and a stretch even to call it three hours,
which I sure as hell did, but that was it. And since I'd
wasted so much time with Albrect, I got started so late
that I still didn't get home till nearly six, in spite of
only working a three-hour day.

My five-year-old son, Tommie, was waiting by the

front door. He was wearing his baseball cap and his glove.

"Daddy!" he screamed, running to give me a hug. "Daddy! Daddy! Daddy!"

I picked him up and swung him around. "Hi, Tommie."

"Daddy, can we play baseball?"

I hadn't eaten since early morning. "Right after dinner."

"No, now."

"I'm hungry."

"No, now."

"After dinner."

"It isn't ready yet," my wife, Alice, said, emerging from the bedroom. "Everything's on the stove ready to go, but you didn't call so I didn't know how to time things."

"Sorry, I should have called," I told her. "How long will it be?"

"Well, we're having chicken, rice, and asparagus. The rice will take a while, say forty-five minutes."

I sighed, cursing myself for not calling. "O.K., Tommie, let's go play baseball."

"Yay, Daddy!"

"Go make a pee-pee while I change, and we'll go to the park."

"I already did."

"Did he?"

"That was a while ago. Go again, honey."

"Go make a pee and we'll go to the park," I told him.

He ran out of the room. I went into the bedroom and began to change out of my suit. I had a brief respite while my wife got things started on the stove, but everything must have really been ready to go, because in no time at all she came in to keep me company.

The problem with my wife, and it is a problem, is that she really *likes* me. At least that's the impression that she gives, and I have no way to prove it false.

And more than just liking me, she *respects* me. She thinks I'm intelligent, and capable, and worthy, and she wants the *best* for me. In short she drives me nuts.

The other part of the problem is I like her too. She's a very nice person, and is generally pleasant and agreeable. That's not to say she doesn't have a temper— when provoked she can be a regular hellcat, and her sarcasm is a wonder to behold, but such outbursts are rare and always for good reason. But most of the time she's just nice.

And that's the trouble.

Take my job, for instance. If she simply bitched about how few hours I was getting, and how little money I was making, and how we couldn't possibly live on it, that would be fine. I could give it right back to her and we could have screaming arguments of the type where everything gets said but nobody really gets hurt, and afterwards you feel better about it.

But my wife doesn't do that. She doesn't *complain* about how little I'm making. She *sympathizes* with me for making so little. She *laments* the fact that such a fine person as me should be stuck in such a dead-end job. She *encourages* me to quit the job and find something else. And she *supports* my decision, whatever it may be. The end result, of course, is just the same as if she had simply bitched and moaned, with the added aggravation that her position is invulnerable and I have nothing to complain about.

I have never been able to figure out if she is as naively nice as she seems, or if she knows she is driving me nuts. I have tried to discern this information by means of such subtle questions as, "Do you know you're driving me nuts?" but they never result in any concrete answers, and only serve to lead the conversation through various detours, all of which eventually lead it back to the same thing.

My gut feeling is my wife must know what she's doing. When she urges me to get out and find another job, she says things like, "You're good with people," which I take to mean that she thinks I am afraid of people, and have to be encouraged to go and meet them. She says, "You're good on the phone," which I hear as, "If you had the gumption to pick up the phone you might accomplish something." She says, "You're too good for this job," which I hear as, "Why are you so lazy, and timid, and stupid that you can't find something else?" But since she never says the things I hear, I can never answer her. The end result is I often want to strangle her.

"So how'd you do today?" she asked, as I hung my pants over a hanger and began to unbutton my shirt.

"A broken leg in Brooklyn. Three hours."

Her face fell in dismay. "But it's six o'clock."

"It came in late."

She shook her head. "Oh, Stanley," she said, sympathetically. "How awful for you. To sit around all day long waiting and then wind up with three hours. This job. This awful job."

"It's not that bad," I mumbled. I pulled on a T-shirt and began looking for my shorts.

"It's not fair," she persisted. "It's not fair for them to keep you on call all day long, make you work overtime, and then only pay you for three hours."

"It's the nature of the job," I told her.

A search had not revealed my shorts in the drawer. I headed for our bathroom to see if they had wound up in the hamper.

"It's a terrible job," she said, following me into the bathroom. "You're such a talented writer. It just isn't fair that you should—you're not going to put those on, are you? They're filthy."

"They're fine," I told her, bringing the prized shorts out of the bathroom and putting them on, relieved that the subject had changed.

It didn't stay changed. "I know I encouraged you to take this job," she went on, "because we needed the money. But it was supposed to be temporary. I never would have suggested you take it if I thought it would turn into a dead-end job. How long have you been doing it now, six months?"

I muttered something unintelligible and looked around for my sneakers.

"I was looking in the paper today," she said. "I know there are no jobs for creative writers, but there are jobs in related fields. Editing. Advertising. Proofreading. Jobs where you could use your talents. Wouldn't you rather be doing something like that?"

I discovered I was tying my shoelaces faster than one would have thought humanly possible. "They all require experience," I said.

"And where do they expect you to get experience, that's what I'd like to know? It's Catch 22. You can't get a job without experience, and you can't get experience without having a job."

Fully dressed, I fled for the foyer. Tommie was already there. I straightened his shorts, which he always manages to tug up crooked. He put his glove back on, took my glove out of the gym bag we use for equipment, and handed it to me, along with my baseball cap.

"Here, Daddy," he said.

I put the glove and cap on. I'm originally from Massachusetts, so we wear Boston Red Sox caps, a bold move in New York City. I picked up the bag and opened the front door. Tommie went out and rang for the elevator.

My wife followed us to the door and stood there, holding it open and looking out into the hallway.

"I just feel so sorry for you," she said, picking right up as if the conversation had been continuous, a habit I find disconcerting. "Working such long hours and not getting paid for them. I don't know how you can take it. I mean, am I wrong, or how do you feel about it?"

The elevator arrived. I ushered Tommie in.

"Really," she persisted. "How does that make you feel?"

"Useless," I told her, and stepped into the elevator.

4

I READ THE *NEW YORK POST* ON THE SUBWAY ON MY WAY TO THE OFFICE THE NEXT MORNING. I take the subway to the office because there's no place to park in midtown Manhattan, at least no place cheap. I read the *New York Post* for the sports—they have the late baseball scores. At least, that's what I tell my wife. Actually, it's the closest you can come to reading the gossip mags without actually buying one. My wife buys the *New York Times* and makes fun of my taste, but the hell with her. She watches the soap operas, for Christ's sake.

I was squashed against the express-side door of the Broadway downtown local by a large black man smoking a cigarette, and a fat woman with a handbag the size of a steamer trunk, when I found it. It was on page four, but that was just by luck. If a fairly prominent TV star hadn't died the same day it might have made page one.

"BUSINESS EXEC MURDERED AND MUTILATED," ran the headline. "The body of Martin Albrect, executive vice president of Fabri-Tec Inc., a prominent Manhattan firm, was discovered late last night in a midtown Manhattan parking lot. The body had been mutilated."

The article did not elaborate on the specifics of the mutilation, but I could guess. The N.Y.P.D. must have been tactfully withholding the information that Mr. Albrect's penis was in his mouth. That fact alone could have pushed the story up to page one. After all, the TV star had merely died of cancer and, in all probability, with his genitalia intact.

Despite the fact that I was crowded unmercifully in a stifling, non-air-conditioned subway car, I suddenly felt very cold. I also felt nauseous. I also found I was having trouble breathing, and it wasn't just the clouds of cigarette smoke the large black man was spewing out in my direction. I also felt incredibly claustrophobic, and the fact that the article about the demise of Martin Albrect was continued on page thirty-two didn't help. Getting from page four to page thirty-two seemed a Herculean task. My fingers felt numb and useless. Useless. I riffled the corners of the pages, located number thirty-two. I steeled myself for the effort of refolding the paper. I raised my arms aloft above the crush of shoulders, and began jockeying for the room to open the paper and fold it in on itself again.

The train pulled into the Times Square station, shoving me into two young businesswomen, one of whom said, "Hey!" and the other of whom said, "Shit!" I grunted, "I'm sorry," as the express doors opened and the surge of commuters thrust me out the door onto the platform. Automatically, I turned and followed them up the platform toward the 42nd Street exit, folding my paper to page thirty-two as I went.

The police hadn't released many facts about the incident, but there were some. The body had been found in a parking lot on Tenth Avenue near 47th Street. It was found around 2:00 A.M. by a young man and his date returning from a disco to pick up their car. The parking lot had been closed for hours. It was one of those outdoor lots where, for a few extra bucks, you could get a park-and-lock spot that wouldn't be blocked after closing. The indications were that the murder had taken place somewhere else, and the body had been driven to the lot and dumped. Martin Albrect was described as a successful sales executive for Fabri-Tec Inc., a textile manufacturer with offices on West 40th Street. He was a bachelor and lived alone in his apartment on East 81st Street. He was not known to be linked in any way with organized crime.

I finished the article and discovered I was standing on the northwest corner of Broadway and 42nd Street. I felt instinctively for my wallet. By some miracle it was still there. This marked, I realized, the first time I had ever made my way through the Times Square subway station without transferring my wallet from my hip to my front pants pocket, and keeping my hand pressed firmly against it. I folded the paper, joined a stream of traffic, and headed uptown.

My office is just east of Broadway, Seventh Avenue—actually, on 47th Street, right in the diamond district. My father-in-law, years ago, had used the office as his principal place of business, selling plastic bags to the jewelers there. He jobbed the bags then, buying at dealer discounts from the large manufacturers, and then underselling them to their own customers. He made enough money doing it to expand his business. He manufactured the bags now, and had his own factory down on 30th Street. The 47th Street office was still carried on the company books as a business expense, but he rarely used it and, in one of those infrequent moments when he had almost believed I was going to be able to support his daughter by writing, he had offered it to me as a place to work. I'd been using it ever since, first for writing, and then as a base for my pseudodetective agency when writing revenues ran thin.

I waited the usual eternity for the elevator, rumbled up to the third floor, and walked down the narrow hall to my office. In crime novels, detectives always have doors with frosted glass, through which the vague outlines of slinky women can be seen hesitating in the hallway, before making up their minds to enter, or through which the sinister silhouettes of suspected gunmen tip off the hero to the threat of danger. My door was solid wood. A metal plaque on the door read: "STANLEY HASTINGS DETECTIVE AGENCY." It covered up the original, old, hand-painted sign which

read: "COHEN BAG CORP." The plaque had been
given to me by friends as a joke, and I had hung it on
the door, partly as a joke, and partly, as I said, because I need to receive mail. The door had a small
mail slot at the bottom, and when I opened the door I
discovered the post had, indeed, come. Three pieces
of junk mail. I let it lie there, closed the door behind
me, and switched on the light.

The office was a small room with one window looking out over an air shaft. It was not the type of place
that was conducive to entertaining clients, but then I
had never *had* a client until Mr. Albrect had stumbled
upon me the day before.

The office was furnished with two desks, three chairs,
a typing table, and a file cabinet. One desk was where
I did my writing. The other was where I ran my
detective business. The typewriter, on wheels, served
both masters.

The answering machine was on the detective's desk.
There were no messages, and for once I was glad. No
messages meant no work, but I wasn't ready for work
yet. I slumped into the desk chair, and spread the
newspaper out on the desk in front of me. I read the
article again. It said the same thing it had the first
time.

Martin Albrect was dead. He had come to me for
help. I hadn't helped him. Now he was dead. There
was no other way to look at it. But I did my best to
come up with one.

I hadn't refused to help him, after all. I had merely
pointed out why I wasn't the best man he could have
picked for the job. And he had agreed. Unhesitat-
ingly, wholeheartedly agreed. Agreed so thoroughly
that he had walked out, abandoning the thought of
whatever small amount of help I might have been to
him, and preferring to face his crisis alone.

And I had toyed with him. Made fun of him. Made
up stupid comic book names to ridicule his story.
Amused myself with him. Done my damnedest not to
take him seriously.

I felt I ought to do something, but what? In the first place it was none of my business. In the second place, there was nothing I could do. I could go to the police, I suppose, but what could I tell them? I had a story, but no names, no places, no facts. What was I gonna tell 'em, the guy who killed Albrect was probably Bambi or Pluto?

No, there was nothing I could do. And that was the problem. That was what was gnawing away at me. Because if I were a *real* detective, I could do something. I didn't know what. But something. If I were a real detective, I'd at least *know* what I could do. But I wasn't a real detective. I was a failed writer and successful ambulance chaser, who'd never had the gumption or the balls to be anything else. So there was nothing I could do.

And yet I really wanted to do something. It really mattered to me. Not for Albrect—Albrect was just a bungling clod who'd brought it on himself. No, I wanted to do it for me.

Just for me.

The phone rang and I picked it up.

"Three-four-one-four," I said, reciting the last four digits of my phone number, a neutral greeting that allowed me to reveal myself as the Hastings Detective Agency if I found I was dealing with someone from whom the announcement would not evoke laughter.

"Good morning, Stanley," came the perennially cheery voice of Susan, one of Richard Rosenberg's secretaries. Richard Rosenberg was the lawyer I worked for. Susan and Kathy were the secretaries who called me with new assignments. Susan was always cheerful. Kathy was always sour. I was never sure which irritated me more.

"Hi, Susan," I said. "What's up?"

"I have a new case for you," she announced in the manner of one informing someone they have just won the lottery.

Like Pavlov's dog, I reached for a pen.

"The client tripped on a crack in the sidewalk in

front of her building and broke her leg. She'd like to see you today. She's home now, and I told her you'd be giving her a call. The number is 718—"

Seven-one-eight was the message I'd been waiting for. Even since the phone company split the area code for New York City, the numbers 212 and 718 held special meaning for me. Two-one-two meant Manhattan or the Bronx. Since our clients are usually not particularly wealthy—people who call a lawyer they see advertised on TV rather than their own or some friend's recommended lawyer are generally less than wealthy—most of our Manhattan clients were from Harlem, and most of our Bronx clients were from the South Bronx. In either case, it usually meant slums or housing projects, areas in which I was liable to be the only white man for blocks. I'm not prejudiced, but I'm not crazy either.

Seven-one-eight meant Queens or Brooklyn, and though there are bad neighborhoods there too, the odds of getting a good one are a little better. And somehow, they just seem safer, probably unrealistically so, but they do. So 718 was the announcement that always came as a relief. It was kind of like not getting hit over the head.

Susan went on to confirm that the client lived in Brooklyn. A Mrs. Rabinowitz on Ocean Parkway, out by Coney Island. Better and better. An elderly Jewish woman living in a tenth-floor apartment in what was bound to be a perfectly respectable building. This was a dream assignment. Safe, secure, and way the hell out in Brooklyn. I could put it in for four hours and forty miles, easy.

I told Susan I'd take it and hung up the phone. I leaned back in my chair, took a deep breath, and blew it out again. I knew I had to pick up the phone and call Mrs. Rabinowitz, but not just yet. First I had to get my head clear. This is a godsend, I told myself. This is exactly what I needed—a nice, cushy, routine assignment, a nice bit of busywork to immerse myself in. Business as usual.

The only thing stopping me from picking up the phone was the nagging thought of the late Mr. Albrect. The late Martin Albrect—I'd been right to doubt the Morris—unless the *Post* was wrong, which was quite possible.

Put it out of your mind, I told myself. Fuck Albrect. He was a fool, and he got what was coming to him. Get your mind on Mrs. Rabinowitz. That's your business. This other business, it's got nothing to do with you.

"Yeah," I said aloud. "It's got nothing to do with me."

5

THE RECEPTION AREA AT FABRI-TEC INC. WAS LARGE
AND LAVISH. The walls were lined with plush couches,
where the clientele could wait comfortably to be ushered into the presence of the powers that be. Current,
rather than backdate, magazines filled the coffee tables, just in case the wait should prove to be long. A
coffee maker and cups were also set up for that purpose. From the decor, Fabri-Tec seemed to be doing
well.

They had economized, however, on the personnel.
A lone, gum-chewing girl appeared to be it. She was
manning the reception desk, the company switchboard,
which was a permanent fixture on the left hand corner
of the desk, and an electric typewriter on a portable
typing table not dissimilar to mine. A half-typed letter
was in the machine, which hummed faintly. Several
lines on the switchboard were lit up and several others
were flashing. The receptionist, a blonde in her mid-
twenties, was pushing buttons on the switchboard,
saying, "Fabri-Tec," listening for a few seconds, and
then saying, "please hold." The corner of a movie
magazine protruded from beneath the blotter, doubt-
less stashed there for a happier and less busy time.

I was obviously an added aggravation to the receptionist, but in between phone calls she managed to
force an artificial smile. "May I help you?"

I smiled back at her. "Yes," I said. "I'm Nathan

Armstrong from the Whitney Corporation. I have an appointment with Mr. Albrect."

The receptionist paled and her smile froze. "Oh," she said. After a pause she added, "Oh."

The receptionist seemed to have several functions at Fabri-Tec, but apparently informing prospective buyers that company sales executives had been found dead with their dicks in their mouths was not one of them. She rose to her feet, murmured, "Excuse me a moment," and vanished into the inner recesses of Fabri-Tec Inc., leaving countless impatient callers stranded on hold.

The phone rang three more times while she was gone. I didn't answer it. After all, I had my own problems.

The receptionist returned with a smartly dressed young man of about thirty-five, an aggressive go-getter with the word "salesman" written all over him. He didn't wait for the receptionist to attempt an introduction, which was probably wise under the circumstances.

"Hi, I'm Michael Murphy, executive vice president."

He extended his hand and I shook it, wondering how many executive vice presidents a company of this kind had.

"Nathan Armstrong, Whitney Corporation," I told him.

There was no reason for him to doubt it. I always wear a suit and tie in the practice of my profession. Richard insists on it. That's because his TV ad promises a free consultation with a lawyer right in your own home. That, of course, is bullshit. No self-respecting lawyer is going to go running around to people's homes trying to sign up accident cases when he can hire some schmuck like me to do it. So I have to wear a suit and tie and pass myself off as a lawyer. I never actually say I'm a lawyer, and if anybody specifically asks, I'll admit that I'm not. I just walk in wearing a suit and say I'm Mr. Hastings from the lawyer's office, and the clients just assume I'm a lawyer and that's all there is to it. So I figured if the suit could make me a lawyer, it could damn well make me a businessman.

Murphy seemed to buy it. "Won't you come in," he said, ushering me around the reception desk and through huge oak double doors.

We passed through a short hallway and into an immense room teeming with stenographers. We zigzagged through them unobserved. Deafened by headsets, none of the typists so much as glanced up.

I found the typing pool somewhat reassuring. To tell the truth, I was a little apprehensive, or perhaps scared shitless would be more accurate, about whether I could pull off my little impersonation, seeing as how I had never done anything even remotely like it before. After the intimidating opulence of the waiting room, which had all but convinced me that I hadn't a prayer, it was nice to discover that the grand and glorious Fabri-Tec, Inc., was a company run by mortal men, capable of designing their work space so that executive vice presidents and the buyers they were attempting to impress had to pass through the typing pool in order to get to their offices.

I followed Murphy out of the typing pool and down a long hallway to a door marked "MICHAEL J. MURPHY, EXECUTIVE VICE PRESIDENT." I counted three other executive vice presidents on the way, and we weren't even halfway down the corridor.

Murphy opened the door and ushered me into what proved to be his outer office, manned by a grim and efficient-looking secretary behind a desk.

"Hold my calls, Mildred," Murphy said, and led me into his inner office and closed the door.

While Murphy's outer office had been furnished for business, with files, typewriters, and supply cabinets, his inner office was furnished to impress and entertain. Aside from the desk, on which there was not a single scrap of paper, only a phone and an intercom, the office boasted a couch, coffee table, three comfortable chairs, a bar, a stereo, and a TV complete with VCR.

"Sit down," Murphy said, gesturing to the couch. "Would you care for a drink."

"Little early for me," I said, sitting on the couch. "But you go right ahead."

"I don't want one either," Murphy said. He sat in one of the chairs. "Now, you say you have an appointment with Mr. Albrect?"

"That's right." I looked at my watch. "In five minutes, in fact."

"And you came up here from Miami to meet with him?"

"That's right."

Murphy took a deep breath. "I'm afraid Mr. Albrect is not going to be able to see you."

"Oh? Why not?"

"I'm sorry to have to tell you this, but Mr. Albrect is dead."

"What!" I exclaimed. "You're kidding! I just spoke to him a couple of days ago. From Miami. Are you sure?"

"Yes. I'm afraid so."

"Oh, that's terrible. I can't believe it. He didn't have any health problems, so far as I know. Maybe a little overweight. What was it, his heart?"

"No."

"Well, what was it?"

"He had an accident."

"An automobile accident?"

"No."

"Well what then?"

Murphy shook his head. "I'm sorry to have to tell you this. The police found his body late last night in a parking lot. He'd been murdered. Shot to death."

I stared at him in what I hoped would pass for shock. My mouth was open, but I held my breath for a second or two, then let it out in a whoosh. I closed my mouth, opened it again, and began breathing in short, shallow breaths. In a small, shaky voice I said, "I think I'll have that drink now."

I was afraid I was overdoing it, but Murphy immediately jumped up and poured me a brandy. I took a big swallow, coughed, choked, and came close to spitting it out. I swallowed, exhaled, shook my head, and took another smaller sip, hoping like hell my wife wouldn't catch it on my breath when I got home.

Murphy watched me solicitously. "Are you all right?" he asked.

"Yeah, yeah, sure," I said. I forced a small, nervous chuckle. "Then I guess our meeting is off," I said in the manner of one making a feeble attempt at a joke to try to cover the embarrassment of an awkward situation.

Murphy picked right up on it, good salesman he. "That is probably a shrewd deduction," he said with a grin.

We shook our heads and chuckled for a bit.

"Well," I said, "what the hell am I going to do now?"

"Don't worry," Murphy assured me. "This is, of course, a bit of a shock, but we've already begun transferring all of Marty's accounts to other executives."

Ah! Marty. Score one for the *Post*.

"Now," Murphy continued, "seeing as how you've come all the way from Miami, this will be given a top priority. In fact, I shall insist on handling it myself."

He made the pronouncement in the manner of one bestowing a great favor, and I couldn't help wondering, what with there being so many executive vice presidents and all, just what Murphy's place on the hierarchical ladder actually was—had he outranked Albrect, or had Albrect's demise kicked him up a rung?

"I'm not sure you can," I told him. "Albrect and I had a special understanding."

"Our customers always have a special understanding, Mr. Armstrong. Now, if you'll just tell me what your understanding was, I'm sure I'll be able to help you."

I looked at him skeptically. "You're familiar with our account?"

"The Whitney Corporation? Yes, of course. I've never handled it personally—it was Marty's account—but I'm certainly familiar with it."

I still looked skeptical. "All right, then," I said. "You say you're familiar with the account? Then tell me, what is our usual order?"

Murphy went to his desk and pressed the intercom. "Mildred," he said, "please bring me the Whitney account."

She was fast, I'll give her that. Either the account was cross-filed in his office, or he'd sent her for it the moment he learned I was in the building, but, in any case, Mildred delivered the file in ten seconds flat. After she'd scooted out again, Murphy crossed his legs, opened the file and said, "Now then, you asked what is your standard order?"

"That's right."

"That would be 25 thousand units."

"How often?"

"Once a month."

"At what terms?"

"For 25 thousand units we allow you the 50 thousand bracket price less 2 percent discount for net cash."

Among the numerous jobs I have had throughout my less than distinguished writing career, was teaching algebra for one term at a private boarding school. I was 28 at the time, and the only algebra I knew was what I remembered vaguely from my junior year at high school. To make matters worse, I was pressed into service because the real algebra teacher died halfway through the school year, so the class was a whole term ahead of me when I began. Not having the faintest idea what I was doing, and not wanting to let it show, I soon developed my own method of teaching. Every time I hit a problem I didn't understand, which was often, I would send the class genius to the board and have him do it, which he always could. I would learn the procedure by watching him, and then when he was done I could sharpshoot, offering criticism such as, "Yes, that's very good, but in step #3 you could have combined terms before you multiplied instead of after," which, of course, while true, had no effect on the actual answer, which was invariably right. By that device, my own version of the Socratic method, I was able to get through to the end of the term without ever having to actually admit to the students that I hadn't the faintest idea what I was talking about.

I was using this old teaching method now. Murphy, my class genius, had been called upon to recite, and I was preparing to sit back and sharpshoot.

"The 50 thousand bracket less 2?" I said.

He checked the ledger sheet again. "That's right."

"Well, now—" I began.

My beeper went off. Its high pitched "Beep, beep, beep" filled the room. Christ! I'd forgotten I had the damn thing on. Now Richard's office was beeping me. I reached quickly into my jacket and shut it off.

"What the hell was that?" Murphy said.

Before I could answer, the beeper went off again. It always went off twice when they beeped me. The second beep was supposed to be a safety check, which seemed pretty stupid to me. If the first beep didn't work, the second one wouldn't either, and if you heard the first beep, you didn't *need* the second one.

The system of double beeping had never irritated me more than it did now.

"What is that?" Murphy said as I shut off the second beep.

"Just my office beeping me."

Murphy stared at me. "From Miami?" he asked, incredulously.

"No, no," I told him. "The branch office here in Manhattan. I have to call in. Could I use your phone?"

"Certainly," he said, pointing to the desk. "Dial nine for an outside line."

I dialed 9, got an outside line, and called Richard's office.

Kathy answered the phone with her dulcet snarl.

"Hi," I said. "You beeped."

"You're damn right, I beeped," she said. "Mrs. Rabinowitz just called. She said you never called her."

"I called twice and the line was busy. After that I got no answer."

"Oh yeah? Well, she's been there the whole time. Waiting for you."

"Maybe you gave me the wrong number."

Kathy was incensed. "I didn't give you the number. Susan gave you the number."

"Well, maybe it's wrong. Let's double check. What number do you have?"

Reluctantly, she read me the number.

"Ah, that's it," I told her. "You had the last digit wrong."

"*We* had it right, damn it!" Kathy shrieked. "*You* wrote it down wrong."

She hung up on me. I hung up too, and turned to Murphy. "I'm sorry," I said, "but I have to make a private business call. Is there a pay phone I could use?"

I wasn't sure if making private business calls was standard procedure in the textile industry, but if it wasn't, Murphy never blinked an eye, just directed me to a pay phone in the lobby, which indicated either my request wasn't that unusual, or else Whitney Corporation was one hell of a good account.

I went down to the lobby, called Mrs. Rabinowitz, apologized, told her I was tied up at the moment, and made an appointment for four in the afternoon. In the elevator on the way back up, I went over the information I'd already gleaned, preparing myself to tap dance with Murphy.

He was sitting waiting patiently when Mildred let me back into the office, further indication that Whitney Corp. was a good account.

"Sorry for the interruption," I said breezily, going right to my chair and sitting down, as if making an extra effort at efficiency to make up for taking up so much of his time. "Now then, we have 25 thousand units a month at the 50 thousand bracket less 2. Right?"

"Right," Murphy said.

"Fine," I said. "Well, here's the deal I had with Albrect. I wanted to increase that order to 50 thousand units a month."

Murphy, who had shown only polite interest, perked right up. "Really?"

"Really."

"At what price?"

"The 100 thousand bracket less 2."

"Well," Murphy said with a smile. "That seems a perfectly normal request. I see no problem with that."

"There is one," I told him.

"Oh? What's that?"

"I'm not really buying them for Whitney Corp. I'm buying them for myself."

Murphy stared at me. "Run that by me again."

"It's perfectly simple," I told him. "I'm a jobber. I want to buy from you at the 100 thousand price so I can undercut you with your own product and score a profit on the Whitney account."

Murphy was visibly confused. "Wait a minute. Wait a minute. I thought you worked for Whitney Corp."

"I do."

"You buy for them."

"That's right."

"And you want—let me see if I understand you correctly—you want to buy for yourself and then turn over the merchandise to your company, thereby making an additional profit for yourself in the process."

"That's right."

"You'll be taking our account with Whitney Corp. and getting us to provide the merchandise at a lower rate by combining it with another order that you will also get at a lower rate, which you will also turn over for a profit, probably by undercutting us with one of our other customers."

"You got it."

Murphy shook his head. "Mr. Armstrong," he said, "that is illegal."

"Well," I said, "let's say it's unethical."

Murphy still couldn't believe his ears. "Wait a minute. Let me see here." He picked up the account folder again. "All right, now look. Our 50 thousand bracket price is $4.90 a towel. Our 100 thousand bracket price is $4.80 a towel. So instead of selling 50,000 towels to two different accounts at $4.90 a piece we'd be selling them to you at $4.80 a piece and losing $5,000 a month."

Bingo! My class genius had done the math for me. Now I knew what the figures were. I also knew what the product was, which couldn't hurt.

"That's right," I told him.

"And," Murphy went on, "in order to do it, we would have to be party to what you, yourself, describe as unethical."

"This is true."

"Mr. Armstrong," Murphy said, shaking his head. "Why in the world would Mr. Albrect ever agree to such an outlandish proposal as that?"

"Because he needed the money," I told him.

Murphy just stared at me. I sat and waited. It was all bullshit, of course. I hadn't the faintest idea what I was talking about. I knew a little bit about jobbers and bracket prices from my father-in-law, but that was about it.

The actual logistics of it didn't matter, though. As far as I was concerned, the only thing that mattered was whether or not Murphy was greedy.

He was.

"What do you mean, 'he needed the money'?" Murphy asked, after a pause.

I had him.

"He needed the money," I told him. "He was hard up for extra cash. In return for handling this little deal for me, Albrect was going to pull down a grand a month. Apparently, he could have used it."

I sat back and let that sink in. A grand a month. I could see his mind racing. He probably had some bills—who doesn't? Who couldn't use an extra thousand dollars a month.

Murphy could. He said slowly, "And you're offering me the same deal?"

"Bingo, right on the button," I said.

"And just how was this supposed to work?"

"Easy. You increase the Whitney Corp. order from 25 to 50 thousand a month. You still bill the Whitney Corp. on the books, but the actual bills would be sent to a different address. To me. I would pay them in the name of the Whitney Corp. from a special account."

"I see. And how would I know that—excuse me—that your credit was good?"

"You'd have to check me out, of course."

"By calling your bank?"

"Of course not. You can't do it through normal channels. You would have to do what Albrect did."

"What was that?"

"Come to Miami and check me out."

"Oh," he said.

"When's the next time you're going to be in Miami?"

"I don't know. None of my accounts are in Miami. Maybe, with Albrect gone—but we haven't worked that out yet."

"Then this will have to wait," I told him. "I'm due back in New York in three months. I can bring you references then. I admit that's not the same as if you got them yourself, but it's the best I can do."

"I see," he said. He did not sound happy.

"Wait a minute," I said. "I know you can't take a chance on me on a thing like that without checking me out, I understand that. But Albrect did check me out, and he got a complete credit check in writing before he said he'd O.K. the deal."

"So?"

"So wouldn't that satisfy you?"

"Maybe. Where would it be?"

"In his office. Where else?"

Albrect's office was identical to Murphy's, with the exception that, where Murphy's was immaculate, Albrect's was a holy mess. Files, letters, circulars, price lists, catalogues and memos were strewn everywhere, including the couch, the chairs, the coffee table, and the bar. A mound of it reposed on his desk.

It hadn't taken much to persuade Murphy to search the office. The police had given it a once over, told the company to lock the office, and left. They'd never know we'd been in there. Besides, they'd never promised Murphy a thousand a month.

"The police do this?" I asked as we ploughed through the mound on Albrect's desk.

He shook his head. "This is the way they found it, this is the way they left it. Albrect's office was always like this. I thought he kept it this way deliberately so that people'd think he was always busy."

"He seems to have succeeded," I said.

Murphy was sifting through litter on the bar when I came across a small black notebook, tucked in the bottom corner of Albrect's top right desk drawer. I palmed it, shoved it into my jacket pocket, kept on looking.

It was nearly two hours later when we called it quits. I hadn't found anything else I considered significant and, oddly enough, we had not found any written record of Albrect's credit approval of Nathan Armstrong.

"Well, that's it," I said. "We're just gonna have to put this on hold till next time."

Murphy's regret was genuine. "That's really a shame," he said. "I don't see why I can't check your credit over the phone."

"You wouldn't understand," I told him. "It involves talking to some people you can't talk to on the phone. What I mean is, they wouldn't talk to you. I took Albrect to them in person and they were able to satisfy him that my credit was good. But it took a face-to-face meeting and a personal introduction."

Murphy didn't want to let go. "Well, maybe I could go without a credit check," he said.

Christ! I realized I'd better ease off the sales pitch before I wound up with 50 thousand fucking towels. Fortunately, Murphy let it drop.

"Well," I said. "This trip's a total washout for me."

"Yeah. It's a shame."

"It's not just the order. See, I'm an old riverboat gambler from way back, you know. Albrect told me there was a casino operating right here in Manhattan. He was gonna take me there tonight."

"Is that right," Murphy said with a grin. "Well, Mr. Armstrong, things aren't as bad as you think. I'd be delighted to take you there myself."

"Oh, you know the place?" I asked.

"Know it?" he said. "Hell, I'm the one who told Albrect about it."

Son of a bitch! First rattle out of the box. Murphy was Dumbo.

6

THE LOCKSMITH TURNED THE KEY IN HIS HANDS, looking it over. "It's the key to a safe deposit box," he told me.

That was interesting, seeing as how the key had been tucked in the plastic fold of the cover of Albrect's address book.

"You mean in a bank?" I asked.

"I don't know where else you're gonna find a safe deposit box."

"Can you tell me which bank?"

"Nope."

"Well, what *can* you tell me?"

"Well, it ain't any bank around here."

"How do you know that?"

"Cause I never seen this blank before. If it was for a bank around here, I would have this blank."

"What do you mean by around here?"

"Huh?"

"How large an area you talking about? Where the bank wouldn't be?"

"It wouldn't be in Manhattan. It wouldn't be in New York City. It probably wouldn't be in New York State, and when I say New York State I mean Eastern New Jersey and Southern Connecticut too."

"Who doesn't," I said.

"You wanna buy something?"

"Whaddya sell?"

"Keys and locks."

"The only lock I'm interested in is the one that key fits."

"That I haven't got."

"You know where it isn't from. Any way to find out where it is from?"

"Could be."

"Depending on what?"

"What it's worth."

"It's worth ten bucks."

He picked up the phone, dialed a number. "Jerry, Sam. I got a blank here for a safe deposit box, key 35732, can you tell me who makes 'em. . . . Uh huh . . . yeah. Thanks."

He hung up the phone, looked at me, said nothing. I interpreted his silence correctly and laid a ten-dollar bill on the counter.

"Bailsey Manufacturing," he said.

"Great," I told him. "Now can I get 'em to tell me who they made those blanks for?"

"I doubt it."

"Well, can I go there and ask?"

"You can if you want," he said. "The company's in Florida."

I came out of the 42nd Street locksmith shop into the blazing heat of Times Square. The freaks were out in force. I slipped the key in my pocket, transferred my wallet, and caught the subway uptown to get my car.

The key was undoubtedly the most interesting thing in Albrect's address book, though there were a couple of close seconds. One was a rather cryptic notation on an otherwise blank page: "7th and Burke N.W. 4:00." The other was an address in Manhattan. The book held many Manhattan addresses—some belonged to women, some to businesses, some to friends—but only one was in the East Village, and only one carried a name that was unmistakably ethnic.

Now, I must admit I'm not great at identifying people's backgrounds from their names. I know other people are. They'll hear a name and go, "Oh, black" or "Oh, Jewish," or whatever. As I said, I'm not good at that, but, nonetheless, if Guillermo Gutierrez wasn't Hispanic, I'd eat my hat.

I drove to the address on East 7th Street between Avenues B and C. It was a five-story walk-up building in a row of similar structures, all in what could generously be described as poor repair. My building was brown, with cracked concrete steps leading up to a wood and glass door. Half the panes of glass were missing and the other half were cracked. Security didn't seem to be a major concern here, since both this door and the inner door were propped open.

Though there were tenants hanging out on the front steps of many of the other buildings on the block, no one was in evidence here. I went inside and up the stairs.

Guillermo Gutierrez lived in 5B, which proved, as I had feared, to be the top floor. There was no cross-ventilation in the building, and I was dripping sweat by the time I reached the fifth floor. I knocked on 5B and got no answer, again no surprise. I tried the door. It was locked. In the movies, detectives have a set of skeleton keys or know how to pick a lock. Failing that, they kick the door down. I have none of those talents. If a door is locked, I can't get in.

I went back downstairs. The door in the back of the hall on the first floor was open, and I figured that to be the super's apartment. I thought about knocking on his door and asking him about Gutierrez, but decided against it. You start asking questions and people get suspicious and clam up on you.

I went out to my car, opened the trunk, and took out my briefcase, the pure black imitation leather one that was supposed to help give the impression that I was a lawyer. I opened it up, and took out my Canon Snappy 50, the camera I use to take pictures of broken legs and cracks in the sidewalk.

I closed the briefcase, locked the trunk, and reset the code alarm on my car, the computerized $250 warning system and ignition cutoff switch without which my '84 Toyota would not have lasted a day in the neighborhoods I visit.

I went back inside, pulled out the switch for the flash attachment, and was relieved to see that, although the batteries were weak and it took a while to warm up, the light indicating the flash was ready finally went on. I began taking flash pictures of the staircase, just as I would if I were doing accident photos for a personal injury case.

In some of the cases I handle, there is no defect where the client fell down, and therefore no liability. In those cases, Richard will sometimes send me back to try to get a camera angle on some small crack or crevice so that it looks like a precipice. I'd have had no such problem here. One of the stairs was cracked in two, one of the risers was separated from the stairwell, and a good six feet of the handrail on the wall was missing. I concentrated on these defects, and had some pretty good liability shots in the can before the flash attracted the super out of his apartment.

The super was a skinny Hispanic of about 45, with short black hair, and a small, close-trimmed mustache. He was dressed in a white sleeveless undershirt and shorts. He was hot, tired, and hostile. His attitude gave the impression that my presence in the building had caused him to have to move, and for that he hated me.

"Hey, what you doin'?" he asked.

"Taking pictures."

"I see that. Why you takin' pictures?"

"Someone fell down the stairs and hurt himself."

"Oh yeah? Who?"

I took out my notebook, made a show of looking up the name. "Guillermo Gutierrez."

The super snorted. "Oh, him. So why you take pictures?"

"This guy fell down the stairs and hurt himself. He's gonna make an insurance claim."

"You gonna sue?"

"We don't use the word sue. We call it 'making a claim.' "

"You call it anything you like. You gonna sue, you gonna sue. Who you gonna sue?"

"I don't know. That's not my department. We might have a claim against the owner of the building, or the landlord, or the real estate agent."

"You gonna sue me?"

"You the super?"

"That's right. You gonna sue me?"

"No."

"You sure?"

"I'm sure."

"How you know that?"

I smiled at him. "Cause you ain't got no money."

He looked at me for a moment as if deciding whether or not to be angry. Then he laughed. "Hey, you all right." He laughed some more. "Who are you, anyway?"

I took out my I.D. as a private detective. It was in a brown leather folder that opened up to show a photo I.D. of me in my suit. At the top it said "SPECIAL INVESTIGATOR." Below, in smaller print, "LICENSED BY." Below that, in big print again, "STATE OF NEW YORK." Below that, three lines: one, small print, "THIS IS TO CERTIFY THAT"; two, typed in a blank, "STANLEY HASTINGS"; three, small print, "IS EMPLOYED AS A SPECIAL INVESTIGATOR." Below that, small print, "SHIELD NO." and a blank, left blank, since I am not a cop. Finally, below that, the authorized signature of the private detective who had gotten me the license.

Technically, the license only empowered me to work as a private detective for his agency, which I didn't, and not to run my own agency. But technically, I didn't run my own agency, as I had no employees, and I had a perfect right to do what I was doing, and if anyone ever complained, the worst that could have happened would have been I might have had to take down the signs on my door and in my lobby, which were there mainly to amuse my friends anyway.

At any rate, it was a genuine I.D., and it was invaluable in my work. I'd go into a bar where a woman fell and broke her leg, show it to the owner, tell him I was investigating an insurance claim, and he'd assume I was from his insurance company and let me take pictures of anything I wanted, never dreaming I was actually working for the person who was trying to sue—excuse me—making a claim.

He took the I.D., looked it over. A silly grin came over his face.

"You private eye?" he said.

"Guilty as charged."

"You shoot people?"

"That's just on television," I told him.

"Yeah, TV," he said.

I decided to trade on the image. "Look," I said. "I've been trying to get in touch with this guy, Gutierrez, for four or five days. He doesn't answer the phone. He doesn't answer the door."

"What you want him for?"

"You like to get paid?"

He stared at me. "What, are you nuts? I like to get paid? Sure I like to get paid."

"Yeah, well I like to get paid, too. And I don't get paid until I find the guy."

"What you want him for?"

"He has to sign some papers for his lawyer."

"That's all?"

"That's enough."

He shrugged. "Maybe. You talk to Rosa?"

"Who's Rosa?"

"His girlfriend."

"What's her name?"

"Rosa."

"What's her last name?"

"I don't know. Her name's Rosa. Only name I know."

"Where would I find this Rosa?"

"She usually here."

"Well, she's not here now."

"No?"

"No. Where else might she be?"

"She live around the corner." He made a circular gesture indicating around and to the south. "On B."

"You know her address on Avenue B?"

"No. Right around the corner. Over the candy store."

"Which candy store?"

"Only one on the block."

"You seen her around here lately?"

"I don't know."

"You seen Gutierrez around here lately?"

Again. "I don't know."

"O.K., look," I said. "I'll talk to this Rosa, but right now I'm talking to you. And I gotta tell you, I'm a little worried about Gutierrez. See, he got hurt in the fall, you know. Now, just between you and me, I talked to Gutierrez before and, I can tell, he takes a little drugs, you know?"

He looked at me sideways. "No, I don't know."

"Yeah, well I know. Look, I'm not worried about that. That's none of my business. But here's the thing. He's hurt from the accident. He can't move well. So maybe he takes a little drugs. Maybe he takes a little too much drugs, you know. He ought to get out of there and get help, but he's hurt, he can't move. So he just lies there. He can't answer the door. He can't answer the phone. He's in trouble, but there's nothing he can do."

The super was staring at me. "So?"

"So he dies. I don't get his signature, so the lawyer can't sue. The lawyer can't sue, so I don't get paid."

"Too bad."

"And too bad for you. The cops wanna know what kind of a super you are, you let people take drugs and O.D. in their rooms, and lie around dead for days, and you don't do nothing about it."

"Not my fault, some guy takes drugs."

"Yeah, but if you don't help me, then I gotta go to

the cops, tell 'em I think some guy O.D.'d and the super won't do nothing. Then they come here and hassle you. If the guy's dead, they hassle you a lot more."

The super had ceased to be my friend. "Why the hell you wanna do that?"

"I don't wanna do that. I'd hate like hell to do that. I just wanna get paid."

"So what you want?"

"You're the super. You got keys to all the rooms here. You go upstairs with me, we knock on his door. We get no answer, you open the door and we see if our friend is lying there and can't get up."

"You kidding?"

"Hey, I'm not a cop. I don't give a shit if there's a bunch of drugs up there. That's none of my business. I just want to get paid."

"How I know you're not a cop?"

I had him. At least, I was pretty sure I had him. The thing is, I had never bribed anyone before, and I was somewhat hesitant about doing it, but that's where I figured we'd gotten to. The way I figured it, the super didn't care if I was a cop or not, or if Gutierrez was dead or not, or whether he opened the guy's door or not. All it came down to now, assuming I'd read the situation correctly, was how much money it was going to take to get this basically lazy guy who just wanted to go back and watch TV to climb four flights of stairs in this stifling heat. If, of course, I was right.

What made me hesitant, of course, was what if I was wrong? What if I pulled out a wad of money and, instead of taking it, the guy got offended and froze up on me? In that case I would feel like an asshole, and I wouldn't know what to do next, which is a hell of a position for a private detective to find himself in.

I needn't have worried. My assessment was dead on. I opened the bidding at five dollars and closed it out at ten.

Guillermo Gutierrez's apartment was about what I expected. A dirty, ill-furnished, one-room apartment with a kitchen alcove and a small bath. I couldn't help wondering why a guy who obviously moved huge quantities of drugs for exorbitant amounts of money would choose to live in squalor like this. The answer, of course, was obvious. He was investing all of his capital in his arm.

I couldn't search the apartment with the super there watching me like a hawk, so I didn't find anything interesting, but I hadn't expected to anyway. I just wanted a little confirmation. I found it on the floor just outside the door into the bathroom. A faint reddish tinge on the floorboards, which were cleaner there than anywhere else in the room, as if someone had made an effort to mop something up. I didn't point it out to the super, nor did I suggest to him that he notify the police that the occupant of the apartment was, to the best of his knowledge, missing. But I would have given long odds right then and there that, whatever information Rosa might have notwithstanding, I wasn't going to be seeing Guillermo Gutierrez in the near future.

7

THE SECURITY AT ALBRECT'S UPPER EAST SIDE APART-
MENT HOUSE WAS A TRIFLE BETTER THAN IT HAD BEEN
AT GUTIERREZ'S LOWER EAST SIDE ONE. I'd known I
was in trouble the minute I walked into the lobby. A
uniformed doorman was stopping all visitors and calling upstairs on a house phone to get the tenant's
permission before letting anyone up. There was actually a line ahead of me. I watched a young man receive approval to visit a Lisa Hartman, and a middle-
aged woman be confirmed as a suitable caller for a
Mrs. Ruth Goldstein. I jotted the names in my notebook and left.

I went outside and did some serious thinking. This
was not going to be easy. First I had to get past the
doorman, then I had to get past the door. My talents
did not seem particularly suited to either task. I racked
my brain for an answer. I didn't get an answer, but at
least I got an idea.

I went to a pay phone on the corner and called
Leroy Stanhope Williams. For me, this was a radical
departure. You see, Leroy was one of Richard's clients.
I had never called any of Richard's clients before on
anything other than Richard's business and, quite
frankly, I was sure I'd never want to. You see, it is an
occupational hazard of my profession that one soon
becomes contemptuous of the very people one is supposed to be helping. Often, I have to stifle the urge to
say, "Madam, you are fat, lazy, stupid, and incompe-

tent. You fell down because you are overweight and clumsy and too dumb to look where you are going. And now you want to sue someone for something that is obviously your own fault." I never actually say that, but I often have the urge.

Leroy Stanhope Williams was an exception.

The first hint I got that Leroy Stanhope Williams was something special, aside from the three names, was that his address in Queens was listed as a private house. Of course, that could have meant nothing. Many clients listed their address as a private house, but when I got there it turned out they had an apartment in the basement they illegally rented from the owner, whom they wanted to sue for not fixing the cellar stars. Or, it turned out they actually did live in a private house, but the front door was a sheet of plywood, if you leaned against the walls the ceiling would come down, and the only reason the place hadn't been condemned was that no one in his right mind would have wanted the property.

Leroy's house was different. It was a three-story frame house, newly painted white with blue trim, on a small but immaculately kept lawn with actual grass and a flower garden. A smooth, clean concrete walk led up to a small front porch, framed by windows with ornate, decorative blue grillwork.

As I went up the steps to the front porch, the first thing I noticed was that there were three locks on the front door, the regular lock and two deadbolts. Then I noticed that the grillwork on the windows, though ornate, was also functional. It was, in effect, bars, and all the windows had them, even those on the upper floors. Great. Some doddering 80-year-old man, hiding from the world. The door would undoubtedly open two inches on a safety chain, and I'd have to slide my I.D. through before I got in.

I rang the doorbell. As I did so, I noticed the eye of an infra-red beam set into the doorjamb. That caught me up short. I looked at the windows again, and discovered a thin wire embedded in the glass running around the perimeter of the panes. This was something else. I could understand some paranoid old fart investing in a couple of deadbolts, but an electronic burglar alarm system?

I was still thinking about that when the front door swung open, not on a safety chain, to reveal a black man on crutches, standing in the shadows of the front hallway.

I inquired, "Leroy Stanhope Williams?" and he nodded. "Stanley Hastings from the lawyer's office." He nodded again and ushered me in with a gesture, momentarily holding that crutch with only his armpit. I walked by him through the dimly-lit foyer and into the living room, where I stood and gawked.

I must admit, I don't know anything about art; in fact, I'm not even sure what I like, but I must say I was impressed. I think that even without having seen the security system, I would have known that the paintings on the walls were originals, the statues genuine, the antique pottery authentic, the gold pieces solid not plate, and the jewelry real.

While I looked around, Leroy lowered himself into a wheelchair, and raised his broken right leg up onto the support in front of him. When he was settled, he turned to me, raised his hand in one flowing gesture to the couch, and said, "Please be seated."

A character study in three words and a gesture. The gesture was theatrical or regal, take your pick, but it was certainly grand. The voice was resonant, cultured, and refined. It had an almost British hint to it, which could have merely meant he was a foreigner from some British province, but somehow I didn't think so. Something about him said New York.

I murmured, "Thank you, Mr. Williams," and sat. Usually, I identify my clients by name as I come in the door to make sure I'm talking to the right person, and after that just call them "you," but I just naturally called him Mr. Williams. In fact, it took an effort not to call him "Sir."

And he was not old, that is to say he was younger

than me, perhaps somewhere around thirty-five. It's hard to guess a man's height and weight when he's sitting in a wheelchair, but I guessed he was about my build, not too tall, not too short, not too fat, not too thin, just about average. His skin was chocolate brown. Bemused eyes, and a high, sloping forehead gave him an intellectual look which, coupled with his pattern of speech, made him remind me of a young Roscoe Lee Brown.

I pulled myself together, took out my papers, and got down to the task. Leroy had been hit by a car. It turned out he had all the necessary information and more, including the name and address of the driver, license and license-plate numbers, driver's insurance carrier, names and precinct number of the officers on the scene, and even the names and addresses of two witnesses. How he managed to get all that while lying in the street with a broken leg is beyond me, but he had it and, as I would have expected, he supplied it all succinctly and precisely.

Things were going so well I was quite surprised when we bogged down on one of the simpler parts of the form. When I asked Leroy what his occupation was there was a long pause. I would not have been surprised to hear "Classics professor from Columbia University" or "New York Supreme Court judge," but what Leroy actually said was "electrician."

I believe I gave him a look before writing "electrician" in the proper blank. Then I moved on to the question that I always hate to ask people, but which is a necessary part of the form.

"And how much do you make as an electrician?" I asked him.

This time Leroy gave me a look. "Why do you have to know that?"

"For the suit," I told him. "We want to show an earnings loss. You're losing a lot of work with that broken leg. We can get the money back for you."

"I see," he said. He didn't look happy about it.

There was another long pause, during which Leroy

looked as if he were wrestling with something and trying to make up his mind.

At length he sighed. "All right. Look. You're a lawyer," he said, making the usual assumption which, as usual, I did not jump in to correct. "I have to be honest with you, right?"

"It's not a bad idea," I told him.

"All right, then. I am not really an electrician."

"Oh? What are you?"

"I'm a thief."

"I beg your pardon?"

"I'm a thief."

"A thief?"

"Yes." Leroy leaned back in his wheelchair and cocked his head in my direction. "And you see I have a terrible earnings loss because, now, if I were to steal something, I would not be able to get away."

I looked at him closely. He was smiling, and there was a twinkle in his eye, and for a moment I thought I knew what it meant. He was putting me on. His eyes were twinkling because he was *not* a thief, because everything he was telling me was a complete fabrication. I immediately realized this assumption was wrong. He was *not* putting me on. His eyes were twinkling because he *was* a thief, because everything he was telling me was absolutely true. And suddenly I realized I was talking to a person one usually meets only in works of fiction, a gentleman jewel thief, a modern day Arsine Lupin, operating out of Flushing, Queens.

I pursed my lips, nodded my head thoughtfully, and deadpanned, "That must be a considerable inconvenience," and he had the good grace to smile.

After that we had a grand old time. I countered his I'm-not-really-an-electrician-I'm-a-thief confession with my I'm-not-really-a-lawyer-I'm-a-detective confession, and we spent the afternoon talking shop.

I found out how Leroy had come to call Richard, which was interesting, since Richard's clientele were not often in his class. It happened that Leroy's criminal attorney was the lawyer to whom Richard, who did no criminal work of his own, often referred clients. So when Leroy had broken his leg, the attorney, who handled no litigation, had reciprocated by sending him to us.

Leroy told me something about his background. He was born and raised in Harlem, and grew up on the streets. He had been arrested several times as a teenager, and had eventually been sent to a reform school in upstate New York. The school had been Leroy's salvation. He had done so well there that when he emerged he got a scholarship to N.Y.U. He majored in fine arts, and by the time he graduated he had developed a taste for the finer things in life which, unfortunately, he was unable to afford. And so he had taken his street education and college education, and managed to combine his talents.

In the end, I crossed out the word "electrician" on the fact sheet and wrote in the word "thief," assuring Leroy it would make no difference and, sure enough, Richard took the case.

It took Leroy less than thirty seconds to open the door to Albrect's apartment. That was the easy part. The hard part was getting the two of us into the building, and I must say it encouraged me considerably to find out I was able to do it.

Here's what I did.

After I called Leroy, I hunted up a candy store, bought a Whitman Sampler, and had it gift-wrapped. Then I went back to the office, found a summons I'd been given to serve, and went out and had it Xeroxed. I bought a bottle of Liquid Paper, the red one "for copies," and whited out the name and address of the defendant on the summons. Then I Xeroxed it again. I took the new copy and typed in the name "Ruth Goldstein" and the address of Albrect's apartment house. Then I Xeroxed that. The end result was a pretty official-looking summons.

I met Leroy in front of Albrect's building and gave him the Whitman Sampler. Leroy had dressed down for the occasion, in jeans and a T-shirt. The jeans looked a bit new for the part, and I couldn't help wondering if they were something Leroy had had in some drawer but had never worn, or whether he had rushed out and bought them after I called.

I went in first. The lobby was empty, and the doorman gave me his full attention. After all, I was wearing my suit.

"Yes?" he said.

"I have a delivery for Ruth Goldstein."

"Your name, sir."

"Stanley Hastings."

The doorman called up on the house phone and relayed the information. "She doesn't know you," he said.

I raised my voice. "I'm an officer of the Supreme Court of the State of New York. I have a summons for Mrs. Goldstein."

The house phone immediately began making squawking noises. It was still squawking when Leroy strolled in with the Whitman Sampler.

"Package for Lisa Hartman," he announced.

The doorman, still listening on the phone, said, "I'll take it," and held out his hand.

"Hell you will, bro," Leroy said. "I ain't gettin' done outa ma tip."

To be honest, Leroy's attempt at talking jive left a little bit to be desired, but I wasn't about to complain, and the doorman wasn't about to notice.

The doorman was overmatched. Leroy and the Supreme Court might not have intimidated him, but Mrs. Goldstein sure did. The beleaguered man waved Leroy on up, so he could give her his full attention.

After considerable negotiation, I went up, too. I'd known I would. In the long run, Mrs. Goldstein just had to find out what it was all about.

I hadn't stuck around while she found out what it was all about, since I knew damn well that as soon as she turned to page two she was going to discover she was being sued for owning a building on Patchen Avenue in Brooklyn where someone had fallen down and broken their wrist due to a faulty riser on the stair. I had signed that case myself, and from what I remembered of the neighborhood, I was sure Mrs. Goldstein wouldn't have been caught dead anywhere near Patchen Avenue in Brooklyn, so I made damn sure I was out of sight around the corner of the corridor before she got to the second page.

Moments later, I joined Leroy in front of Albrect's door. Leroy clicked the lock back, stood up, smiled, and said, "There you are."

"I really appreciate this, Leroy," I told him. "Could I compensate you for helping me out?"

Leroy held up his hand, palm out. "That will not be necessary," he said. He fished in his pocket and produced a dollar bill. "Miss Hartman has already taken care of it."

We shook hands and Leroy took his leave, commenting that it would be just his luck to be apprehended breaking and entering when he had no intention to steal. He was heading for the elevator as I let myself into the apartment.

Albrect's apartment was a large one-bedroom that probably set him back $1200 a month. I proceeded to take it apart. I wasn't sure what I was looking for; I just knew it would be something Albrect didn't want anybody to find. I tried to put myself in Albrect's shoes and imagine what I would do if I were Albrect, but that made me nauseous. Instead I just tried to figure out what Albrect might do if he had something to hide. The inside of the mattress or the pages of a book would probably seem like nifty hiding places to him. I pulled out the mattress and searched it, but there were no incisions. I started in on the books. I was halfway through the second shelf when I found it. It was pressed between the pages of "Portnoy's Complaint," but I tried to attach no undue significance to that. I mean, hell, I like to pull the old pud every now and then myself, even after ten years of marriage. So I concentrated on what I'd found.

It was a photo I.D. bank card made out to Martin Albrect. It seemed to me Albrect looked a little nervous in the photograph, but I might have been projecting. After all, I knew Albrect was dead, I knew he'd hidden it, and I knew one other thing. The card was for a Miami bank.

8

MY WIFE'S FACE WAS A PICTURE OF DESPAIR AS I RANG
FOR THE ELEVATOR. "You re really going out tonight?"
she said.

"We need the money, and I had another slow day."

"How slow?"

"A signup in Brooklyn. Ocean Parkway."

That was a half-truth. I'd gotten the assignment all
right, but I hadn't done it. By the time I'd finished
with Albrect's apartment it'd been too late to go out
there, and I'd called and changed the appointment to
tomorrow morning.

"What do you have to do tonight?"

"I got two summonses in Brooklyn and a signed
statement in Queens."

"Can't you do them during the day?"

"I've tried. People aren't home during the day."

"I know. I just hate you going out at night. It's bad
enough you going into those neighborhoods during the
day."

"It's perfectly safe," I lied to her. "No one's ever
bothered me."

No one had ever bothered me, but a couple of
junkies had once assured me if I went into a particular
building I would be mugged, and I would not have
had to look much farther than them to find the
potential muggers. I'd wound up calling the client on
the phone and having him come downstairs, broken leg
and all.

"I know," she said, "but there's always a first time. I worry about you."

She does, and I'm sure it's her constant worrying about me that helps fuel my own paranoia. It's bad enough going into those neighborhoods without always being reminded how scary they are.

"Look, I gotta run," I said. "My appointment with the witness is at eight."

"Just be careful," she said.

The elevator arrived and I stepped in and heaved a sigh of relief as the door closed behind me. Jerry, the young elevator man proceeded to regale me with how well the Mets were doing, and how poorly the Red Sox were doing, all the way down to the first floor, but I barely listened. I had an eight o'clock appointment, all right, but it wasn't with a witness in Queens. It was with Michael Murphy, alias Dumbo, of Fabri-Tec Inc., who was taking me out for an evening at an illegal casino.

Since I'd told Murphy I'd meet him in front of the Sheraton, where I was presumably staying, it would have been easier for me just to take the Broadway IRT downtown, but I was afraid Alice might take Tommie out for pizza and notice my car still parked on our block. I got in the car and drove up to the Chemical Bank at 113th Street, which has a cash machine. I'd never been to an illegal casino but, smart detective that I am, I figured money might come in handy.

The line at the machine wasn't that long. I double-parked, hopped out, pulled out my Chem Card, and five minutes later the machine spewed out 200 dollars in nice crisp twenties, the maximum withdrawal you were allowed in any one day. I noticed on the receipt that my bank balance had dropped from $329.15 to $129.15.

The nice thing about the cash machine was that my wife wouldn't know I'd used it until the statement came at the end of the month. Just so long as she didn't write too many checks and discover she was overdrawn.

I drove down into the eighties, which I figured was safe enough, found a parking spot on West 87th Street, and left the car. I caught the IRT at Broadway and 86th Street, rode down to 50th Street, walked to the Sheraton, and was standing right outside when Murphy drew up front in a cab at 8:05.

"Hop in," he said. "Next stop, Playland."

I got in and the cab headed downtown. Murphy and I exchanged a little small talk, but I could see something was on his mind.

"I've been thinking about your proposition," he said finally.

I'd been afraid of that. It was one thing to spew out a bullshit line of goods to try to get something out of somebody, but it was something else to keep up the facade after they'd had time to think it over.

"Oh yeah," I said.

"Yeah," he said. "There's gotta be a way to check the references."

"There is," I told him. "Just hop on the big bird to F-L-A."

"I can't do that," he said, and I was extremely grateful. "I mean without doing that. There must be some way I can check you out from here. Some way you can assure me of payment."

"No problem," I told him. "I'll just win 50 G's tonight at the table, and we'll use that as collateral."

We laughed about that, and while it didn't satisfy him, it put off the conversation until the taxi drew up in front of an old factory building on Crosby Street. I got out and stood on the sidewalk while Murphy paid off the cab. If there was a casino in the area, I wouldn't have known it. The place looked dead.

"Right this way," Murphy said, taking my arm and heading for the front of the factory building, which had to be one of the darkest buildings on the block, which was saying something. Next to the door was an old rusted bell button which looked as if it had been years since it had been connected to anything. Murphy pressed it. Nothing happened. No ring from deep within the building. No light flashing on. I had a faint flash of paranoia, wondering if somehow Murphy had figured out who I was, if this was somehow his idea of a bad joke, or worse, if he was somehow more deeply involved in this than I thought he was and had been given instructions to "take care of me."

Before I had too long to dwell on this, there came a clanking sound from overhead. I looked up, and saw an old-fashioned, open-sided freight elevator slowly descending from the 4th floor. There was a guy in it, operating it, and while he wasn't pulling a rope hand-over-hand to make it move, the actual mechanism couldn't have been much more sophisticated than that. The elevator clanked to a stop and the guy opened the door.

"Hi, Jack," Murphy said. Then, indicating me, "He's with me."

We stepped inside and Jack closed the iron gate. He pulled the lever and the platform lurched slowly upward.

The elevator squeaked to a stop on the 4th floor. Jack opened the iron gate on the opposite side from where we got in and we all stepped off into a small, dimly lit alcove. Jack pressed against the far wall, which proved to be a door, and let us into another small, dimly lit alcove. Jack closed the door behind us, made sure it was tightly latched, and then opened a similar door on the far wall.

I was immediately assaulted by noise and light. I don't know what kind of soundproofing they were using in the building, but it must have been fantastic. The din coming out of the casino was incredible. Rock music only served to underscore the sound of voices, whir of wheels, click of balls. The place was mobbed. I just stood there a moment, staring. Then Murphy put his hand on my shoulder and guided me through the crunch of people into the room.

"What's your pleasure?" he shouted in my ear.

"Roulette," I shouted back.

I was glad Murphy had asked. To tell the truth, not only had I never been in an illegal gambling joint before, I had never been in a legal one, either. My entire gambling experience consisted of poker. I did know, though, that in roulette you bet on the numbers, on red or black, or odd or even, or something like that, and I figured I could fake my way through it, whereas, if Murphy got me at the crap table, I'd be lost.

With some relief, then, I followed Murphy over to one of the roulette tables, and we elbowed our way into positions by the board and watched as the ball revolved around the wheel and settled in number five.

"Five, black, low and odd," said the croupier, or something to that effect. I know five is low and odd, but whether it's red or black I don't remember. At any rate, whichever it is, he said it, and then raked in over three-quarters of the outstanding bets.

Murphy pulled out a wad of money and I followed suit, peeling five twenties off my roll and trying to look as if this was just the tip of the iceberg in terms of a sizable bankroll. Murphy bought ten-dollar chips, so I did too, though my heart longed for fives. We began placing bets around the table and, to my great relief, in the beginning I won a little. Nothing much, of course—I'd miss on the number but hit red or black, or odd or even, and I did it often enough that my bankroll began to grow a little. As soon as it did, I began exhibiting the poor gambler's signs of nervousness, cashing in chips, leaving myself short and having to buy new ones, pulling money out of different pockets, counting it, putting it back. This is bad form, I know. In the song "The Gambler," Kenny Rogers says, "Never count your money while you're sittin' at the table," but I think that's bullshit. I've found from playing poker that the best procedure is to count your money all the time, over and over again, keeping up a running patter about how poorly you're doing and how much you're losing. I've found that by doing this, no one ever has the faintest idea how well I'm actually doing and, even in games where I've been the only winner at the table, I've been able to cash in and leave with everyone thinking I was over a hundred dollars down. I don't mean to give the impression that I usually win at poker—I don't, I usually lose. All I'm saying is, the few times I have won, I've found this procedure to be fundamentally sound.

Sound or not, it was irritating Murphy, even more so because he happened to be losing.

"What're you cashing in for?" he groused. "You only have to keep buying new ones."

"You're right," I said. "I'm a lousy gambler. But I really love the game, you know."

"Yeah. I know what you mean," he said.

The croupier swept away all of Murphy's bets and paid off two out of three of mine, even and the first twelve numbers. I'd lost on red.

A tall, thin man with razor-cut black hair, a soap opera star plastic profile, and a six hundred dollar suit with white shirt open at the neck displaying a bunch of gold chains, threaded his way through the crowd to Murphy's side.

"Hey, Murphy," he said, clapping him on the back. "How's it going?"

"Bad, Tony," Murphy said. "Can't get a nibble."

"Your luck will change," Tony told him. "Who's your friend?"

"Tony, this is Nathan Armstrong, a business acquain-.tance from Miami. Nathan, this is Tony Arroyo. This is his little club."

"Ah, Bambi," I thought to myself as I smiled and shook his hand.

"Armstrong's a business acquaintance of Marty Albrect's," Murphy added by way of explanation.

It seemed to me Tony's eyelids flicked before he smiled and said, "Oh yeah? How come you didn't bring Albrect along with you?"

Murphy looked at him. "Oh. You haven't heard."

"Heard what?"

"Jeez, Tony, I hate to tell you this. Albrect's dead."

"What? Dead? You're kidding."

"No, I'm not. He was killed. Just last night. Shot to death in a parking lot.

"Oh, my God," Tony said, shaking his head. "Well, it figures. I used to warn him. He was never careful, you know. Always flashing a wad when he was flush. Always talking too much. I knew he was going to get rolled one of those nights. It had to happen. You can't say I didn't warn him."

"Sure, Tony," Murphy said. "I heard you say it."

Listening to the conversation convinced me of two things. First, if Tony was involved in Albrect's death, Murphy didn't know it, and second, Tony's involvement was a given. I'd have bet my life on it. Tony did a pretty good job of being surprised at the news, but he didn't quite pull it off. He wasn't that good an actor. I ought to know, because I used to be an actor myself when I first got out of college, and I wasn't that good an actor either. If I had been, I would have made a living at it, and I never would have become a writer, and if I'd never become a writer, I never would have become a private detective, and if I'd never become a private detective, I never would have found myself in the position of standing around an illegal gambling casino talking to the guy who ran the place, who—I was damn well sure—also happened to be at the very least an accessory to murder.

"Well," Tony said, turning his attention back to me. "You say you're from Miami?"

"Yeah."

"You up here on business with Albrect?"

"That's right."

"Well, that's a kick in the face, ain't it? So, how's this affect you? You gonna be in town long?"

"Not any more," I said. "I'm going back tomorrow morning."

"You driving down?" Tony asked casually.

My stomach suddenly felt hollow. This was it. All I had to do was say, "yes," and things would start happening. I knew it. Albrect had been driving pick-

ups from Miami. Albrect was dead. They needed someone else to do it. Bambi was looking for someone,
putting out feelers. He'd asked me the question. All I
had to do was say "Yes."

"Gosh, no," I said. "Take forever. I'm flying, of
course."

"Of course," Tony said. He patted Murphy on the
back, nodded to me, nodded to the croupier, and left.

From that point on I lost. I couldn't swear that
Tony's nod to the croupier had anything to do with it,
but it had to figure. I was there for one night. There
was no reason to let me win so they would get me
hooked and take me for a fortune later. And I wasn't
going to develop into the driver they needed for the
Miami run. From the casino's standpoint, there was no
reason to let me win at all, and from then on I didn't
even come close.

Due to my creative bankrolling, I still had 150 dollars of my stake money tucked in my side pocket when
I was able to shove my last chip on the table and
declare I was broke.

Murphy was disappointed. "It's only midnight," he
said. "This place doesn't close till four. Let me loan
you a little stake. We can straighten it out in the
morning."

"Nope," I said. "When your luck's bad, it's bad.
Believe me, tonight mine's bad. And I want to get a
little sleep before my flight, anyway. I can't sleep on
airplanes. Too nervous, I guess. Anyway, don't let me
spoil your fun. Thanks for the invite. I'll give you a
call from Miami when I get back."

Murphy seemed glad to be off the hook. "You sure
you can get uptown all right? It's not easy to get a cab
around here."

I grinned. "If I'd won I'd be worried about it. You
can't mug a loser. I'll be all right."

"You got cabfare?"

"Always save cabfare. See you."

Jack took me down in the freight elevator and spewed
me out into the darkened street. Despite the bravado

of my statement to Murphy, I wasn't too keen about being out there at midnight. I stepped along briskly in the deserted street, and felt the old 718 surge of relief when a solitary cab with the light on came around a corner and picked me up.

I took the cab back uptown to get my car. I discovered I'd parked right in front of Murder Ink., the detective bookstore. How symbolic, I thought ironically. Yeah, sure, me and Phillip Marlowe.

I drove back downtown to 7th Street and Avenue B to check on Gutierrez's girlfriend. I'd been there once already, right after I finished with Gutierrez's apartment, but she'd been out. I parked on the corner across the street, and had just gotten out of my car, when a girl emerged from a doorway halfway down the block and began walking down the street away from me. From that angle, I couldn't tell which door she'd come out of, but it seemed to be damn near the candy store. I quickly locked the car, neglecting for once to turn the code alarm on, and hurried down the block to the candy store. An old lady was sitting on the front steps. She didn't look like a bag lady, but she didn't look too many steps up the social ladder either.

"Is Rosa around?" I asked her.

I expected her to tell me to go to hell, or go see for myself, but she didn't. "She just left," she said, jerking her head in the direction of the girl I had seen coming out of the building. The girl had just reached the end of the block and was starting to cross Avenue B.

I could have yelled her name and run after her. That certainly would have made more sense to the old lady than what I actually did do, which was turn around and walk as briskly as I could back to my car. But I didn't really care what the old lady thought, and somehow the idea of shouting at and running after a young lady who'd never seen me before in her life, at one in the morning, didn't strike me as the height of investigative technique. I pulled out from the curb and sped down Avenue B. I was about to make a right turn on

6th Street to follow the girl when I suddenly realized it was a one-way street in the opposite direction. There were no cars around at that time in the morning, and I probably could have made it down the block without incident, but somehow driving the wrong way down a one-way street didn't seem the best way of being inconspicuous. Even if the girl were a stoned-out junkie, she couldn't help but notice me. I looked down the street, saw that the girl was walking right along, and figured it was a safe bet she was headed for Avenue A. At any rate, I'd have to chance it. I sped on down to 5th Street, ran the light which had just turned red, hung a right on 5th, and gunned it over to Avenue A, where I turned right again, running another light, sped up Avenue A to the corner of 6th Street, pulled into the curb, and killed the lights and motor. I was close enough to the corner so that I could see about a quarter of the way down the block. The girl wasn't in sight yet, but before I had time to start worrying about it, she came into view, stepping right along. She reached the corner and looked up and down Avenue A, obviously searching for a cab. There were none. She dug in her purse, fished out a pack of cigarettes, and lit one. I might have driven up and offered her a ride, except for two things. One was I probably would have scared her to death. The other was the way she was dressed. She was right under a street light, and I could see her pretty well. She was wearing a very short skirt, fishnet stockings, and high heels. A bright red blouse, loose and clinging, showed off a pair of absolutely fantastic breasts, which were obviously unhampered by any undergarment. And her face was made up much more heavily and garishly than she could ever have possibly needed. Now I'm not the smartest, or most experienced, or astutest detective in the world, but I had a pretty good idea of where she was going and what she was doing, and I wanted to see if I was right.

A cab came along and she flagged it down and got in. I followed the cab uptown to 48th Street and

Broadway, where she got out and paid it off. She went to the corner and stuck out her leg. Within five minutes a man stopped to talk with her.

I followed them up the block to one of those cheap hotels where they rented the same room ten times a night. She and the guy went in. He was out twenty minutes later, and she was out in twenty-five. She headed back to Broadway.

I had the whole setup now, and it was just what I had figured. Without Gutierrez to keep her in drugs, she had to make it on her own, so she was tricking to get enough money to score.

I wondered if she knew anything that could help me. I realized it would have been the easiest thing in the world to make the contact. I had 150 bucks in my pocket I'd saved from the casino. All I had to do was walk up to her and say, "Hi." I mean, I'm human, for God's sake, and she sure did have glorious boobs. But, on the other hand, I'd probably catch something. In fact, with my luck, I'd probably catch everything. How would I explain it to my wife? Herpes, syphilis, and crabs, all caught in the line of duty. I'd probably get AIDS too, as a sort of bonus.

I sat in my car and watched Rosa work the street. She was good at it. She had no trouble hooking them, and no trouble getting rid of them either. In the next hour and fifteen minutes she turned three more tricks. That must have been enough, because the last time she came out of the hotel, instead of taking up her position on the corner, she went straight to the pay phone and made a call. I wasn't anywhere near close enough to hear what she was saying, but I knew she got an answer because I could see her head bobbing up and down and her lips moving. She was on the phone less than a minute. She hung up, walked out onto Broadway, and hailed a cab.

I followed the cab to an address on East 64th Street. It was a townhouse just like all the other buildings on the block, except it was the only one with the upstairs light on. Rosa got out of the cab, went up the steps to the front door, and rang the bell. About thirty seconds later a man opened the door and let her in. The light was poor, and the best I could make out was he was young enough to have dark hair, and he wore a maroon robe.

The door closed behind them. I sat in the car with my lights out, waiting. I had what I wanted now. I figured this guy had to be Rosa's connection, and therefore Gutierrez's connection, and therefore the guy the coke had flowed through before the deal went bad. Perhaps he was even Pluto himself. I had the guy's address and I could check him out at my leisure. But I decided to wait anyway. I didn't figure Rosa would be long. Just a quick score and out of there. The connection wouldn't be tempted by her body, great knockers notwithstanding. He'd recognize the uniform, just as I had, and wouldn't be keen on banging her after coming off an evening of turning tricks. Besides, a big coke and skag connection in an East Side townhouse who was up at 3:00 in the morning would undoubtedly have one or two fifteen-year-old nymphets sitting on his face and plunging his drug-inflamed tool into every orifice. And Rosa, having scored, would be eager to get on home. Despite the fact she had let the cab go, I figured she'd be quick.

She was out in five minutes. She walked briskly to the avenue and caught a cab downtown. I figured she was on her way home, but I tagged along just to make sure. She was. The cab let her out in front of the candy store, and she went straight inside and up the stairs, nodding as she passed to the old lady, who was still sitting on the front steps and who showed no signs of moving. I didn't know what *her* story was, but fortunately, as far as I knew, it didn't concern me, for which I was thankful.

I checked my watch. It was nearly 3:30. I drove back over to Crosby Street and parked a block away from the casino. About a quarter of four the elevator began disgorging loads of tired gamblers. At 4:15 Tony Arroyo came out. As soon as he appeared on the sidewalk, a limo that had been parked in the shadows roared into life and pulled up in front of the door. Tony got in and the car pulled away. I followed more carefully this time. It was one thing to tail a hooker in a taxi. It was something else to follow a guy in a chauffeured limousine, particularly when that guy is probably connected with people who have a habit of cutting people's cocks off.

If the chauffeur had the faintest idea he was being followed, he didn't show it. He drove straight uptown and pulled up to a luxury apartment building on East 58th Street, one of those buildings that is so posh it has a circular driveway for cars to pull in to drop off tenants right at the front door. Tony got out and went in and the limo drove off.

I sat and looked at the building for a while. A thought kept nagging at me, and finally I couldn't resist. I drove to the corner, parked, got out, and went to the pay phone. I dialed information, and asked if they had a Manhattan listing for a Tony Arroyo. Yes, they had a Tony Arroyo on East 58th Street. They even gave me the address. It was the building I had just seen him go into.

It figured. Tony could have had an unlisted number, or the phone company could have refused to confirm the address but, no, it was right there for the asking. Some detective. I stake out a casino at four in the morning, follow the guy home, worrying the whole time about being spotted by his chauffeur, and what do I learn? The same thing I could have got by just picking up the phone and dialing information in the first place.

But that didn't really matter. And it didn't really bother me. After all, all the running around I'd been doing wasn't that important, and it didn't really accomplish anything. It was just jerking off. It was just me trying to keep busy and pretend I was doing something, to make up for the fact that I had muffed the really big play, the golden opportunity I had had back in the casino when Tony had asked me if I were driving down to Miami. It had been right there, and I had blown it, muffed it, chickened out. Oh, I could justify my decision a lot of ways. If I said I was driving to Miami, I'd have to go through with it. How could I do that? I don't have the time. I don't have the money. What could I tell my wife? What could I tell Richard?

But that didn't really wash. I didn't have to go to Miami. There would be ways to get out of that. Hell, I didn't even have to agree to the proposition, assuming that Tony got around to making me one. All I had to do was say "Yes, I'm driving to Miami," and see what happened next. But I hadn't done that.

I always knew I had my limitations. I'm not particularly strong, but I've always been athletic. In high school I was the high scorer on the basketball team, the shortstop on the baseball team, the first man on the tennis team, and the goalie on the soccer team. But those are all skill sports, sports requiring coordination and finesse, but not great strength. I could never have played football. They'd have eaten me alive. Anything requiring confrontation, aggression, or assertion was just beyond me.

My wife was right, I realized, in her presumed opinion of me. The reason I never made it as a writer, or an actor for that matter, was that I never had the stuff. I never had the courage to get out there and hustle, to confront new situations, to meet new people, to assert myself, to get ahead. And it wasn't just fear of failure. It was fear, plain and simple. Just fear. When push came to shove, when the chips were down, I was a bloody fucking coward.

It was a hell of a realization to come to at four-thirty in the morning on a dark, deserted street corner in midtown Manhattan.

9

I FELT LIKE HELL RIDING THE SUBWAY DOWNTOWN THE
NEXT MORNING, and it wasn't just the fact that I'd
gotten approximately an hour and a half of sleep. I felt
like hell because I was on my way to my office to
check my mail and pick up my messages before I
headed out to Brooklyn to sign up Mrs. Rabinowitz
and her broken leg, when in my heart of hearts what I
really wanted to be doing was catching an early morning flight down to Miami to check out what was in
Martin Albrect's safe deposit box. That's what I should
have been doing. That's what any fucking detective
worth his salt would have been doing. But I couldn't
do it. Even if I had the guts to say "fuck it," to leave
Mrs. Rabinowitz in the lurch one more time, to kiss
off the day's work and head South, I simply couldn't
do it. Because, unlike any detective I've ever heard
about, I didn't have the money. Even if I went to the
cash machine and drew out every penny left in my
account, that, added to what I had left from the casino, wouldn't be enough. I had a Master Charge card,
but it had a $1500 limit, and I'd been hovering in the
high 1400's for the last year and a half. If I presented
it at the airlines, the computer would register "tilt,"
and the nice girl at the airline counter would take out
a scissors and cut my card into little pieces right then
and there, as she had been trained to do.

What made this even more frustrating was the fact
that I was sure I could do it. I was sure it would work.

I had Albrect's key and I had Albrect's bank I.D. card. True, the card had Albrect's picture on it and not mine, but that didn't seem too serious a problem to me.

Half to see if I could do it, and half to torture myself, I stopped at a shop on 42nd Street and had my picture taken in the automatic photo booth. I went into another little shop and asked them if they could make me a photo I.D. They said "sure." I gave them Albrect's I.D. and my photo, and ten minutes and five dollars later I was walking out of the place with a bank I.D. absolutely identical to Albrect's, with the exception of the fact that it had my picture on it.

As I had expected, having the I.D. only made it worse. I was in a hell of a frame of mind when I put my key in the door and unlocked the office.

The mail was already there lying on the floor. It would be bills. Whenever the mail came early, it was always bills. This time there were three of them, and they couldn't have come at a worse time. What with my casino withdrawal, it was going to be touch and go whether I could cover them.

The first bill was from the Penny Copy Center—$7.80 for Xeroxing a hundred copies of my time sheets, the daily vouchers that I turned in bi-weekly to Richard's office in order to get paid. Not too bad. The second wasn't a bill at all, just an appeal from some charity. I threw it in the wastebasket. The last one was the killer. It was the Master Charge bill. Shit! I'd fogotten all about it. The Master Charge bill always came a little bit after all the other monthly bills, and I'd forgotten it hadn't come yet this month. They only gave you ten days to pay, too. This was going to put a big hole in the account. I sighed and ripped it open.

It wasn't a bill. It was a letter. Stripped of its delicate phrasing and cheerful terminology, what it actually said was this: because I was fully charged to the limit on my account and had been for some time, because I was a poor schmuck who could never afford to reduce the principal of the debt, but dutifully every month forked over the exorbitant interest charge, because I was in every aspect exactly the sort of sucker these people made their enormous profit from, they were delighted to inform me that they were raising my credit limit from $1500 to $2000.

10

MY PLANE SET DOWN IN MIAMI AT 12:45. I rented a car
at the airport, followed the stream of traffic, and headed
for what I presumed was downtown Miami. I'd never
been to Miami before, and I had no idea at all what
the city was like. I stopped at the first stationery store
I came to and bought a Hagstrom map, god love 'em.
More than a few times a Hagstrom map had bailed me
out when I couldn't find a client's address. I checked
the address on my bank card, and found I was heading
in only slightly the wrong direction. I made a couple of
turns, and ten minutes later I was driving by the First
National Bank of Miami, big as life.

I looked around for a parking space, but the bank
was in a metropolitan area where signs were proclaim-
ing no parking under penalty of death. I cruised around
for about ten minutes trying to find a meter. I must
have passed a dozen garages and parking lots on the
way. I told myself I was doing this to save money.
Bullshit, myself answered back. You're just stalling
because you don't want to go into the bank, just like
you're afraid of any new situation. I had just about
sold myself on giving in and entering a garage when I
found a parking meter not two blocks from the bank. I
pulled in, and put a quarter in the meter. It was a
one-hour meter, and I wondered if that would be
enough. Asshole, I told myself. If it goes well, you'll
be out in no time. If it doesn't go well, you'll be

arrested for forgery, extortion, and attempted grand larceny, so why are you sweating a parking ticket?

I straightened my tie, took out my briefcase, and walked to the bank.

I couldn't see very well through the window, just enough to tell that it was big and it was busy, both of which were good. I went inside and found it was a bank, similar to the banks in New York. A long line of people were queueing up and making their way through a labyrinth of ropes as they waited for the tellers, three-quarters of whose windows had signs that said "CLOSED." To the right of them was a fenced-off area where bank officials of various ages, sexes, and races sat behind desks with name plaques on them. The bank officials were talking on the telephone, talking with each other, eating sandwiches, reading periodicals, and for the most part doing their best to ignore the somewhat shorter line of people waiting to do business with them.

At the far end of the bank was a glass door on which the gold letters, "SAFE DEPOSIT" were emblazoned. I went to the door and looked in. Unfortunately, the blank wall of a small hallway to the left was all I could see. This was too bad. I would have liked some reassurance—for instance, a room with four or five people manning the desk. This was not just paranoia. Albrect must have rented the box within the last couple of months. I had to hope the guy I was about to talk to wouldn't be the guy who rented it to him, wouldn't know damn well who Martin Albrect was, and know damn well I wasn't him.

There was a button on the wall next to the door. I took a deep breath and pressed it. Seconds later, a buzzer sounded. I pulled the door open and went in.

About ten feet down the corridor was a small alcove where a lone, elderly man with bifocals and a stubby cigar sat at a counter.

"Yeah," he grunted.

I slid the I.D. card and the key across the counter. He slid the key back at once, a gesture that eloquently told me he was dealing with an idiot who didn't know the system, that he dealt with idiots who didn't know the system often, and that if people had half the brains they were born with, his job wouldn't be such a pain in the ass.

He took my card, looked it over, put it in a small machine similar to a Master Card charge machine. He slid a form into the machine, pulled the handle across, and printed the information from the card onto the form. He took the card out of the machine and slid it back to me. He took the form out of the machine, picked up a pen, and made a big "X" on it where I was supposed to sign, just in case, as he suspected, I was a total idiot who couldn't read the word "Signature." He turned the form around and slid it over to me.

I had practiced signing the name Martin Albrect all the way down on the plane, and had gotten pretty good at it. It was a little different doing it without bumping along through air pockets, but I managed a pretty good facsimile.

It didn't matter. I could have written John Doe on the form for all this guy cared. He pressed a button on his desk, and a security guard appeared from a door down the hall. For a second I thought they had me, but the old guy just handed the security guard a key, said "Box 372," and the guard nodded and started down the hallway with me following.

With our two keys, the guard and I unlocked #372, which proved to be a rectangular box about a foot wide, a foot high, and two feet deep.

The guard brought the box into a private alcove. I followed with my briefcase. I half expected the guard to look at my briefcase and say, "You can't bring that in here," but then I remembered this was my safe deposit box and I could damn well put in or take out any goddamn thing I wanted. The guard withdrew and closed the door.

I lifted the lid and looked in. In the box were an envelope and a package. I picked up the envelope first. It was unsealed. I pulled out the contents. It was money. One thousand dollars in crisp, new hundred-dollar bills. I counted it twice, put it back in the envelope, and stuffed the envelope in my jacket pocket.

I took out the package. It consisted of a large manila envelope, folded in half and held with string. It was heavy, weighing, I guessed, about two pounds. I squeezed it, and the contents gave slightly. It was somewhat like squeezing a bag of sugar.

I put the package in my briefcase, closed the safe deposit box, opened the door, and summoned the guard. Together, we put the box back and locked it in place.

The old man buzzed me through the door again, and I walked out through the bank. No sirens went off. No police appeared to handcuff me and take me away. I went out the front door and walked the two blocks to my car. I still had 40 minutes on the meter. Well, someone else could have 'em. I got in the car, drove to a Sheraton Motor Lodge, and rented a room.

If the fact that I had no luggage other than a briefcase bothered anybody, it didn't show. The bellhop escorted me to my room, accepted my dollar tip with the gracelessness of someone who is being paid something for nothing, and withdrew.

The room had two double beds, a color TV, a couple of dressers, and a round table with four chairs.

I put my briefcase on the table, sat down, opened it up, and took out the package. I slid the string off, and unfolded the manila envelope, which was both clasped and sealed. I couldn't be bothered with it. I tore the end off and slid out the contents—a large, heavy-duty, Ziploc plastic bag. I knew the bag well. My father-in-law still sold them. He didn't manufacture them—the Ziploc bag was a patented item upon which he couldn't infringe—so it was one of the few bags he still jobbed. He sold a lot of them in his day, but he sold 'em empty. And if I was right about the contents, this one bag was worth more than any goddamned Ziploc bag order he ever filled.

The bag was rolled up and held by heavy-duty rub-
ber bands. I slid them off and unrolled it. Inside were
huge chunks of a white, rocky, crystalline substance. I
pulled apart the top of the bag, stuck my finger in, got
a few small chips on my finger, and stuck it in my
mouth. It was bitter, which was a good sign, and it
numbed my gums, which was another good sign, so I
figured it must be coke. But then I remembered a
friend of mine telling me that some of the things they
use to cut cocaine, procaine for instance, had the same
properties as cocaine. So this could either be coke or
cut. The only difference was, one got you high, and
one didn't. I had to be sure, so I figured the only way
to be sure was to sample some.

This presented a bit of a problem. Even if I'd had a
razor blade, which I didn't, the coke was so hard and
compressed that chopping a line fine enough to snort
was going to be quite an undertaking. I sealed up the
package, locked it in my briefcase, and stashed the
briefcase under the bed.

I went out and hunted up a head shop. I was a little
nervous about it. I couldn't help wondering if narcs
kept watch on head shops and tailed people who bought
drug paraphernalia, but logic told me no. They'd have
to follow everyone.

I went in and told the guy at the counter I wanted
something to grind up a crystalline substance. He gave
me a look not unlike the one given me by the guy at
the safe deposit counter in the bank, then showed me
a three-piece plastic grinder that was just the ticket.
When I told him it would do, he asked me knowingly
if I'd be interested in a straw. I allowed as to how I
would, and he showed me one. It was gold-plated on a
gold neck-chain and went for $85. I asked if he had
something simpler. The cheapest straw he had was of
a baser metal—price $9.95.

I decided to pass on the straw. I stopped at a news-
stand down the street and bought a can of cold soda
for 65 cents. The proprietor put it in a paper bag with
a straw. Outside, I threw the paper bag and the can of

soda in the garbage, and put the straw in my jacket pocket.

I walked back to the hotel, went up to my room, and made sure the door was securely locked. I took the briefcase out from under the bed, put it on the table, opened it, and took out the plastic bag. I unwrapped the grinder, took it out, and unscrewed and took off the grinder top. I removed a couple of smaller chunks from the bag. They were so hard I was afraid they would break the screen. I took out my pocket knife, and crunched them up against the top of the table, and then scraped the results onto the screen of the grinder, screwed on the top, flipped out the lever, and began to twist. The sound was somewhat grating as with each bumpy revolution the plastic blades on the grinder pressed the tiny rocks into the screen. The grating gradually lessened, and the grinding got smoother. I stopped, unscrewed the bottom of the grinder. It was covered with a fine, white powder about a quarter of an inch deep. I dumped some of it out on the smooth surface of the table, took a matchbook cover, compliments of the hotel, and fashioned a decent-sized line.

I took the straw out of my pocket, unwrapped it and, with my pocket knife, cut it in half. I murmured, "Cheers," stuck the straw in my right nostril, leaned over the table, and snorted the line.

I must admit that my experience with coke had been rather limited. In fact, it consisted of the time a guy at one of the poker games had persuaded me to try a line. It was not a particularly memorable experience. Aside from a general sense of well-being which lasted about a half an hour, I don't remember feeling anything much at all. I just remember thinking that, as far as cocaine was concerned, I really couldn't see what all the shouting was about.

In light of that experience, I was in no way prepared for what happened next. My head shot back, my eyes teared, and my breath shot out in a whoosh. Jesus Christ! That's not coke. What the hell is it?

Then I realized. The coke I'd snorted at the card game had passed through many hands, and been cut and recut many times, so it was doubtful if it was even a tenth as pure as the line I'd snorted now. This stuff was, as Coca Cola puts it, "The Real Thing."

I'd just had time to work this out when the coke hit me. Christ, did it hit me! My whole outlook changed. I could rule the world. Suddenly, I wasn't douche-bag, ineffectual detective; I was super-cool, super-successful, super-stud detective. Hell, I'd come to Miami, hadn't I? Walked into the bank and walked out clean with ten C-notes and a key of pure snow. All deduced and tracked down from the vague ramblings of a paranoid client who couldn't or wouldn't get to the point. God, I was doing great. Hey, I thought, give me a shot at Tony Arroyo's proposal now. Give me another chance to play that scene and I'll show you some cool moves. Christ, I'd have the dope ring rounded up and Albrect's murderer in jail by this time tomorrow.

11

LIKE ANYONE CAUGHT IN THE GRIP OF DELUSIONS OF
GRANDEUR, I was sure I could get away with anything.
Which is why I called my wife from the hotel phone to
tell her I'd be late for dinner. Hell, I charged it to my
room number, so she wouldn't even catch on when the
telephone bill came next month. It was a piece of
cake.

There's nothing that brings you down faster than a
good dose of reality, which in my case is usually a
good dose of my wife. As I've said, my wife is a very
nice person unless she's provoked, and this time I had
the misfortune to catch her provoked. She was really
pissed off.

"Where the hell are you?" she asked.

"Working," I told her. "I'm out on a case."

"That's not what your office says. They've called
here three times. Some client out in Brooklyn is having a shit fit because you never showed up. They've
been beeping you all day, but you don't answer."

Not surprising. My beeper has a 75 mile radius,
which made it fairly useless in Miami. I'd left it in the
office.

"Oh shit, my batteries must be dead," I said. It was
a terrible excuse. When the batteries went dead, the
beeper automatically began emitting a sickly, wailing
beep to inform you of the fact. But my wife didn't
know that.

"Yeah, well then why didn't you call your office, for

Christ's sake. And what's all this about some client in Brooklyn you stood up?"

"I didn't stand her up. I went there and she wasn't home. It's the same old bullshit. I wasn't going to stand around there waiting for her so I went out on some other assignments. I've been calling her. First I got no answer. Now every time I call the line's busy, which must be her wearing out the phone bitching that I'm not there yet. It's the same old bullshit. What are you getting so upset about?"

"It's the same old bullshit, but it's not *my* bullshit. Why the hell are they calling me?"

"Because you're there," I said.

"Oh, great! Good answer. Listen, will you get your act together and get some new batteries and call your office and tell 'em to leave me alone?"

"No problem," I told her. "And I'll get ahold of the client and straighten it out. I'll have to go out there, which means I won't be home for dinner."

"What a surprise," she said, and hung up the phone.

Well, one down and two to go. I called the office, fed them the same bullshit story. I got Susan, which was a blessing this time, as she was more apt to be sympathetic, and less apt to be suspicious. Still, the beeper story didn't sit well. Susan knew how it worked and knew my batteries couldn't have just gone dead.

"Listen," I said. "Do me a favor. Cover for me. The truth is, I forgot to turn the damn thing on."

She laughed at that and I knew I was home free. I assured her I'd get right on the Rabinowitz case and hung up.

I called Mrs. Rabinowitz and made up another bullshit story. A three-car accident on the Major Deegan. Two people killed. No, I hadn't been involved, but I had seen the whole thing and the police had dragged me in as a witness after the tow trucks and ambulances had finally left and they'd gotten all the traffic unsnarled. Yes, I should have called, but you know what cops are like. Mrs. Rabinowitz probably didn't know what cops were like, but she probably had some fairly fixed notions. At any rate, she went from overtly hostile to mildly sympathetic in the course of the conversation, and promised not to call my office and get me in any more trouble in return for my agreement to be there at eleven the next morning.

When I got off the phone I felt suddenly exhausted. After all, I'd had less than 2 hours' sleep, and I'd taken a mammoth hit of cocaine which was starting to wear off. I thought of taking another hit and decided against it. A friend of mine once told me that when you do coke, no matter how much you have, you always do it all. I wasn't sure if that was true or not, but seeing as how I had a good kilo on me, it didn't seem like a very good time to find out. After all, I had an eleven o'clock appointment the next morning. What I needed to do was call the airport and catch the next plane to New York.

I looked at my watch. It was 3.30. That reminded me of something, but for a moment I couldn't think what. Then I remembered. "7th and Burke N.W. 4:00." It seemed too much to hope for. On the other hand, it seemed stupid to pass up. I pulled out the Hagstrom map and checked the location of the intersection. It was a good distance, but I could probably make it.

I locked up the briefcase again and stashed it under the bed, took the map, went down to the garage, got my car, and headed out.

It was 3:55 by the time I reached the corner of 7th and Burke. I cruised through the intersection slowly, checking out the corner. I couldn't believe it. There on the corner, large as life, was a businessman in a three-piece suit and tie, holding a suitcase.

I found a parking spot halfway down the block. I parked the car, got out, and walked back to the corner. I walked slowly, to give myself a chance to size the guy up.

The first thing I could tell about him was that he had red hair. I figured a tough detective would call him "Red." Red was about 30. He wore horn-rimmed glasses. He was overweight, and he was perspiring, but who wouldn't in Miami in a three-piece suit. I had on a light summer suit, and I felt hot. But Red was clearly nervous. He kept fidgeting with the suitcase, shifting it from hand to hand. I figured it was his first. More than that, I figured it was probably a one-shot deal. Red didn't look like he had the stamina to go it more than once. Moreover, if he were a regular, the job would have been filled and Tony Arroyo wouldn't have been making overtures to me the night before.

I had figured all this out by the time I hit the corner. Then I had a problem. I couldn't just stand there staring at the guy. I suppose I could have turned and looked in the store window, but somehow that seemed hopelessly theatrical, and the only window at hand in the corner drugstore seemed to be devoted entirely to feminine napkins.

I should have turned around and headed back to my car, but at that moment the light changed, and as the pedestrians on the corner started across the street, I just naturally went with them. It didn't seem such a bad idea at the time. There was a phone on the far corner, and I could pick up the receiver and pretend I was making a call, and be in a great position to watch Red across the street.

I had no sooner done that than a black Cadillac pulled in at the corner. The driver opened the door and stood up, leaning on the open door of the car. He was a big, solid, muscular Hispanic with shaggy black hair. Floridian #1! He jerked his thumb at Red. Red threw the suitcase in the back seat, got in, and the car pulled out.

There was no time for me to get back to my car. Even if there were, I was pointed in the wrong direction. I dropped the phone, stepped out into the street, and hailed a cab.

Luck was with me. One stopped at once. I hopped in, slammed the door, leaned forward, pointed, and said the words I'd dreamed of saying all my life, ever since I was a small boy: "Follow that car."

The driver, who couldn't have been more than 20,

had probably never heard those words said in his life either. He turned around in his seat.

"Are you kidding?" he said.

I whipped out my I.D. and flashed it under his nose. "I'm a private detective," I said. "There's ten bucks in it for you if they don't get away."

The cabbie's eyes widened. "No shit!" he said. He slammed his foot to the floor and the cab shot away from the corner and hurtled down the street.

"Hey, don't let them know they're being followed," I said.

"Why should they think that?" he said. "Hell, I always drive like this."

We caught them in five blocks, and the cabbie was forced to slow to a more reasonable pace.

"This is more apt to make them suspicious," he told me.

"I can't help that. Just stay about a block behind 'em, but don't let 'em out of sight."

"Right, boss."

We followed the car out of town to a residential area. The houses started getting larger and further apart.

"Pretty ritzy neighborhood," the cabbie said.

"Yeah."

"Drug deal?" he asked.

"The reason you're getting ten bucks on top of the fare," I said, "is not just because you're a good driver. It's because you've got a lousy memory and you're not nosy."

"Right, boss."

The Cadillac pulled into a driveway on a tree-lined lot that fronted what had to be a two-and-a-half-million dollar house. I had the cabbie stop half a block away, giving them time to get into the house.

"All right," I said. "Pull by slow, not so slow that anybody gets suspicious, but slow enough that I can get the house number."

"You got it."

We cruised by the driveway. I copied the address into my pocket notebook.

"Now what?"

"Go down to the next intersection and turn around."

The cabbie did so, pulling a beautiful U-turn just as the light changed.

"Now what?"

"Pull into the side and park."

We parked about a block past the driveway to the house, facing back the way we came.

"Should I kill the motor?" the cabbie asked. "We gonna be long?"

"I don't think so," I said.

I was right. Less than ten minutes later the Caddy came out of the driveway and headed back the way it had come. We pulled out and followed along, keeping a block behind.

Floridian #1 drove straight back to the corner where he'd picked Red up, and let him off again. Red still had the suitcase, but I would have bet you it didn't have the same thing in it as when he'd started.

The Cadillac pulled away from the curb and the cabbie started to follow, but I stopped him. The car wasn't important any more. I had the license number. I could trace Floridian #1. I had the house number. I could trace Floridian #2. Red was the one I wanted now.

Red lugged the suitcase half a block to where he'd parked his car. More coincidence. It was right in front of where I'd parked mine, but I wasn't going to take the chance of hopping out and switching cars now. I stuck with the cab.

Red got in his car, drove to the Essex Hotel, and pulled into their underground garage. He rolled down his window and flashed his hotel key at the attendant, who waved him on.

A large sign on the garage entrance said "REGISTERED GUESTS ONLY." Even if it hadn't, the taxi wasn't going to pass muster.

"What now, boss?" the cabbie said.

"Back to where his car was parked," I told him.

"Why?" he asked. I just stared at him. "Right you are, boss," he said.

We turned around and headed back.

The cabbie dropped me off right next to the space where Red's car had been parked. Another car was now in the space.

"That's gonna make it harder, isn't it?" the cabbie said, jerking his thumb at the car. I said nothing, but counted out the fare into his hand and laid a ten on top of it. I got out of the cab and stood on the sidewalk. The cabbie sat there watching me. He wanted to see how I looked for evidence. I looked at him and jerked my thumb down the street. Slowly, reluctantly, he drove away.

As soon as he was out of sight, I got in my car and pulled out. I turned a few corners, just to make sure no one was following me. When I was sure the cabbie wasn't lurking around somewhere trying to learn a little more about my investigative technique, and sure Floridian #1 wasn't backtracking me with the thought of turning me into a eunuch, I stopped at a pay phone and made a few calls.

12

I DON'T USE ELECTRONIC SURVEILLANCE IN THE COURSE OF MY BUSINESS. In fact, I don't even *do* surveillance in the course of my business. I don't even follow wayward wives around to get evidence in divorce cases. Of course, I knew about electronic surveillance, and I even had a few catalogs of electronic surveillance equipment that the companies that make that sort of stuff would send me from time to time just because I was listed as a detective agency. But I'd never really looked at them, other than thumbing through them now and then on a slow day. So I was out of my depth when it came to buying that sort of equipment, and both I and the guy in the store knew it.

"You want a what?" he asked in response to my request.

"I want a tracking device. The sort of thing you attach to a car that tells you when the car is moving and where it's going."

"You want a transmitter," he told me.

"Is that what I want?"

"Yeah, that's what you want. You want a transmitter and a homing unit. The homing unit emits a beep when the car moves and shows you the direction it's heading."

"That sounds about right," I said.

"We have several units of that type," he said. "Starting at $79.95 and going on up."

"Depending on what?"

"Signal strength, for one thing. At $79.95, you can cover a five-mile radius. You wanna go higher than that, you're dealing with a larger transmitter with a higher frequency, and of course the price goes up."

The unit I wanted went up all the way to $249.95. It had a fifty-mile radius and could pinpoint a car ten miles away within an area of about ten blocks. Following the signal vector, and turning right or left as it increased and decreased, sort of in the manner of playing the children's game of "hotter and colder," would enable you to locate any stationary transmitter in a matter of minutes.

I lifted the transmitter part out of the box.

"How does it attach to the car?"

"It's magnetic. Clamps right on underneath. Just stick it on to the gas tank."

"What if it falls off?"

"It won't. It's very strong. It's fully guaranteed."

"You mean if it falls off I get my money back?"

"That's right."

"What about the car?"

"What *about* the car?"

"Right," I said. "All right, I'll take it."

I paid for the transmitter with three of Albrect's hundred-dollar bills. I felt bad doing it, but my Master Charge wasn't going to stand this one, even with a $2000 limit. And after all, I was sort of doing this for Albrect. Besides, he didn't need the money.

I packed up the unit, picked up my car, and drove to the Essex Hotel. I registered at the front desk, paying with another hundred-dollar bill. It was easier the second time. I took my room key, went back out, got in my car, and drove around to the indoor garage. I flashed my key at the guard and he waved me in. I found a parking spot, locked my car and got out.

It took me fifteen minutes to find Red's car, which was parked down on the third level. I took out the transmitter, looked to be sure no one was in sight, bent down, and pressed it against the bottom of his gas tank. As the guy had assured me, it stuck like glue. I tried tugging at it, but it seemed fairly secure.

I went back up to the first level and got in my car. I took out the receiver and switched it on. Sure enough, I was getting a beep. The only trouble was, the direction vector was having trouble figuring out where to point. That's all I need, I thought. The one faulty unit in the store. Then I remembered. I tilted the receiver on its side, and the vector, happily reassured, pointed straight down at level 3.

I switched off the unit, stuck it in the glove compartment, got out, and locked the car. There was an elevator against the far wall of the garage. I went over and rang the bell. The elevator arrived promptly. I got in and rode up to the lobby.

I went to the front desk, slid my key across the counter, and said, "I'd like to check out."

The desk clerk stared at me. "Check out? You just checked in."

"That's right. Now I want to check out."

"Is something wrong with the room?"

"I don't know. I haven't been up to the room."

"You haven't been up to the room?"

"No."

"I don't understand."

"It's perfectly simple. Here's my room key. I'm checking out."

"Are you asking for a refund?"

"Certainly not."

The clerk was making an effort to understand. "You say you haven't used the room? You're saying we're free to rent it again?"

"Well, you're welcome to try," I said. "Some guests may be more picky than I am."

I smiled at the discomfited room clerk, and headed for the elevator. God, I felt cocky. Three days ago, such jive repartee never would have occurred to me, and even if it had, I wouldn't have had the guts to do it.

Taking the elevator back down to the garage brought

me back down to earth. Doing it made me realize I could have just walked through the lobby, gotten in the elevator, and gone down to find Red's car without ever having rented the room at all. So I wasn't the sophisticated, suave, smooth private investigator I'd thought I was; I was still the same old naive, bumbling asshole, groping his way in the dark, that I'd always been.

I got in my car, drove out of the garage, and back to my first hotel. I took the receiver out of the glove compartment, and went up to my room. I pulled the briefcase out from under the bed, opened it, and assured myself that the receiving unit would fit in it. Then I started to pack up to go.

Which presented me with a problem. What to do with the cocaine. The bank was closed, so I couldn't put it back in the safe deposit box. I couldn't leave it in the hotel room unless I rented it for a week, which seemed a poor idea, prices being what they were. Even then, I'd have to find some way of getting back down here in a week's time, which wasn't going to be easy.

I toyed with the idea of wrapping it up and mailing it to my office in New York, but somehow that seemed like a poor idea. Surely packages from Miami would be highly suspect. And simply the idea of having my name on a package of those contents was more than I could deal with.

That left me with two alternatives: throw it away, or take it with me on the plane. You can't throw it away, it's evidence, I told myself. Bullshit, myself cried. You just don't want to part with it. I had to admit that that was true. Somehow the idea of throwing something worth twenty or thirty grand, whatever it might be, in the garbage, went sorely against the grain. So the only thing to do was take it with me on the plane. What an unattractive proposition! Consider the fact that Tony Arroyo, Pluto, Floridian #2, and the rest of the boys, heavy hitters indeed, had found taking it on the plane so risky an operation that they were willing to pay huge chunks of money to poor schmucks like Martin Albrect to drive it up instead. Granted, they weren't really giving him anything—they were fleecing him at the roulette table and making him drive to pay it off, but the underlying principle was the same. And, of course, they were doing it as a regular thing. I'd only have to do it once. And they were moving much larger quantities. Still, the quantity I had would be large enough for the drug enforcement boys. I could envision the phone call I would have to make: "Yeah, honey, I'm in jail. What's the charge? Drug trafficking. No. Not possession. Not sale. Trafficking. Transporting large enough quantities of regulated substances to be considered a major cog in the drug traffic machine of America. Bail? Do we happen to have $100,000 in the account?"

It was not a pretty prospect, and it tipped the scale. I was *not* going to take it on the plane. Which meant I had to throw it away.

Or did it?

Vaguely I recalled a principle from my old math days. I'm sure the wording is all wrong, but it went something like this: if you find yourself working on a problem where every conclusion that you reach is unacceptable and wrong, reexamine your hypothesis.

My hypothesis was that I had only two alternatives: throw the kilo away or take it on the plane.

13

THE GUY IN THE ELECTRONICS STORE RAISED AN EYE-
BROW. "You again."

"Yeah," I said. "The bad penny."

"Let me guess. The transmitter fell off and you
want your money back?"

"Not at all," I told him. "In fact, I'm so impressed
with it I decided to give you some more of my business."

He shrugged. "If I worked on commission I'd be
thrilled. Whaddya want?"

"The magnets that hold that thing on. They're terrific. I wonder if you have them *without* the transmitter, perhaps attached to some small bag or other."

He didn't, but what he did have, and what I eventually bought, were suction cups, the kind with the lever
on the top that clamps down to lock them in place, the
kind you see cat-burglars use in the movies. I bought
four of them, and a small canvas backpack with buckles and straps.

I took the stuff back to the hotel room and put it
together. When the levers were closed on the suction
cups, it formed a perfect loop for the straps to go
through. I shortened the straps as far as they would
go, so the thing wouldn't hang down any more than it
had to, and the end result wasn't bad. I figured it
would do.

I took the kilo of coke out of my briefcase, and put
it in the backpack. It wasn't a bad fit. I buckled it shut

and tested the flap. It was O.K. If the buckles stayed
put, there was no way it was going to fall out.

I put the whole shmear in my briefcase, went out,
hailed a cab, and had it take me to the Essex Hotel.
This time I didn't bother to register for a room I didn't
need. I just walked through the lobby and took the
elevator down to the garage.

I had a moment of panic when I didn't see Red's
car, but then I spotted it behind a Lincoln Continental
that had come in since the last time I'd been there.
I went to the back of Red's car and bent down.
The transmitter was still in place, though why it
should have moved when the car hadn't is beyond me.
I gave it a tug anyway, just to be sure. It didn't
budge.

I glanced around to make sure no one was coming,
then popped open the briefcase and took out the four
suction cups and the canvas bag. One at a time I
snapped the cups in place on the underside of the car
next to the transmitter. I threaded the straps from the
bag through the levers as I snapped them closed. The
whole operation seemed an eternity, but took about
30 seconds. I snapped the briefcase shut, jumped up,
and did my impression of a guy minding his own
business looking for his car, just in case anyone was
coming. No one was.

I bent back down and inspected my work. It wasn't
bad. The straps were short, and I'd pulled the suction
cups as far apart as they'd go, to keep the straps up
tight. The bag hung down, of course, but not that
much. It cleared the ground by a good 6 inches. Of
course if you bent down and looked you'd see it, but
you had to be looking for it. From a standing position
it didn't show at all.

I left the Essex, took a taxi back to the Sheraton,
and went up to my room. I packed the tracking unit in
my briefcase and the grinder in the paper bag the
suction cups had come in.

I checked out, got in my car, and drove to the

airport. On the way I stopped and threw the paper bag with the grinder into a trash can on a street corner. It still had four or five good lines in it. Some bag lady was in for one hell of a time.

14

THE NEXT DAY I FOUND OUT WHY COCAINE IS SO PSYCHO-
LOGICALLY ADDICTIVE. There is no hangover quite so
bad as a coke hangover, at least none that I know.
You've been up so high, and suddenly you're down so
low. Who wouldn't want to feel good again when
they're feeling so bad?

Of course, it was a surprise to me. I'd gotten high in
Miami, and come down in Miami, and I thought that
was all there was to it. Naive me. The next day is a
real kick in the ass, and I felt like shit that morning as
I drove out to Brooklyn to see Mrs. Rabinowitz.

The case, however, was, as I'd imagined, a dream
assignment. Nice old apartment building, clean lobby,
automatic elevator, Jewish tenants. Mrs. Rabinowitz
was even pretty nice, considering I'd stood her up
three times. And for once, the case was simple and
straightforward. The roughest part of the form I had
to fill out was the blank marked "HISTORY." There
were five blank lines under it, but often they weren't
nearly enough, since clients' complicated and sprawling accounts of their mishaps often spilled over onto
the back page, filled it, and continued on into the
pages of the yellow legal pad I carry for taking witness
statements. Mrs. Rabinowitz's said, in its entirety:
"Client tripped on a hole in the sidewalk and fell
down."

Also, many clients have a medical history that could
fill a small novel, with frequent visits to a number of

hospitals, a myriad of doctors, none of whom agreed with each other, and courses of treatment to be followed and understood only by those with degrees in medicine—preferably specialists. Mrs. Rabinowitz had broken one leg, gone to one hospital, once, where one doctor had put it in one cast.

I was done in half an hour. I'd have been done in half the time, except Mrs. Rabinowitz interrupted me incessantly in her eagerness to hear the grisly details of the automobile accident that had delayed me the day before. She seemed a nice old lady, so I created a particularly gruesome version, giving firsthand accounts of severed limbs, copious quantities of blood, and even—though suspecting I was pushing it a bit—a decapitation. Mrs. Rabinowitz ate it up, and I was glad, for she was a game old lady, and even accompanied me downstairs on her crutches to point out the defect in the sidewalk that had felled her. It was a few buildings down the street from her. It was a beauty, and I was able not only to get pictures, but also the street number of the building it was in front of. All in all, a profitable morning. Richard would be happy.

I offered to see Mrs. Rabinowitz back to her building, but no, she was heading for the drugstore on the corner, so I said goodbye and got out of there fast. I knew she was on her way to pick up the *Post* and the *Daily News* to look for pictures of the accident on the Major Deegan, and I didn't want to stick around and see her disappointed.

My beeper went off just before I got to my car. That was a blessing. Usually the damn thing went off when I was on the Grand Central Parkway or some such highway where I'd have to get off and drive all over creation to find a phone. When I did find one, it would either be broken, or be occupied by some Spanish-speaking woman who was planning her life. And once I did find an unoccupied working phone, I would discover that there was no easy way of getting back on the highway from where I was.

I went to the pay phone on the corner. It was

unoccupied and working. I dialed 0, 212, and the office number, waited for the tone, and then punched in the office calling card number.

Kathy answered with a snarl. "Well, it's about time."

"You just beeped me," I protested.

"Today I just beeped you. What about yesterday? What about Mrs. Rabinowitz?"

"It's all signed. No problem."

"No problem for you. I've had it on the books for three days with Richard wanting to know how come it wasn't done."

"Then he's gonna be real pleased when you tell him it is. And he's gonna love the accident pictures."

"He can love his grandmother, for all I care. I just want the case closed."

"It's closed. Look, did you just beep me to compliment me on my performance, or was there something else?"

"I have a new case. Any chance you'll have it done before Monday?"

"I'll have it done before lunch."

"Oh yeah? Then how the hell you gonna get off charging 3 hours on it the way you always do?"

"That was a figure of speech. So I have a late lunch. Just give it to me, will you?"

She gave it to me. 212. Death. 5th Avenue. Not so bad. But a pretty high number. Ten bucks said it'd be above 110th Street. I pulled out the Hagstrom map. Sure enough, I owed myself ten bucks. Right around 114th Street. The apartment number was the kicker. 14G. A project.

I've been in some pretty grungy four-story walkups in Harlem with rotting floorboards and unlit hallways, but I think I like housing projects even less. A friend of mine in the detective business once told me he figured when the city set about to build the low-income housing projects, they got a mugger, a rapist, and a murderer together to help design them. I wouldn't disagree. Projects have front doors that anyone can get in, long, narrow dead-end hallways to get cornered in, alcoves for unsavory types to lie in wait in. The room numbers are so flimsy and fastened so poorly to the doors that they never last more than a few months, leaving any poor outsider desperately trying to locate an apartment, stranded forever in the aforementioned mineshaft-like corridors, hoping like hell if he rings a doorbell the person who comes to the door either is the person he's looking for, knows the person he's looking for or, failing either of these, doesn't kill him.

I was in for a surprise. The building wasn't that bad. The lobby was fairly clean. My client's apartment number was on her door, which I located easily. She turned out to be a perfectly nice young black woman, who kept a clean, if modestly furnished, apartment and had a five-year-old son who had broken his wrist, not, as is so often the case, through some negligence of her own, but because someone at his day care center had slammed a door on the kid's hand.

I felt like a schmuck. I also felt relieved. It was a damn good interview, and the only thing that made me the least bit uncomfortable was when her son got into my briefcase, which I had left open on the floor, and pulled out the receiving unit of my electronic tracking device.

"What's this?" he said.

I looked up, saw it, and realized that today at least it had been business as usual, and the only effort I'd made in the direction of continuing the Albrect investigation had been in sticking the unit in my briefcase.

The unit was on, of course, primed to inform me of Red's impending arrival.

I smiled as I took it away from him. "That's a tracking device, so my office can keep in touch with me."

The young mother frowned. "Don't they just beep you?" she said, pointing to my belt.

"Sure they do," I told her. "But this tells 'em where I am, so if they get a case they can beep the agent closest to the area."

"Agent?" she said. "I thought you were a lawyer."

Parnell Hall

I smiled. "No, ma'am, I'm not," I said, and launched into my "I'm not a lawyer, I'm an investigator" spiel.

I got out of there with the sign-up, but I was lucky. The girl was nice, sharp, intelligent. I felt like a fool, but it was good. When you realize you're a schmuck, you might as well realize you're a big one.

But the kid finding the unit really bothered me. Not that he found it, but rather, that it was on and nothing had happened yet. How long did it take to drive from Miami, anyway? How would I go about finding that out? Add up the miles and make an estimate? How would I go about finding out how many miles it was? What kind of detective was I, anyway? I had the answer to that. A schmuck. An asshole. The real question was, when the fuck was Red going to show up?

15

RED SHOWED UP THAT NIGHT AT THREE IN THE MORNING. Oddly enough, it was my wife who proclaimed his arrival. She shook me out of a sound sleep, and said, "What the fuck is that?"

I was groggy, and it was a few moments before I realized what she was talking about.

"What?" I muttered.

"That!" she said, in the helpful way she has of clarifying what she has just said by repeating it in a louder and more strident tone of voice.

Then I heard it. From the living room was coming a faint, but annoyingly high-pitched "beep, beep, beep."

"Oh, it's my beeper," I said. "It does that when the batteries get weak."

I stumbled out of bed and groped my way toward the living room, hoping my wife was sleepy enough that she wouldn't notice the blatant contradiction between that statement and what I'd told her concerning my beeper just the other day. A disgusted "Mmmmmph!" and slamming of the pillow as she turned over assured me that she had not.

I hurried into the living room, switched on the light, and pulled the unit out of the desk drawer where I'd stashed it. This made the beeping louder, but I quickly turned the volume down. I checked the vector. It was pointing south and slightly west. The object it was tracking was heading north. That made sense. Red would be coming up the New Jersey Turnpike.

I'd stashed a bag of shoes, socks, pants and shirt in the foyer closet. I took it into the living room and quickly dressed. I shoved the tracking unit into my briefcase. I got my keys from the cabinet in the foyer. I switched off the light, and groped my way to the front door. I squeezed out, trying to let in as little light as possible, even though the bedroom was a few turns of the hallway away. I closed the door quietly behind me and rang for the elevator.

I had to ring three times. The night man looked groggy when he opened the door. He had been sleeping. Tough luck for him. I'd been sleeping, too.

I ran to my car and got in, pausing only to shut off the code alarm and lock the door. I opened the briefcase on the seat beside me and checked the tracking device. Red was still southwest of me and heading north. He figured to be around Newark. He was heading slightly northeast now, and somehow the thought flashed: "Holland Tunnel." That's what I would do if I were hitting Manhattan at approximately three-thirty in the morning. I pulled out, sped down West End Avenue to 96th Street, and got on the West Side Highway heading south.

There was virtually no traffic at that time in the morning, no bottleneck at the ramp at 57th Street where the elevated section of the highway now ends. Even stopping for lights, I made Canal Street in record time.

So did Red. By the time I got there he was right alongside me. The only trouble was the vector indicated he was still heading north. Shit! The Lincoln Tunnel.

Ordinarily, a U-turn at the Canal Street exit on West Street would have been a problem, but not at three in the morning. I wheeled around and began racing Red to the tunnel.

It was a dead heat. Unfortunately, the race didn't end there. Red was still heading north. The George Washington Bridge! You dumb schmuck, I thought.

Three in the morning and you're going all the way up to the goddamn G. W. Bridge.

I sped on uptown, keeping pace with Red as he drove up the other side of the river. After ten minutes or so his vector turned and pointed east and I knew he was coming over the bridge.

Which presented a terrific problem. Due to the construction taking place on the ramps to the bridge, the only way you could get on the West Side Highway heading south was if you were coming over the bridge from Jersey. So Red could get on the Highway and I couldn't.

Under the circumstances, I did the best I could. I positioned myself on Riverside Drive next to the bridge entrance ramp and waited to see what Red would do. If he just kept going straight, taking the Cross Bronx Expressway to either the Harlem River Drive or the Major Deegan, I could zoom up the ramp and come out right on his tail. But if he took the West Side Highway, I was going to have to hustle.

All I could do was wait, watch the vector, and hope. I tracked Red's progress as he hit the bridge. I could even tell when he stopped for the toll booth. Then he came over. He was right on top of me. Then the vector started turning in a circle as he hit the exit ramp. That could mean only one thing: the West Side Highway.

I slammed my car into a U-turn and sped down Riverside Drive. I had a start on him, cause he had to get out of the exit loop, but I had some looping of my own to do. I gave it the gas and took a left fork off Riverside Drive onto a side street that, oddly enough, was also called Riverside Drive. I zoomed down it like a bat out of hell and ran the light at 158th Street, where a zillion roads merged, *two others* of which, so help me god, were *also* Riverside Drive. I hung the hard right, and shot down the hill. I swerved under the *real* Riverside Drive and under the Highway, hung a hard left, and hit the highway entrance just in time to see a lone car whiz by. I was going so fast I nearly veered out and hit him. I hit the brakes hard, wrenched the wheel back the other way, screeched onto the highway, and fishtailed. I let off the brake, and the car straightened out. I risked a glance at the tracking unit. It was him all right. He was right ahead of me, heading south. Great work, I thought. Talk abut inconspicuous.

I dropped back and let him have a good lead, so he could have a chance to stop thinking about the guy at whom he'd undoubtedly shouted, "Asshole!" We passed 125th Street, 96th Street, and 79th Street, which meant he couldn't be getting off until at least 57th Street. I had a chance to say, "Asshole!" back at him. Not only had he gone all the way north to go south again, but if, as I suspected, he was headed for Tony Arroyo's place, he had also chosen to take the West Side Highway down and then drive all the way across town, instead of taking the Harlem River Drive and the FDR like a normal person.

My assumption proved to be correct. Red got off at 57th Street and drove straight to Tony's building. He pulled into the circular driveway, took out the by now familiar suitcase, and went in. From my vantage point in the street, I could see him through the lobby window talking to the doorman. The doorman called upstairs on the house phone, and, after a brief conversation, waved Red up.

I would have loved to have gone over and checked out the bottom of Red's car to see if the kilo of coke was still among the present, but the driveway was brightly lit, and with the doorman standing right there it was out of the question. I had to content myself with staying put and seeing what happened next.

Red was down in five minutes, without the suitcase. He got into his car and drove off. I let him go. I had his license number and I had his car bugged. I could get him any time I liked. Even with the kilo of coke aboard, he had ceased to be a main concern.

I sat in the car and waited. Twenty minutes later a familiar looking limo pulled into the driveway. Tony

Arroyo came out of the building, carrying the suitcase. He got in the limo and drove off. I pulled out and followed.

I don't mind admitting I was scared to death. It was one thing to follow Tony's limo when he was driving home from a nice night at the casino. It was something else to follow him when he was carrying a king's ransom in contraband. One might suspect he might be slightly more curious as to whether or not anyone was taking an interest in him.

I hoped like hell he was heading for a particular address on East 64th Street. First, because it was close. Second, because it would have tied everything up. I would have traced the two separate drug operations from both ends back to where they crossed, to where it had all gone wrong, to where Albrect's future had suddenly become such an iffy proposition.

It would have been nice, but it didn't happen. The limo didn't turn up toward 64th Street; it headed for the East River. So Rosa's connection wasn't Pluto. Well, win some, lose some. If I didn't get killed, I'd probably find out who *was* Pluto.

The limo took the ramp onto the Queensboro Bridge. I followed at what I hoped was a safe distance. Far below me lay the East River, where Guillermo Gutierrez presumably still resided. Better him than me.

On the other side of the bridge the limo took Queens Boulevard to the Brooklyn-Queens Expressway, took the B.Q.E. south to the Long Island Expressway, and headed east on the L.I.E. It was a hell of a route to take. I'd have gone through the Midtown Tunnel and been on the L.I.E. in the first place. But it occurred to me that Tony's driver probably didn't get paid for his knowledge of the city; he probably had other talents that helped him earn his keep. The thought did not sit well, and I dropped back another hundred yards.

The limo turned south onto the Grand Central Parkway, took the Grand Central to the Van Wyck. It was heading for JFK Airport, which didn't make any sense at all. You drive the stuff all the way up from Miami, and when it gets here you get on a plane?

Tony wasn't going to the airport. The limo got on the Belt Parkway heading east and got off at Sunrise Highway. It stayed on Sunrise Highway for a while, and I realized we had left Queens and were now in Nassau County.

We drove a little further, then turned south and started following some smaller back roads. This made things a lot trickier. I had to stay closer to see which way they turned, and if they made too many turns they were going to realize I was on their tail.

We were going through a very poor section, which suddenly turned into a very rich section, as if someone had just pushed the "wealth" button, and suddenly I knew where we were. Woodmere!

I'd served a summons in Woodmere once, and I had reason to remember it because it had been a thorn in my side. I hadn't signed up the case myself, so I didn't know anything about it other than the information in the summons I was supposed to serve: a 12-year-old boy had fallen down on the front steps of a building in Yonkers, owned by G. & D. Realty, and broken his arm, and his mother wanted a million dollars cash. Could you write me a check now, Mr. Real Estate Man?

The address of the real estate company was on the summons, so I drove up to Yonkers to serve it. When I got there, though, the address turned out to be a wooden door with a diamond-shaped glass window on the street level between two stores. There was nothing on the door other than the street number, nothing to indicate what, if any, businesses resided within.

I looked through the window. There was a narrow hallway with a flight of stairs leading to the presumed businesses above. On the wall just inside the door were a half-dozen mailboxes, but the angle wasn't good enough for me to read the names on them. There were no bells outside the door, no way of attracting the attention of anyone within. And the door, of course, was locked. Considering my expertise with locked doors, I was somewhat at a loss as to what to do next.

I was pondering my next move when a woman came down the street, pulled out a set of keys, and unlocked the door.

I stepped right up as if she were just the person I'd been waiting for, said, "Thank you," and held the door open as she went in. She gave me a look, but I was wearing my suit and tie, and didn't appear to be that dangerous rapist the whole county was looking for, so she continued on in and up the stairs.

I followed, stopping at the mailboxes, There were several small businesses listed, none of them G. & D. Realty; none, in fact, realty companies at all. Nor was there a listing for either a Mr. Golden or a Mr. Dursky, the two partners of G. & D. Realty named in the summons.

I went upstairs and pounded on every door. Nobody had ever heard of G. & D. Realty, or any Mr. Golden or Mr. Dursky.

Things were not looking good. I went outside, found a pay phone down the street, and called Richard's office.

I had the bad luck to get Kathy, who reluctantly looked up the information: yes, they had pulled the tax record for the building where the boy was injured; yes, the owner was listed as G. & D. Realty; yes, the address was the one on the summons; yes, the partners were Golden and Dursky; no, the tax record didn't list home addresses; no, she didn't have any other information, why didn't I stop bugging her and go serve the damn summons?

Why indeed?

I was so angry when I got off the phone that it didn't even register when a mailman walked right by me on his appointed rounds. He was halfway down the block before I came to my senses and caught up with him.

He was a black man of about 55 and, contrary to the postal employee stereotype, intelligent, friendly, cour-

teous, and helpful: yes, he delivered mail to the building in question; yes, G. & D. Realty received mail at
that address—the mail was put in the box marked
Craft Associates; no, the mail did not necessarily come
care of Craft Associates, but anything addressed to
G. & D. Realty went in that box.

He had nothing for G. & D. Realty or Craft Associates that day, but he had mail for the building and, of
course, a key to get to the mailboxes, so I followed
him in.

Craft Associates was one of the doors on the third
floor where I had found no one in. I pounded on the
door again, not expecting anything, and sure enough,
no one was in again. I hung around about fifteen more
minutes and called it a day.

I went back three more times on three separate
days, at different times of the day, which is the legal
requirement, and then did a nail-and-mail. What that
consists of is taping a copy of the summons to the
door, and then mailing a copy of the summons to that
address. I got a two-inch roll of masking tape and
plastered the summons to the door of Craft Associates, and then drove down to Richard's office to turn
in my bill.

Which Richard refused to pay. "Are you crazy?" he
screamed in his high-pitched, nasal you're-ruining-my-
life tone of voice. "Are you nuts? I have a million-
dollar case here, and you're kicking it out the window.
If these guys are so slick they don't even put the name
of their company on their office, which is nothing
more than a mail-drop, do you think they're gonna fall
for a nail-and-mail?" Richard put his fingers and thumbs
together, held his hands to the sides of his face, and
said, as if addressing a child, "They never got it.
They'll claim they never got it. I'll have to prove they
did. I can't do it. I lose a million-dollar suit."

"Yeah, but—"

"You gotta understand, you're dealing with sleazebags
here. They're tricky, and they know all the angles.
You send it regular mail, they never got it. You send

it registered mail, it's a red flag to them, they never pick it up." Richard shook his head. "How did you send it?"

"I didn't send it yet. See—"

"What?!"

"I was going to send it out from here. See, I need to Xerox another copy to—"

Richard couldn't wait for me to finish. "Get it back! Get it back!" he said, practically jumping up and down. "They read that, it does nothing but let them know we're on to them. We'll never serve them, then. Get the hell up to Yonkers and get it off the goddamn door!"

I broke all speed laws back to Yonkers but, of course, it was gone. I could see tape marks and traces of adhesive left on the door, but that was it.

I had a copy of the summons in my pocket, so I pounded on the door again, but with little hope. Of course, there was no one there.

I hated like hell to go back and report to Richard, but there was nothing else to do. On the way back I kept trying to think of some way I could make up for the fact that I'd really blown it. The best I could come up with was staking out the front door and waiting to see who showed up to pick up the mail.

"Great!" was the way Richard, dripping sarcasm, responded to the suggestion. "Wonderful idea! You think I wanna pay you ten bucks an hour to sit and stare at a mailbox? You wanna do something useful, get up to the County Clerk's office and see if you can dig up the corporate papers and get these jokers' home addresses."

So I drove up to White Plains and spent six hours at the County Clerk's office going through volume after volume of listings. Talk about wasting time, I thought. Wait'll Richard sees *this* fucking bill. And then I found it. There was no listing for G. & D. Realty, or G. & D. anything for that matter, nor was there any listing for Craft Associates, but there was a listing for a limited partnership, Craft Partners, with the same address as G. & D. Realty and Craft Associates. The partners were listed as Marvin Golden and Jonathan Dursky.

I copied down the numbers from the log, filled out a form, gave it to the clerk at the desk, and five minutes later I was looking at a partnership agreement called Craft Partners between Golden and Dursky. Home addresses were listed.

I Xeroxed the document, and set out on my Golden and Dursky hunt. Golden's address was in Englewood Cliffs. Dursky's was in Woodmere.

Now the thing about summonses is, people don't want 'em. You can't call up a guy and say, "Hey, I got a summons for you, you want me to bring it on out?" You have to drop in on them, hope they're home, and hand them the thing when they come to the door. That's why, with Englewood Cliffs, New Jersey, right over the George Washington Bridge, and Woodmere way the hell on the South Shore of Long Island, I tried the New Jersey address first. If I hit pay dirt there my job was over, since I could serve both summonses on either partner.

In all, I went four times to the Englewood Cliffs address, which turned out to be a luxury high-rise so posh you practically had to show your membership in the local country club to get in. I never got past the front desk. Three times I was told Mr. Golden wasn't there. The fourth and last time, the doorman called upstairs and someone answered the phone. The doorman wouldn't let me talk to this person, but instead relayed messages back and forth. I said I had a delivery for Mr. Golden. I was asked who I was and what I was. I said I was an officer of the Supreme Court of New York, and I had papers for Mr. Golden. I was asked what kind of papers. I said it was a summons. I was asked from whom. I told them—they would know anyway, from the copy I'd taped to their door. The doorman then hung up the phone and informed me that Mr. Golden was not at home.

I just stared at him. I knew he was lying, and he

knew I knew he was lying, but what the hell could I do about it? I didn't even know what Golden looked like. He could walk right by me in the lobby, and I wouldn't even know it. And the doorman sure wasn't going to tell me. Jesus Christ, I thought. What sleazebags. These guys are so slick and crafty and rich that they know all the angles. They're smart enough to hide behind their phony corporate names and addresses and mail drops and doormen. They've consulted their lawyers and know the statute of limitations is running out on the case, and all they have to do is keep ducking me for a few more weeks and it will be too late to file suit, and they'll have won. The fucking sleazebags.

I was determined to get them. For one thing, I owed it to Richard. I had fucked this thing up for him, and now it was up to me to make it right. For another thing, Richard never paid for an assignment until it was completed, and I had already invested almost twenty hours in the damn case, for which I wouldn't get a dime until the summons was served. But most of all, I had to get them for me. My self-esteem as a private detective, never particularly high, was at an all-time low, and I was feeling particularly stupid, incompetent, bungling, useless.

I swore I'd get them.

I'd failed with Golden, but I still had a shot at Dursky. His address in Woodmere would be a private house, no doorman to contend with. But he'd be forewarned. He'd know I'd tried to serve Golden, that I had Golden's address, so he'd assume I had his address, too. He'd be expecting me. He'd take precautions. He wouldn't open the door.

For a service to be legal, there must be physical contact. It can be slight—you can touch the guy with the summons and drop it on the ground and that's fine—but there has to be some. So Dursky had to open the door.

I'd never gone to such lengths to serve a summons before, but I was desperate. And what I did made me feel almost like a real private detective, at least for a little while.

I dug through my desk drawers and found a old telegram someone had sent me back when Tommie was born. The envelope was a little faded, but I figured it would pass.

I borrowed an old UPS book from my father-in-law's business. With it folded open and a carbon in place so you couldn't see the UPS emblem, it could pass for a Western Union receipt book.

I got up early the next morning, put on a jacket and cap, which I figured was as close as Western Union messengers would come to wearing a uniform these days, and drove out to Woodmere with the telegram and receipt book. I got there a little after seven, figuring if a guy as wealthy as Dursky got up and went to work any earlier than that, perhaps he deserved to keep his money.

The address in Woodmere turned out to be a sprawling three-story stone mansion on an ungodly large lot. I parked my car in the street, and walked up the twisting drive to the house.

The front door was a massive thing of carved oak. It had a peephole in the middle, a large brass door-knocker, a mail slot, and three substantial-looking locks. The locks were my main concern. If I were to succeed, they would have to open.

I rang the bell. There was long wait, during which I thought, Jesus Christ, maybe nobody *is* at home. Then I heard movement behind the door—slow, shuffling steps, and then the sound of the metal plate covering the peephole being slid back. A thin voice said, "Who is it?"

I held up the telegram in front of the peephole. "Telegram for Jonathan Dursky," I said.

"Slide it through the slot," came the voice.

I held up the receipt book. "Sorry," I said. "You have to sign for it."

The plate on the peephole slid back in place. There was a pause, during which I held my breath, and then

I heard the reassuring click of the deadbolts being unlocked. The greatest hi-fi system in the world never sounded so good. One, two, three . . . they were done, and the door swung open.

Standing there was a frail, doddering old . . . woman!

I couldn't believe it. I'd blown it again. What an idiot. It'd never occurred to me that someone other than Dursky might come to the door. This old lady might be his wife or his housekeeper or his mother or his grandmother. It really didn't matter. Whoever she was, she wasn't him.

And before the words were even out of her mouth, I knew what she was about to say.

"Where do I sign?"

It was too much. I felt like saying, "Forget it," and getting back in my car and driving away. But I had worked too hard and come too far to just let it go. And so I said a stupid thing. A hollow, transparent lie.

"You can't sign for it. He has to sign for it."

She looked at me with a look that told me I had just said a stupid thing. "But I'm his wife," she said. "I always sign for him."

"Not with me, you don't," I said, improvising wildly. "We've had trouble with unauthorized people receiving telegrams, and my boss is cracking down. I could lose my job over this."

She just stared at me for a few seconds.

Then she slammed the door. One by one, the deadbolts clicked back.

I turned around and sat down on the top step. I wanted to cry. Twenty hours down the tubes. Richard's case down the tubes. Stupid, stupid, stupid. What ever made me think Dursky would come to the door himself? Why hadn't I thought of something clever enough to get me into the house, to guarantee personal contact, to guarantee my getting to him? Now he was doubly warned and we'd never get him. He'd sit in his house till doomsday, rather than open that door, and—

Behind me, once again, came the familiar click. I

sprang to my feet and turned around. Another click. And a third. And the door opened.

Standing there in the doorway, leaning on a walker, was an emaciated old man—eighty-five if he was a day. He looked so fragile and helpless that I felt a pang of remorse at having tricked him. Then I remembered how rich and shifty and tricky he was, and what a fucking sleazebag he was, and how he deserved everything he was about to get.

"Jonathan Dursky?" I asked.

"Yeah," he said. "Where do I sign?"

I slapped the summons into his hand. He knew at once what it was, and knew he'd been had. He jerked his hand back as if the summons were hot, and slammed and locked the door, leaving the summons lying on the ground at my feet. It didn't matter. I had touched him with it, and it was a legal service. The sleazebag was mine.

I filled out my affidavit, and sent in a whopping bill to Richard, 22 hours and 264 miles. I felt terrific. I was on top of the world.

A week later I was up in the office talking to one of Richard's paralegals about serving the summons, since it had now become my favorite story, and he asked me who the client was, and when I told him, he said, oh yeah, he remembered the case, in fact, he'd helped develop it. I asked him what he meant. He said it was a case where there was tremendous liability, because the boy's leg was badly broken, and might never heal right, but there was no defect on the steps where he fell down. Since there had been no police on the scene, though, and no ambulance since the mother had taken the kid to the hospital herself, and thus no witnesses of any kind, he had looked around the neighborhood until he found a house where the front steps *were* broken, and he had taken pictures of that, and then looked up the owners, and Richard had filed suit against them.

The guy was pleased as punch when he told me all this, but my world had just collapsed. Golden and

Dursky had nothing to do with the summons I'd just served. They had been picked at random as defendants. Golden and Dursky were innocent. Golden and Dursky weren't the sleazebags. I was the sleazebag. I was the sneaky, tricky, son of a bitch who had managed to nail two innocent men.

These happy thoughts raced through my head as I followed the limo to a house in Woodmere not unlike the one where I had served the summons. The limo pulled into the driveway and stopped. I eyed the street number on the mailbox as I drove by. I kept on going. It was late, I was tired, and stopping would have been risky. I'd done enough for one night. I had Pluto's address now. Like Golden and Dursky, he wouldn't get away.

16

I OVERSLEPT THE NEXT MORNING, which wasn't surprising, since it had been nearly six when I finally got home and sneaked back into bed. I woke up in a terrible mood, had a screaming argument with my wife over nothing at all, and stormed out of the apartment. I had breakfast at a greasy spoon on Broadway, and tried to pull myself together. When I finished it was after nine, so I stopped by the bank and deposited $200 of Albrect's money in our account. Now I had a $200 withdrawal and a $200 deposit that weren't reflected in the checkbook, but at least the balance would be the same.

I took the subway down to my office. I fell asleep, and overshot my stop, which isn't easy to do standing up, but I was really tired. I woke up at 34th Street, thinking I was at 42nd Street, and started to get off the train. I immediately knew something was wrong. The Penn Station stop is like no other stop on the entire subway system. It is the only express station where you cannot transfer directly from the express to the local, even though the trains stop right next to each other. You have to go downstairs from one, and back upstairs to the other. At Penn Station, you get out the local side of the local train, rather than the express side. There is no platform between the two trains. There is, however, a platform between the uptown express and the downtown express, so it is perfectly easy to transfer from one of those trains to the other, though there is no reason at all why anyone would ever want to do so, unless, of course, they had missed their stop.

I had missed my stop, but I was on the downtown local, which didn't help me at all. As soon as the door opened on the local side, I knew I'd screwed up, so I decided to stay on the train. I took it down to Chambers Street and walked over to the Department of Buildings.

I gave the address of Rosa's connection to a young man at a computer, who punched it in and gave me the block and lot number for the building. I filled out a form requesting information on the ownership of the building with that block and lot number, handed it in, and sat down to wait. Fifteen minutes later my name was called and I was presented with a computer print-out of the ownership and tax record of the building. For the past ten years the building had been owned by a Mr. Alan Donaldson, who also listed it as his permanent address. Bingo. Another of the players-to-be-named-later identified.

Of course, it would have been more valuable to have identified Pluto, a Most Valuable Player, than Donaldson, a utility infielder, but to do that I would have had to drive to the County Clerk's office in Nassau County. I'd never done an investigation there, so I wasn't even sure where the County Clerk's office was, but anywhere in Nassau County was further than I felt like driving.

I took the subway back uptown to my office. I paid attention this time, and managed to get off at the right stop. When I got to the office, I called up Fred Lazar, the guy who'd gotten me the job with Richard in the first place, and reminded him how I'd once taken a signed statement for him when he was busy with some girl or other, and how he'd always promised to return the favor. He remembered the incident because he remembered the girl, and was only too willing to help. I told him it was a big favor I wanted, that I needed an address checked in Nassau County. He laughed and said that was no big deal, he could do it with one phone call. I wanted to kill him—if there was some way to trace property ownership without going through all the shit I usually went through, I was going to feel like a real fool. Fortunately, there wasn't. He just happened to be screwing some girl in the County Clerk's office.

I told him I'd be out for the day, but just to leave the info on my answering machine.

I hung up and checked the answering machine for messages. There were none, which wasn't surprising, since I'd forgotten to turn the thing on. I did so now. I turned my beeper on too, since I'd also forgotten about it. It seemed like I was forgetting everything these days.

I also turned the telephone ring off. I was going to be out for the day, all right, but I wasn't leaving my office. I was going to sleep.

I had one last chore to perform, however. I got out the tracking unit to check on Red. After all, the guy was carrying around my kilo of coke.

I switched the unit on. Nothing happened. The red light went on, indicating the batteries were good and the unit was primed for action, but that was it. No beep. No vector. Nothing.

I dug out the instruction manual and pored through it. I discovered the unit had a safety check button on the side. I pressed it, and the unit immediately began to go "beep, beep, beep," and the vector arrow popped on and described a 360-degree arc, and then everything shut off again, just as the manual said it would. So the unit was working. So where the hell was Red?

There were several possibilities, none of them good. He might have found the transmitter. Could they trace me through it? No. I'd paid cash. The most they could establish was where it was sold. That would lead them back to Florida, which wouldn't be that bad. But they'd know someone was on to them. They'd know Red had been tracked to Arroyo, and they could figure Arroyo had been tracked to Pluto. That would piss them off immensely, and probably make the operation too dangerous to continue, even if there was anything left to salvage.

And if they'd found the transmitter they'd also found the coke. What would they make of that? Who cares? It would probably confuse the hell out of them, but it was kind of incidental. The most it would mean would be I'd lost my chance of framing Pluto with it, if that had ever been a viable idea to begin with. It almost certainly wouldn't be if they knew I was on to them.

The other possibility was that the transmitter had fallen off. Not as bad, but not too good, either. On the plus side, I'd be entitled to a refund on the unit if I ever got back to Miami. On the minus side, one of the players in my little drama would be driving around with a kilo of coke on the bottom of his car, and I'd have no way to find it.

That caught me up short. Christ, I must be tired. What did I mean, no way to find it? I had the guy's license number.

I went over and picked up the phone. A reassuring "beep, beep, beep" stopped me in my tracks. Thank god. Red was back.

I slammed down the phone and lunged for the unit. I saw at once something was wrong. No vector arrow. Christ, where the fuck was—

Then I realized. The unit was quiet. It was my goddamn beeper that had gone off. Richard's office was beeping me with a case. Well, screw them. I wasn't going to do it.

I shut off the beeper and picked up the phone, but I didn't call Richard's office. I called Fred Lazar.

Fred was surprised to hear from me ("Christ, I didn't say I could do it that quick"), but I told him I was calling about something else, that I needed another favor. Could he trace a license plate number for me? He allowed as to how he could, and from his chuckle, I inferred that meant he knew a girl at Motor Vehicles too.

I hung up and called Richard's office to tell 'em to

go to hell, but it didn't go exactly as planned. I got
Kathy, who was in a foul mood, even for her.

"Where the hell are you?" she screamed into the
phone. "Do you know it's nearly eleven?"

She was in such a snit, and I was in such a fog, it
was a while before the information managed to filter
through and sink in. Christ! I'd been so wrapped up in
the Albrect thing I'd completely forgotten. Today was
the day I was due at Richard's office to turn in my
cases. I was two hours late.

17

RICHARD ROSENBERG WAS A GOOD TEN YEARS MY JUNIOR. Like me, he had gotten a liberal arts education. Unlike me, when he had discovered his education had left him totally unprepared to deal with the outside world, he had gone back to college and studied law. He was a good student, graduating in the top one percent of his class, and as soon as he passed the bar, he received handsome job offers from several prestigious firms. He turned them all down. His reason was television.

In 1978, when the law was changed and attorneys were finally allowed to advertise, a whole new field opened up. Civil suits, once considered nickel and dime, were suddenly big business. The reason was public awareness. It used to be that if a guy fell down and broke his leg, he figured it was his tough luck. It never would have occurred to him that he was entitled to anything. If it did, he never would have thought of hiring an attorney and, even then, his first thought would have been that he couldn't afford one.

TV changed all that. People who didn't know what the words "contingency basis" meant all knew what the word "free" meant. It meant that your broken leg might be worth money, and that it didn't cost anything to find out.

By the time Richard emerged from college, several prominent law firms, notably Jacoby and Meyers ("It's about time . . ."), and Davis and Lee ("Dial L-A-W-Y-E-R-S"), had built up sizable reputations and practices through TV and radio advertising. Richard looked around and said, "Hmmmm."

He rented an office on West 12th Street and opened the law firm of Rosenberg and Stone. Stone was a dummy. Rosenberg was the whole show.

He took out all the loans he could get and sank the money into twenty-second TV spots. He made three spots, all similar. A typical one showed a black family; the young mother is sitting on a couch holding a baby in her arms. A three-year-old is playing on the floor. The father is sitting next to the young mother, his right leg encased in a huge, white, hip-length cast. The wife, bravely holding back tears, says, "How we gonna pay the rent, Sam? How we gonna pay the rent?"

The answer, of course, was to call Rosenberg and Stone. Their slogan: "No case too big. No case too small." Then there was a lot of other stuff about how it wouldn't cost you anything, and how you could get a free consultation right in your own home.

In the beginning, Richard actually went to those free consultations. He had to. He was a one-man show. Later, as the settlements began to trickle in, he branched out. He moved into a larger suite of offices in the building and hired girls to answer the phones. He hired law students as paralegals to handle the paperwork. And he hired people to do the legwork.

One of the first people Richard contacted was Fred Lazar, who ran a detective agency in Manhattan. It was no go. The most Richard would pay was ten bucks an hour and thirty cents a mile. Fred was out of his league.

Fred and I had been on the Goddard College soccer team together, he at fullback, I in the goal. Together we formed the backbone of the team's defensive unit, which is not really bragging, considering the emphasis they put on sports at Goddard. Anyhow, since we both live in Manhattan, Fred and I occasionally saw each other at New Year's parties and the like. He knew I was out of work and looking for something that would be flexible enough to leave time for writing, so he gave me a call.

I was surprised to hear from him. All his detectives were ex-cops, and there had never been any question of me ever working for *his* agency. The subject had never come up, and never would. But this was something different. It was something he didn't want, and something I could do.

Fred introduced me to Richard, who offered me the same deal he'd offered Fred—ten bucks an hour and thirty cents a mile. There were only two requirements for the job—a car and a detective license.

I had a car.

Fred got me the license. There was nothing to it. I filled out an application. I signed an affidavit attesting that I was not a known criminal, member of the Communist party, or a general nogoodnik. Fred took me down to the 23rd precinct, where I paid ten bucks to get fingerprinted. He also took me to Woolworth's, where I had a color photo taken for two bucks in one of those little booths. "Look mean," Fred told me. I tried and ended up looking stupid. It didn't matter. Fred sent the whole mess off to Albany, and two weeks later he handed me a notarized photo I.D., the one I use to impress people like Gutierrez's super.

That's all there was to it. Richard gave me a half-hour crash course on how to sign up clients and take pictures, handed me a briefcase full of sign-up kits, maps, and a camera, and off I went.

For a while it was fun. Hey! I'm a private detective! Me. Stanley Hastings. With a real I.D. and everything. Christ, if I weren't married, I bet I could hang out in singles bars and get laid all the time. Stanley Hastings, P.I.

The thrill lasted about a month. During that time I was the lion of any social gathering, since all my friends wanted to know what it was like for an ordinary person, one of them, to be a private detective. But the excitement quickly waned. Soon, aside from the anxiety I built up about going into certain neighborhoods, my feelings about the job narrowed down to one specific. It was bloody fucking dull.

On days I had to turn in stuff to Richard, it was also a pain in the ass.

I got off the phone with Kathy as quickly as I could, which wasn't nearly as quickly as I would have liked, but I was so tired the simple expedient of hanging up on her never occurred to me. I ran out to Broadway to the 60-Minute Photomat, and picked up the six rolls of film I'd shot that week. The girl gave me a hassle about my unpaid bill, but I made up some clever excuse like "The check is in the mail," and got the hell out of there.

I went back to the office and began to sort through the photos. Some of them were easy to identify. For instance, the first envelope contained the Rabinowitz photos—four pictures of Mrs. Rabinowitz's injury, and twenty of the defect in the sidewalk. I shoved the whole thing in a different envelope and wrote "Rabinowitz" on the label. Underneath, I wrote "L/A" for "Location of Accident," followed by the specific street address of the defect. Done.

The next one was harder. Six clients all on the same roll.

As I looked at the pictures, my initial reaction was what it always is in these cases: "Who *are* these people?" Even under good circumstances, six clients on a roll gives me pause, but now, with no sleep, and a few other things on my mind, as I stared at the faces in the pictures my eyes began to glaze over.

I shook myself awake and got down to basics. The negatives are numbered, and my paysheets, which list the clients' names and addresses and the time and mileage for each case, are in chronological order, so, theoretically, if I can get one, I can get 'em all.

All right, the little black kid with the scar on his forehead—is that Chakim Frazier from Bedford-Stuyvesant, Brooklyn? Beats me. Reconstruct. Let's see, Throop Avenue, apartment 2R. Yeah. I remember. A three-story frame house, the front door unlocked, 2R stood for second floor right. There were three guys hanging out on the front steps, and I was nervous about going in, but I did, and who lived there? A black kid with a scar on his forehead? No. A black woman with a broken arm. Ah, here's one. Is it her? Sure, this must be Chakim Frazier from old Bed-Stuy. Great. Four shots of Chakim Frazier. Let's match 'em up with the negatives, put 'em in an envelope, and—shit! Another black woman with a broken arm. Which one is Chakim Frazier? Check the paysheets. Ah! Starshima Weaver, Jamaica, Queens. Great. So which is which? Check the paysheets. Starshima Weaver was Thursday afternoon. Chakim Frazier was Friday. Check the negatives. Pictures five through eight, and nine through twelve are the black women with the broken arms, so five through eight's gotta be Starshima Weaver, and nine through twelve's gotta be Chakim Frazier. So who the hell's the kid with the scar on his face? He's one through four. Oh, yeah. I had those four shots in the camera when I turned in my paysheets last time, so I didn't develop them. He'll be on last week's paysheets. Let's see. Ah yes. Hello, Teddy Robinson.

Somehow I got it done. Next, the paysheets themselves. I tallied them up, and filled in the amounts on the recapitulation page. 440 bucks for 44 hours' work, plus $217.95 expenses for gas, tolls, film and developing. If that sounds good, consider this: I turn in my cases bi-weekly, so my average was $220 a week. Try to live on that in New York.

I shoved the whole mess in my briefcase and stumbled out the door.

I took a taxi down to West 12th Street. Ordinarily, I'd have taken the subway, but I was too damn tired. I gave the driver the exorbitant amount it cost for the pitifully short ride, tipped him half a buck at which he neither smiled nor sneered, went in, took the elevator up to the 14th floor, rang the bell, and was buzzed into the office of Rosenberg and Stone.

Richard's outer office resembled a mail-order ship-

ping house more than a law firm. Twin desks, manned
by Kathy and Susan, flanked the doorway. Twin touch-
tone switchboards, 20 lines each, sat on the desks.
Behind them, the walls were lined with file cabinets,
half the drawers of which were pulled open. At the
back of the room, two secretaries typed furiously at
typing stands. Young, underpaid law students scam-
pered back and forth, emerging from the inner office
to the left, pulling documents from the files, thrusting
them at the secretaries, and plunging back in again.
The door to the right-hand office, Richard's, remained
shut.

As usual, Kathy and Susan were both on the phone.
Kathy had four other calls blinking on her switchboard, Susan three on hers.

Kathy immediately put her fifth caller on hold to
bawl me out for being late. Kathy was about 26, with
short-cropped black hair, and a not unattractive face,
considering, of course, that I had never seen her smile.
I never could figure out just what her problem was,
though, uncharitably, it would not have surprised me
too much to find out that she was the type of girl that
was constantly getting fucked and then dumped.

Susan put her call on hold to come to my defense,
which was embarrassing at the very least. Susan, about
22, with shoulder-length straw hair, and cute as a
button in soft pinks and whites was, I imagined, also
uncharitably, the type of girl it might have done some
good to get fucked and then dumped.

I survived the ordeal and was consigned to a chair in
the corner. I had to move a pile of papers off it onto
the floor, causing a paralegal to blanch and rush to
retrieve them. He shot me a dirty look as he scurried
away.

All in all, Richard's office wasn't set up to receive
clients any more than mine was, even less so. But I
knew clients came here. That damn paralegal who had
just sneered at me signed up clients right here in the
office, perhaps in this very chair, any time Susan and
Kathy could talk them into coming in. I resented it, of

course. Every client signed here was a potential thirty-
or forty-dollar job I wouldn't get. That's why Kathy
and Susan were programmed to get the clients in here
if it were at all possible. 'Cause if there was one thing
Richard was, it was tight.

I leaned back in the chair and closed my eyes,
and was doing a fairly good imitation of a man
sleeping, when the intercom buzzed twenty minutes
later, and Kathy bellowed my name and jerked her
thumb toward the right-hand door. I got up, grabbed
my briefcase, and went in.

Richard Rosenberg has always reminded me of a
cross between a toy poodle and a pit bull. A little man
with a pointed nose stuck in the middle of a plump,
jowled face, he had a habit of yapping at you incessantly in a high-pitched, high-strung voice until he spotted his opening. Then he lunged for the throat, grabbing
and holding on till doomsday. He was, as I have
pointed out, frugal to the point of being miserly, and
always bitched and moaned over my bills and be-
grudged me every penny of the small pittance he paid
me. Still and all, as many poor people were finding
out, he was a hell of a good man to have on your side.

When I came in, he was on the phone, obviously
with an insurance adjuster.

"Are you kidding?" he shrilled into the phone. "You
call that an offer? That's an insult, not an offer. You
call that a settlement? We're talking about a six-year-
old girl here, with facial scars. Did you see those
pictures I sent over? The stitches on her cheek? That's
a double layer of stitches, forty-four in all. You know
the kind of scar that's gonna leave? We're not just
talking pain and suffering here, we're talking permanent disfigurement. I mean who's gonna marry her,
huh? Who's gonna give her a job? We're talking earn-
ing potential here, on top of pain and suffering and
humiliation and embarrassment. I file a 2 million dollar suit, which probably should have been 5, and you
come back with an offer like that. If that's how you
feel, let's go to court, but I'm telling you, you know

what will happen then. We're talking about a six-year-old kid. Just let me get one person on the jury with kids of their own, and you know I can do it, and you are gonna pay through the nose."

Richard slammed down the phone, turned to me with no discernible change in his speech pattern, and said, "All right, you're late, let's see what you've got."

I opened the briefcase. Before I'd even fully raised the lid he had the retainer kits out and was pulling out fact sheets.

"O.K., pedestrian knockdown, hit and run, police didn't catch the driver, broken leg, great, it's a No-Fault, money in the bank, next."

He pulled out another sheet. "Starshima Weaver, automobile accident, driver insured, broken arm." He shot a glance at me. "Right or left?"

One thing I learned about Richard was, no matter how carefully I covered a case, he could always find some question to shoot at me to imply there was something I should have included on the fact sheet. I don't think he really cared about the answer; it was just his way of keeping me off balance and keeping himself one-up. This time his gripe was legit. I should have indicated which arm. Fortunately, I remembered from the pictures I'd just I.D.'d.

"Right," I said. Then, inspired, remembering the retainer. "But she's left-handed. She had no trouble signing."

He topped me. "So what? I'll specify in the summons a broken *right* arm, and *they* won't know she's left-handed."

As he whizzed through the rest of the retainers and started in on the pictures, my mind wandered. I was thinking of a case I'd done for Richard early on. It was up in Poughkeepsie, which made it nice, 150-mile round-trip and six hours. It was a case of a young guy, early twenties, who got drunk in a bar and wound up in a fight with some other young guy over a girl. Later that night, the other guy broke into his apartment and beat the shit out of him with a baseball bat. The police got him, charged him with breaking and entering, assault with a deadly weapon, and attempted murder. It was a big case, bigger than my usual trip-and-fall, and I spent a lot of time on it. I got a whole history on the assailant, got the names of the arresting officers, the district attorney, copies of the charges and court dates. I even got signed statements from two witnesses who lived in the building. All in all, I did a hell of a job.

"What's this?" Richard screamed when I showed it to him. "What is this shit?"

"The facts of the case," I told him.

"What facts? What case?" Richard glared at me as if I were an imbecile, which was what I felt like. "You think I'm gonna sue this punk who beat him up? He's got no money. He's got no insurance. How the hell am I gonna sue him?"

Of course, Richard didn't sue him. And I went back to Poughkeepsie, on my own time, of course, since it was my mistake, and did the job again. It was a learning experience. I'd been seduced by the "glamorous" aspects of the case. But actually, the assault and attempted murder, which I'd thought were so important, were incidental. What it was all about was faulty building security—security that had allowed this maniac to get in and beat up our client. The guy who owned the building and who had rented our client the apartment was to blame, and that's who Richard sued.

I was roused from this recollection by the sound of, "Great! Fabulous! What are these?"

I looked over to see Richard leafing through the shots I had taken of the stairs in Gutierrez's building.

"Oh—" I began.

"This is terrific," Richard said. "This is just the type of shot I'm always asking you to get. Good angles, good defects, good perspective. Who's the client?"

"There's no client."

"What?!"

"There's no client. These are just pictures I took—"

Richard was incensed. "You're charging me for pictures you took when there's no client?"

"I didn't charge you for those pictures."

"Well, you charged me for the film, didn't you? There's twelve pictures here; that's half a roll of film. Didn't you charge me for that?"

It was a half hour before I got out of there. I got some new signup kits, and I got some more of Richard's business cards to give clients, and I got my paycheck. It came to 440 bucks, since I handle my own taxes. My check for expenses was for $215.45. Richard had knocked off $2.50 for half a roll of film.

18

I GOT BACK TO MY OFFICE A LITTLE AFTER ONE. Fortunately, there'd been no new cases. I wouldn't have taken them if there had been. I was a wreck.

I checked the answering machine for messages. There was one from my wife: where the hell was I, why wasn't I wearing my beeper, why wasn't the answering machine on before and why was it on now, and where the hell was I again, seeing as how I must have been by the office to turn on the answering machine, and why had I stood up Richard, on payday for Christ's sake, wasn't the money the only thing I was doing this for in the first place?

It was quite a message. I figured Kathy must have called her five or six times.

There were no other messages. I guess Fred Lazar wasn't quite as fast as he said he'd be.

I checked the tracking unit. Still nothing doing.

I reset the answering machine, and made sure the phone ring was off. I left my beeper on, though. I hated to do it, but I couldn't take a chance on Kathy calling my wife again. If they beeped me for a case, I was gonna call and stall the client no matter what.

I lay down on the floor and was out like a light.

I woke up at 5:30 that afternoon. No one had beeped me. I checked the answering machine. No one had called, except for Fred. He had the info, as promised. Pluto was Victor Millsap. Red was Rodney Forrester from East Hampton, Long Island. It was as simple as that.

I checked out East Hampton on the map. It was way the hell out in Suffolk County near the tip of Long Island, which was why I'd never been there, and why Red hadn't been showing up on the tracking unit. He was way out of range.

My relief was boundless.

I took the subway home and got there a little after six. Needless to say, my wife was not in the best of moods. I made up a bullshit story about my beeper being on the fritz, and having three cases in Brooklyn and one in Queens, and having had to juggle Richard in between them. Actually what I did was lie, but somehow "made up a bullshit story" sounds better. I told her I spent nine actual hours on the cases but was putting in for thirteen, that I was sorry to be away all day but we really needed the money. I told her, too, that I was sorry Kathy had called her, but neither I nor any other mortal man had control over Kathy, and I was sorry I hadn't called Richard but how was I to know my beeper was on the fritz, etc., etc. and the end result was I was such a silver-tongued devil that by the time we got Tommie in bed I began hinting about an amorous episode, to which she actually concurred.

As usual, she made fun of the interest I took in her as she undressed. She is always amazed that after ten years of marriage I am still fascinated by her breasts. I guess that's the difference between men and women. My wife is calm and relaxed and amused by my attitude. Personally, I'm always jumping out of my skin.

An added bonus of lovemaking is that afterward my wife is usually happy and content and rolls over and goes to sleep. This night was no exception. By 11:30 she was out like a light. I, on the other hand, was wide-awake and well-rested. I slipped out of bed, pulled on my clothes, and by 11:45 I was on my way out the door.

19

THERE WAS NO REASON TO BELIEVE THAT ROSA WOULD BE AT THE SAME SPOT AT THE SAME TIME AS SHE HAD BEEN THE OTHER NIGHT, but when I got to the corner of 48th and Broadway, there she was, large as life. It was a little after one in the morning. I'd driven down to my office, parking being no problem that time of night, gone in, and made a few preparations. Then I'd left the car there and strolled over to Broadway to check out the corner. And there she was again, just as before. She wore a yellow pullover this time, but the breasts seemed to be the same, and once again there seemed to be no discernible undergarment.

I stopped near the corner and looked at her, as if hesitating and making up my mind. This wasn't hard to do, since what I was actually doing was hesitating and making up my mind. She looked at me and smiled. I smiled back somewhat nervously. I blushed, I'm sure convincingly, and strolled over.

"Hi," I said.

"Hi," she said. It was a wonderful invitation.

I wasn't sure what to say next. She seemed quite familiar with that sort of approach, and took the initiative. "You looking to party?"

"Could be," I said. "How much would it cost?"

"Fifty bucks straight, seventy-five half and half, a hundred around the world."

"Around the world?"

"Yeah."

"What countries you visit?"

"France and Greece."

Hmm. Some itinerary. Book me on a world-wide cruise.

"A hundred bucks?" I asked.

"That's right."

What the hell, I thought, I'm not going to let her keep it anyway. "O.K.," I said. "Take me around the world."

She hesitated a moment, and I realized I'd done something wrong, but I couldn't figure out what it was. Damn, I should have done more research. Then it hit me. I'd agreed to the price too quickly. I hadn't tried to bargain her down. The prices she quoted me were only asking prices. She probably rarely got them. The johns who were actually parting with their money were better businessmen than I.

However, the lure of the C-note was too strong for her to ignore. After a moment, she smiled, took my arm, and led me down the street to the hotel where I'd seen her take her other tricks.

In the hotel, for which the word "cheap" had been invented, I discovered the price of the evening's entertainment had escalated. I had to pay for the room. I registered as John Smith, a clever alias thought of by only half of the establishment's clientele.

Rosa led me upstairs to a small room furnished only by a bed, a dresser, and a chair.

Rosa locked the door, and turned to me. "First the money," she said, holding out her hand.

I took out one of Albrect's hundreds and gave it to her. She inspected it carefully, folded it up, and stuck it in her purse. She put the purse on the bed, straightened up, smiled, put her hands on her hips, and began undulating slowly.

I could have stopped the show there and then, but I figured I should let it go a little further to make sure I had her really hooked good. Besides, I'm only human. I'd been thinking about those tits for days. I contented myself with smiling self-consciously.

Rosa hooked her thumbs under the edge of her pullover and slowly pulled it up over her head. Peace and plenty. Large, firm, protruding breasts, large pink nipples just a half a caress away from being erect. Jesus Christ, remember what you're there for.

It killed me but I did. As she swayed over to me and began to unbutton my shirt, I reached into my hip pocket and whipped out the pair of handcuffs, another joke present, and with what I hoped would pass for practiced skill, clapped them on her wrists, at the same time beginning the Miranda drone, now a staple of TV cop shows, "You're under arrest. You have the right to remain silent. If you give up the right to remain silent—"

Rosa gave up the right to remain silent. "Son of a bitch!" she shrieked, twisting away from me with the fury of a trapped tigress. "Fucking asshole son of a bitch! Shit! Fuck! Cunt! I knew you were a cop! Goddamnit to fucking shit hell!"

I was beginning to regret passing up my evening with this girl. It might have been interesting. Hell, I bet she might have even talked dirty in bed.

"Take it easy," I told her.

"Fuck you, asshole pig!"

I smiled at her. "That's better."

She started a furious retort. Stopped. Thought better of it. Changed her tack to pleading and ingratiating. "Come on, man," she said. "You don't want to arrest me."

"You're right. I don't."

She stared at me. "What?"

"I don't want to arrest you."

"Then what the fuck you doing, man?"

"Let's you and me have a little talk. If it goes all right, I let you go."

"You kidding?"

"No."

"What the hell you want?"

"First of all, I want my hundred dollars back."

She looked as if I'd just told her there was no Santa

Claus. "Oh, shit," she said. She pouted, swung her head back and forth, and shuffled her feet. Then she turned, fumbled in her purse, and took out the folded hundred. Reluctantly, she held it out toward me, begrudging every inch. I took it and shoved it in my pocket.

"All right," I said. "Put your shirt on."

She looked at her shirt on the bed. "I can't do that with these handcuffs on."

She was right She couldn't. Serendipity.

Still, this was business, and I had to concentrate. I took out my key and unlocked the handcuffs. She rubbed her wrists, which I guess is a reflex action, since the handcuffs hadn't been tight. Then she got her shirt from the bed and put it on. Easy come, easy go.

"O.K.," she said. "What do you want?"

"Guillermo Gutierrez."

Whatever she'd been expecting, it wasn't that. She looked as if she'd been slapped.

"What about him?"

"He's your boyfriend," I said. It was not a question, and she recognized it as such.

"So what?"

"He's dead," I told her.

Her eyes widened and her jaw dropped open. She sank down on the bed. Her hands went to her face. "Oh, no!" she said.

It was no good. She was acting, and she wasn't good at all. Her shock at his name had been genuine, but this sucked. She knew he was dead, and the way I figured it, that could mean only one thing.

"Don't give me that shit," I told her. "You know he's dead. You went up to his place and found him there. You panicked and split. You kept waiting to see what would happen, but nothing happened. Finally, you couldn't stand it any more. You went back there. The body was gone."

She was just staring at me. "How do you know this?"

"That's my job."

She just kept staring. "You're not a cop?"

"No."

"Who are you?"

"I'm a private detective," I told her. "I want the guys who did Gutierrez."

"Why?"

"Because the guys who hit Gutierrez also hit a friend of mine. I'm gonna find 'em and I'm gonna bring 'em down."

She believed me. She didn't know I was an asshole. Hell, she watched television, too. She probably thought I could do it.

"What do you want with me?" she said.

"Alan Donaldson," I told her.

Again, I was the Grinch Who Stole Christmas.

"No," she moaned.

"Look," I said. "I know he's your connection. I don't think he's involved in this, at least not directly. I don't want him. It's the higher-ups I want. You cooperate with me, I'll do everything I can to leave him in place."

"Is that for real?"

"That's for real. You in?"

"What do you want?"

"Now you're talking," I said. "Look, I know what your scene is. You're gonna turn three or four more tricks until you've got enough to score, then you're gonna call Donaldson. Frankly, I don't want to wait around that long. So here's the deal. I'll give you the money you need to score, you call him and go score now."

"You shitting me?"

"I'm on the square. How much you need to score?"

She hesitated, and I could see her mind going. "400," she said.

"Don't shit me," I said, "or you go it alone. How much you really need?"

She pouted, shrugged. "Two hundred."

"For what?"

"An eighth of coke."

"Nice price, these days," I told her. I hoped it was.

"Because of Guillermo," she said. "I pay the same as if I bought quantity."

"I can see why you'd hate to see Donaldson go down," I said. "All right, you need two hundred to score. How much have you made so far?"

She pouted, looked at me, shifted her eyes. "Fifty," she said.

"Come again."

She shrugged her shoulders. "All right, a hundred."

"That's what I thought," I told her. "And I'll bet it took you more than two tricks to get it. That's why you took a chance on me. My hundred was all you needed to score."

She looked at me, said nothing. I took the hundred-dollar bill out of my pocket and held it in front of me. She looked at it, but it had kind of lost its thrill for her. She looked back up at me.

"That's all you want me to do?" she said. "Just score?"

"No. You gotta find out something for me."

"What?"

"How low his supply is and when he's gonna score some more."

"Shit."

"That shouldn't be so hard."

"You gonna cut off his source?"

"Hey. A guy like him has lots of sources. I can't protect the whole world."

"Yeah," she said, dubiously.

"Look," I told her. "It's not like you had room to bargain. You cooperate, he stays in place. You don't, he goes down. Now let's go."

We went. She wasn't happy, but she went. She made the phone call from the corner. Then we got my car and drove over there. I let her out at the corner.

"I'm gonna drive down the block and turn the corner, and park. You meet me there."

I gave her the money. She started to get out of the

car. I grabbed her arm. "Remember, you don't show up, he goes down."

She nodded, got out, and closed the door. I watched her walk down the street toward the townhouse. I pulled out and passed her as she headed up the front steps. I turned the corner, parked, and waited.

She was back in ten minutes.

"Well," I asked, as she slid into the seat.

She smiled at me. "Piece of cake," she said. "He's low. He's gonna score tomorrow. He promised me he'd be holding by late afternoon."

I smiled back. "Nice work," I told her.

I drove her home. I figured I owed her that, and not just for the information. Maybe I'm just a sexist pig, but in my book any pretty girl who smiles at me and shows me her tits deserves a ride home.

20

I STAKED OUT DONALDSON'S PLACE AT NINE IN THE MORNING. From what Rosa had told me, it was a pretty safe bet he wasn't going to score until the afternoon, but I wasn't taking any chances. What if he went somewhere else first?

Of course, I was being stupid. Guys who snort coke all night aren't usually up at the crack of dawn, and if they are, it's because they've been up all night and are just getting ready to fall into bed. There were no lights in Donaldson's apartment, no sign of activity of any kind. I had moved my car about ten times, argued with a dozen policemen, and even gotten a forty-dollar ticket from an overzealous meter-maid. And still nothing.

What made things worse was, once again, I had gotten no sleep. After dropping Rosa off, I had driven out to East Hampton to pick up the kilo of coke. That wasn't as easy as it sounds. I have a map that lists the distance places are from New York City, and East Hampton was listed at 106 miles. That's as the crow flies, and I'm not a crow.

The saving grace was at that time of night there was no traffic and I could make good time, and after I took the East Side Drive to the Midtown Tunnel and got on the L.I.E., I was averaging about sixty, and the miles were flying by.

The tracking unit kicked in somewhere around Islip, and I was mighty glad to hear it. It would have been a real kick in the ass to have driven all the way out there to discover that Red was nowhere to be found and was probably on his way back to Florida at the time. The "beep, beep, beep" from the unit spurred me on, and I pushed down harder on the accelerator.

Not long after that I started getting punchy. I had flashes of paranoia that I shouldn't be going so fast, I was going to get busted for drug running. Then I realized how stupid that was. I started cracking myself up, paraphrasing the speech Dub Taylor says to Paul Newman and Robert Redford in "Butch Cassidy and the Sundance Kid": "Morons. I got morons on my team. No one's gonna bust me on my way *out* to East Hampton. I got no *dope* on my way *out* to East Hampton."

You had to be there. I got to giggling uncontrollably and stomping down on the accelerator, and if a cop had happened to stop me, drugs or no drugs, they were going to put me away.

I hit East Hampton about four in the morning. It's a beach town, as the smell of sea air reminded me, and I bet it would have looked great in the daylight, but it was too dark to see, and I was too tired to care. All I cared about was finding Red's house. Fortunately, I had the tracking unit.

So far I'd only used the unit to track a moving object. This was my first time using it to find a stationary one. It was kind of fun. I'd drive along following the vector, and if I missed a turn or made a wrong turn, the vector would change and I'd have to turn around and backtrack until I got the vector pointing ahead of me again. I kept doing this, and it wasn't long before I found myself driving down Red's street with the vector pointing "right this way."

A couple of blocks down the street the vector veered slightly to the right and pointed straight at a car parked in a shrub-lined driveway about two houses ahead of me. I immediately pulled into the curb and cut my lights.

I took a flashlight out of my glove compartment just in case and got out of the car. I stuck the flashlight in my hip pocket, and crept along the sidewalk up to the edge of the shrubs to check out the house and car.

The car was in the shadows, which was good, but there was a light on in one of the downstairs windows of the house, and I didn't like that at all. By rights Red should have been sound asleep, and if he wasn't, what else could it mean except somehow he knew something was up? What if he was watching? What if he was waiting for me? What if he had a dog?

I was a nervous wreck, but I did it. I crept out into the driveway, bent down behind the car, reached under and grabbed—nothing! There was nothing there! I groped my hand around. Jesus Christ, wasn't this where I put it? I lay down on the ground, stuck my head under the car, groped around with both hands. Nothing! I even risked switching on the flashlight. That clinched it. There was nothing there.

My head was racing. What had happened? Could it have fallen off? No, it couldn't have fallen off. The coke could, but not the transmitter, because I'd been following the transmitter here. So the transmitter had to be here, but it wasn't. Impossible. The vector was pointing right at it. It was pointing right at the car and—Jesus Christ! The house! It was pointing at the car and the house, so if it wasn't on the car it was in the house, and that meant that Red had found it, and found the coke. Red knew that something was up and that's why there was a light on in the house, because he, and maybe some of his buddies, were there right now waiting for me, and this was a trap, and they must have seen the flashlight, and—

I was back in my car in nothing flat, surprised to get that far and happy to be alive. I gunned the motor and pulled out from the curb.

I don't know what impelled me to look at the vector as I went by the house. Perhaps I just wanted to see it point to where my would-be killers were.

But it didn't. It didn't swing and point to the house

at all. It kept pointing slightly ahead and to the right. But as I passed the *next* house, the vector swung all the way around and pointed back the other way.

I slammed on my brakes and pulled into the curb. I couldn't believe it. Wrong car, wrong house! How could I? I hadn't checked the vector by driving by the house first. I hadn't checked the license plate on the car. I hadn't even checked the number on the house. *Morons. I got Morons on my team.*

I got out of the car. I was so angry I slammed the door, screw the noise. I strode back to the house I'd just passed. This one was entirely dark. I walked up to Red's car, bent down, and snapped on the flashlight.

There they were, the transmitter and the bag of coke. Two of the suction cups had come loose and were dragging on the ground, and how Red missed them was beyond me, but the bag was still there. There was a big hole worn in one corner where it had dragged on the ground, but the dope was still in it.

I snapped off the other two suction cups. I was going to take the transmitter too, but thought better of it. Maybe I was just trying to make up for the bonehead plays I'd made so far, but it occurred to me Red might make another run, and it might help to know where he went. Besides, I could always find the transmitter if I wanted to take it off later. At any rate, I left it on the car.

I got back in my car and drove home. I held it well under the speed limit, what with a kilo of coke on board, and it was 7:15 when I double-parked in front of my building.

I went upstairs, where my wife was just waking up, and gave her the impression that I had just now gotten out of bed and gone to double-park the car for the alternate-side parking regulations. I shaved, brushed my teeth, went out, had a cup of coffee and a doughnut, and drove downtown. I left my car in the Municipal lot on 54th and Eighth Avenue, which at eighty-five cents per half-hour is great for short stops and prohibitive for all day, ran down to my office, dropped off the kilo of coke, ran back, got in the car and made it down to Donaldson's by 9:00—tired, exhausted, angry, feeling like a fool, and knowing damn well he'd never show before noon.

The first sign of life was about 2:30. The blind in an upstairs window went up. By about three a knockout of a teenage girl came out. Another left at 3:15. What was I doing wrong?

About 3:30 a hired car pulled up in front. It wasn't a limousine, but it wasn't a taxi either. It was car #278 from one of those fleets of hired cars you can call up and order if you move enough coke to be able to afford it.

The driver got out and rang the doorbell, and Donaldson came out. This was the first time I'd gotten a good look at him. He was youngish, say thirty, and of medium height and build. He wasn't ugly, but he wasn't handsome enough to rate two teenage girls. Ah, the wonders of coke. He seemed to look none the worse for his evening of wear.

He got in the car and drove off, with me following. We went through the Midtown Tunnel. This driver obviously was paid just to drive.

I knew where we were going, but I had to be sure. With each turn I got surer and surer. L.I.E., Grand Central, Van Wyck, Southern Boulevard, Sunrise Highway.

The car headed south, twisted and turned, and finally pulled into the driveway of Millsap's house. Bingo. Jackpot. I drove on by and headed home.

I felt pretty good. I had it all now. I'd run down all my leads, tested all my theories, and they'd all checked out. I'd followed the trail, Dumbo to Bambi to Pluto (great double-play combination). I had a line on Floridian #1 and #2, via Red. I knew why Gutierrez and Albrect had been killed, and while I didn't know exactly who had pulled the trigger, I knew what men had ordered it done. Starting from scratch, with only

Albrect's story, so lacking in critical information, to go on, I had figured all this out.

I knew the whole setup now. I had only one more problem. What the hell was I going to do about it?

21

I RENTED THE COSTUME AT A THEATRICAL SUPPLY HOUSE NEAR MY OFFICE. I rented a car from one of the cheaper rental agencies, a mid-size car, not too expensive, not too cheap, nothing to attract attention. I threw the cartons in the trunk and drove out to Woodmere, to Pluto's house.

It had been five days since I'd tracked Donaldson out there. During those five days I'd been busy. The first two, I was mainly busy sleeping, something I sorely needed to do. After that, came a lot of thinking and planning, followed by a lot of research and practice. I spent a day with Fred Lazar, which was kind of tough, seeing as how I couldn't let him know why I was interested in the things I was asking him about, but, although he was understandably curious, I managed to pull it off. I spent another day alone, practicing the things I had learned. I also spent a day working for Richard, which actually consisted of six cases spread out over the five days. So, as I said, I'd been busy.

Now, all my preparations having been made, there was nothing left to do but do it.

I pulled my car into the curb a half a block from Pluto's house, got out, and looked around.

I had been afraid in a ritzy neighborhood like this that all of the telephone wires would be underground, but I was in luck. There was a pole by his driveway from which the phone line ran straight to his house.

160

The pole was unobtrusive, hidden by trees. It was perfect.

I had my telephone repair outfit in the trunk. I was all set, except for one thing. Suddenly I knew how Superman must have felt looking for a phone booth. Where the hell was I going to change?

I got back in the car and drove back to a less posh neighborhood. Still no place to change. I cruised around and finally found a McDonald's on the strip. It was about ten in the morning and the place wasn't too busy. I took the package out of the trunk, went in, and headed for the men's room.

I am well acquainted with fast-food bathrooms. They are a staple of my profession. When you drive around New York City and vicinity all day, one of the biggest problems you come up against is where to take a piss. There really are no public restrooms in New York City. You have to improvise. Regular restaurants are no good, because the minute you walk into one, a waitress with a menu will try to guide you to a table, and when they find you only want to use the bathroom, you become slightly less popular than pond scum.

So fast-food restaurants are the ticket. No one gives a damn about you there, and no one's even going to attempt to wait on you unless you shove your way up to the counter and shout over twenty or thirty other people trying to get served. In my six months on the job, I've probably visited over half the McDonald's and Burger King restrooms in the city. Some of them are better than others, and it has nothing to do with what chain of restaurants they are; it simply has to do with their location and type of clientele. Some of them are spotless. Some turn the stomach. A swollen bladder has made me impervious to most filth. I only pass up a bathroom if, as is often the case, it is out of order and closed, or, as sometimes happens, I find hanging out in it a rather strung-out junkie who looks at me as if slowly realizing I might be his next fix.

This McDonald's restroom fell in the mid-range. It

was open, a plus; unoccupied, a double plus; and filthy, a small minus. I went into the toilet stall and locked the door, another plus.

The toilet was full and unflushed. I would have liked to flush it, but that seemed just as likely to flood the floor as to empty the toilet, so I decided to let well enough alone. I unwrapped the package and changed as quickly as possible, trying to keep the various articles of clothing from going on the floor, or worse, dipping into the toilet. It was hard without a hook to hang anything on and considering how cramped it was in there, but I managed. In less than five minutes my suit was packed in the box, and I was dressed as a telephone repairman, complete with hard-hat and tool belt. I put the box under my arm and left the bathroom.

If the sight of a telephone repairman emerging from a bathroom that had been entered by a businessman in a suit startled anyone, nobody showed it; no one looked at me. I walked out of the place, got in my car and drove off. I felt pretty good about the whole thing until I realized that, in my haste to change, I'd forgotten to take a piss.

I drove back to Pluto's. I parked the car about a block away. It would have been much better if I could have gotten a telephone repair truck, but that was beyond my resources and, even if it hadn't been, I wouldn't have known how to go about getting one. Besides, the suit was just protective coloration. I hoped no one would notice me this time.

I walked up to Pluto's driveway and right to the telephone pole. I put the climbing belt around the pole, snapped it onto the hooks on my belt, and started up the pole.

I'd practiced climbing a pole on Riverside Drive with the belt the day before, but I hadn't had the added weight of the tools, and I hadn't gone much above six or eight feet, not wanting to attract attention and get myself busted for nothing.

I should have practiced more.

Pain. Agony. Oh God, I don't know how to do this.

I'm forty years old and out of shape and I never climbed like this in my life anyway. Oh, let's splurge on the telephone repair truck. I don't care what it costs. Give me a cherrypicker, I can't do this. I don't care if a murderer gets away. Fuck it. Shit. Get me down.

I reached the top. Settled into what I hoped was a secure position. There were two wires running into the house. One would be the phone, one would be electric. I sure wanted to choose the right one. I could see the headline: "PRIVATE DETECTIVE FRIED ON PHONE POLE. *The body of Stanley Hastings, inexplicably dressed as a telephone repairman, was found . . .*"

Stop it! Asshole. You did lights for that summer stock theater, didn't you? What's so damn hard? That's the electric, that's the phone. Get on with it.

I took out of my belt the gadget I'd made. It consisted of two clamps connected by about twelve inches of wire. I clamped them to the phone wire about a foot apart. I didn't light up like a Christmas tree, which was encouraging. Now I could cut the wire without it falling to the ground. I took out my wire cutters, chose a point half-way between the clamps, and cut. It was harder than I'd expected, but I managed to claw my way through. The wire snapped. The clamps held. The two pieces of severed wire dangled about 6 inches from each other. I put the cutters back in my belt and started down the pole.

Going down was a lot easier than coming up, but it was still tricky. I reached the bottom, heaved a sigh of relief, and unhooked the belt. I took a step back and looked up at the wire. It wasn't bad. The clamps were visible, but if you weren't looking for them, you'd never notice they were there.

I hurried back to my car and drove to the McDonald's. Again the bathroom was empty. I changed quickly, became a civilian. I got back in my car and drove back to Pluto's. I pulled off the road and parked in a place a little way down the street from which I could see his driveway. I sat in the car and waited.

I waited over two hours. Jesus Christ, what was the matter with these guys? Didn't they ever use the phone?

Then I started getting worried. What if they *did* use the phone? What if they used it a lot? What if Pluto had tried to use the phone right after I cut the wire. Worse, what if Pluto was *on* the phone when I cut the wire? What if he'd already run out and called the repair service while I was changing my clothes at McDonald's?

Christ, had I blown it again? Probably. It would be just like me. So afraid they'd spot me in my telephone repair outfit that I run out and change my clothes while the whole thing slips away. They must have already called. Any minute now, a telephone repair truck will pull into the driveway and the game will be over.

If they're even home. Hell, I hadn't even thought of that. What if Pluto isn't even home. What if I'm watching an empty house, and—

A car emerged from the driveway and drove past me, headed back the way I'd come. As soon as he was out of sight, I pulled a U-turn and followed. I caught up within three blocks and stayed a safe distance behind. The car hit the main drag, drove two blocks, and stopped at a pay phone on the corner.

The driver got out. He was a tall, dark, hulking man, with one of the ugliest faces I'd ever seen. He went to the pay phone and made a call.

This wouldn't be Pluto himself, I figured, just one of his henchmen. It didn't matter. This was the call I wanted.

Tall, Dark and Ugly got back in his car and drove off. I didn't follow. Instead, I pulled up next to the phone booth, got out, and called Emergency Repair.

"Emergency service," a gruff male voice answered.

"This is Victor Millsap in Woodmere," I told him. "I just had one of my men call in that my phone was out of order."

"Yeah. I got it. Just came in. Don't worry. We'll be right out."

"You don't have to," I told him. "The phone's working again."

"What's that you say?"

"Cancel the order. The phone's working."

"That's not what your man said."

"I sent him to a pay phone. In the meantime, the phone's working again. I'm calling from it now."

"Then what the hell's with the repair call?"

"The phone was dead. Now it's working. Cancel the order."

"Oh, hey, that's gonna be a bitch. I wrote it up. You better let the guys come out there and check it out."

"And then you're gonna charge me for it. No way.'

"We don't charge for repair service."

"I don't care. Listen, I've got important people over for a business conference. I don't want phone repairmen crawling all over the place. Just cancel the order, will you."

"O.K., O.K., I'll cancel it," he said.

The way he said it, I wasn't convinced. I had to be sure.

"What's your name?" I asked him.

"What?"

"What's your name?"

"Frank Parker. Why?"

"Because if your boys show up and interrupt my conference, I want to know who to blame when I call your boss."

"Oh, Jesus Christ," he said. "Listen. I got it in my hand. I'm tearing it up now. You satisfied?"

I was. This time I believed him. I hung up the phone, got in the car, and drove to McDonald's. They ought to be getting to know me by now, I thought as I walked in. Nobody seemed to, though. I went in the men's room and changed my clothes again. This time I even remembered to take a piss.

22

TALL, DARK AND UGLY OPENED THE FRONT DOOR.

"Telephone repair," I said, and pushed by him into the house.

He looked at me as if I were an ill-mannered clod, but he closed the front door, which was all I cared about. I didn't want him to notice there was no truck parked in the driveway.

"How many phones you got?" I asked him. I was using my ill-mannered slob voice, in keeping with the image, all my years in the acting profession not being entirely wasted.

"Three," he told me.

"They all out?"

"Yeah. They're all out."

"O.K. Let's take a look at 'em."

The first one was in the kitchen. I didn't want that one. I took it apart, inspected it, put it back together again. He watched me the whole time. I hoped his constant scrutiny wasn't going to cramp my style.

"Nothing wrong here," I said. "Let's see the others."

He led me into the living room, which was the size of a small basketball court. A better bet, but the decor, rich but starkly modern and impersonal, told me probably not prime ground. Still, it was worth doing. When I got the phone apart, my buddy was still watching me. I turned to him in my best poor slob manner and said, "Hey, buddy, you got a soda or something? I been dying out there."

He gave me a look that could have fried eggs, then turned and headed for the kitchen. His attitude said it all: repairmen may be schmucks, but everyone needs phones.

The moment he was out of the room, I unscrewed the receiver of the phone and inserted the bug. Fred Lazar had given me a crash course in illegal wiretaps and I'd practiced on my office phone, so I was pretty good at it, and I had the phone all neatly back together by the time my friend returned with a glass of coke.

"Thanks, buddy," I told him, and took a huge swallow. I followed with what I imagined to be an artistic belch. "No problem here. Where's the other one?"

"Through here," he said.

He led me through an arched hallway into a large den. Bingo! Television. Pool table. Walk-in bar. Casual clutter. Comfortable couches and chairs. Yup. This was where I'd make my dope deals.

I started taking the phone apart. My buddy was watching. I wondered how I was going to get rid of him now. Chug down the coke and ask for another? Not great. Shit. I should have passed on the living room and saved it for here. What was I going to do now?

I was saved by the front doorbell. Tall, Dark and Ugly reacted to the chime like a trained dog. His head went up and he looked toward the sound, although, of course, there was nothing to see. He turned back, gave me a look, then turned and walked out of the room.

I had the receiver off and the bug in in seconds. I left the phone itself apart in case my buddy came back quick. Then I ducked down under the desk, and looked for a place to plant another bug. I had one on the phone, but I wanted one on the room.

I had just managed to affix it to the underside of the desk, when I heard footsteps. I straightened up and turned my attention to the phone as he entered the room.

I peeked up from my work to see him. It wasn't my friend who had let me in and given me a coke. It wasn't his boss, Pluto, either. My heart stopped dead. It was Bambi, big as life. Tony Arroyo, the only one in the whole operation I'd ever met face-to-face, the only one who only had to take one look at me and the jig would be up. Holy shit. Thank god I remembered to take that piss at McDonald's.

My first thought was that I should have worn a disguise, that any private detective in his right mind would have figured Tony Arroyo might show up and would have worn a disguise. My second thought was that that was a dumb thought. Disguises work great in the movies, where the actors playing the crooks are directed not to recognize the hero, but in real life? A false mustache or a hairpiece and your eye goes right to it. You couldn't think of a better way of attracting attention. My third thought was stop thinking so much and get your fucking head down.

I kept my head down, thankful I was wearing a hardhat. Tony gave me a casual glance, then walked over to the couch, sat down, picked up a *Penthouse* magazine, and began looking at girls' crotches. Better than my face, I thought. As quickly as I could, I started putting the phone back together again.

I had nearly finished when a kid came into the room. He was tall and gawky, with a kind of goony-looking face. He couldn't have been more than 22 or 23, and he had that eager puppy-like quality of youth. I was surprised. It had never occurred to me that Pluto would have children, but then why couldn't dope dealers have kids just like anybody else.

"Tony," the kid said as Tony rose from the couch. "Good to see you. How you doing?"

"Great, Victor. Couldn't be better," Tony said.

Holy shit. There was no mistaking the tone in Tony's voice. Subservience. This kid wasn't named Victor after his father. This was Victor. This wasn't Pluto's kid. The kid was Pluto.

"Look, Tony," the kid said. "I got a problem with

the phones today. The guy's here now. Why don't we go somewhere else?"

That was my cue and I didn't want to blow it. I didn't want them to go somewhere else. I wanted them to talk right here, into the microphone, if you please.

I'd gotten the phone back together. Now I snapped my tool kit shut, stood up, and moved between the two men, keeping my back to Tony.

"Problem's not here," I said. It was hard keeping my accent and keeping my voice from cracking, but I managed. "I gotta check outside."

I pushed by him and out of the door. I could feel their eyes on my back, but I'm sure it was just my imagination. No one notices a repairman. At any rate, no one stopped me.

I met my buddy in the front hall.

"Gotta check outside," I told him. "I'll ring you if I gotta get in again."

He seemed thrilled by the prospect. I went out the front door and closed it behind me.

I hurried down the driveway to the telephone pole. I put my toolbox on the ground, got out the climbing belt, and fastened it on. It should have been easier climbing the pole the second time, but fear made me fumble. Somehow, I finally reached the top. I got out my wire cutters, and as quickly as I could with trembling hands, stripped the wires and made the splice.

I slid down the pole, went back to the front door, and rang the bell. Tall, Dark and Ugly answered the door.

"Found a loose connection," I said. "Should be all right now. Let's check it out."

He followed me to the phone in the kitchen. I picked up the phone and got a dial tone. I held the buzzing receiver up to him triumphantly.

"There you go," I said. "Back in service."

"What about the other phones?" he said.

"They'll all be working," I told him. "It was the main feed."

He didn't want to take my word for it. I supposed it would be his head if I were wrong. On the way out he detoured into the living room to pick up the phone. It worked. He glanced in the direction of the study, but I could see he was as reluctant to disturb the conference as I was. Weighing the two evils, he found it better to let it go.

He let me out the front door, closing it behind me. Nice. No one had noticed the absence of the repair truck, unless Tony was mentioning it to Pluto now. I doubted it. It was not the sort of thing that would come up in conversation regarding the sale of a small fortune in coke.

I wondered what they were talking about. I would have loved to have tuned in on it, but it was just too risky. I got in the car and sped back to McDonald's. I changed in the rest room for the fourth time and emerged a civilian once again.

I threw the costume in the trunk and drove back to my parking spot, half a block from the house. The guys in the store had assured me that would be close enough. I got out and opened the trunk of the car. I set up the two tape recorders in the trunk. The first one was tuned into the phone bugs. When I switched it on, nothing happened, since no one was using the phone. The second one, however, was tuned to the bug in the study, and when I switched it on, the tape, being voice-activated, started rolling. I plugged in the headphones.

Pluto was laughing. "So how's your girlfriend," he was saying. "She know about that little escapade with Marsha?"

"No way," Tony said. "You think I'm crazy?"

I didn't care about Tony's little escapade with Marsha, and I didn't care if Pluto thought he was crazy. All of that would keep for me on tape. Right now, I was at high risk and needed to get the hell out of there.

I thought about taking the package with the costume along with me, but in the end I left it in the trunk. Hell, if they found the bugs on the phone, they wouldn't need the suit to connect them with the telephone repairman. I locked the recorders and the suit in the trunk, and started walking. I moved right along. I wanted to get out of there fast, and I knew that in a neighborhood like this it would be miles before I could get a cab.

23

WHEN YOU COME RIGHT DOWN TO IT, in my regular job, my job for Richard, I'm not so much a private detective as I am a salesman. In a way, I'm not unlike the real estate salesmen in David Mamet's "Glengarry Glenn Ross." I get the "premium leads," that is, the names of people who have called in in response to the TV ads, and I call them, and make appointments, and go and talk to them, and try to close the deal. What I'm selling isn't land, it's an attorney, but the principle is the same. The only difference is, I don't get commissions.

With one exception.

I'd been working for Richard for nearly two months before I found out what IB's were. He'd neglected to tell me, and I probably still wouldn't know if I hadn't happened to overhear a couple of the paralegals talking about them one day when I was up to the office to turn in my cases. Unfortunately, however, when I asked them what IB stood for, one of them said "Incentive Bonus" and the other said "Initiative Bonus," which touched off a huge argument, which to the best of my knowledge has never been resolved, and which did little to enlighten me.

Eventually I found out that while no one was quite sure what the letters stood for, everyone in the office knew what they meant, and were surprised to find out that I didn't. And eventually someone, I think Susan, took time out of the argument to fill me in.

Basically, what it came down to was this. Richard wanted cases. And he wanted lots of cases, as many as he could get. He was much more concerned with quantity than with quality. That's not to say that he wanted cases that couldn't be settled or cases he would lose. He just wanted simple, straightforward accident cases, that could be settled expeditiously for a profit.

What Richard didn't want were the spectacular cases, the kind you read about in the newspapers, the kind where you're suing for hundreds of millions of dollars and the defendants are hiring teams of lawyers, and fighting like crazy, and everything takes a whole lot of time and effort and lasts forever. Because Richard wasn't interested in the notoriety, or publicity, that went along with getting involved in any big splashy case. All he cared about was volume, turning over as many simple, straightforward settlements as possible. When you came right down to it, what Richard wanted to be, basically, was the McDonald's of the legal profession.

Which was where IB's came in. Richard was bringing in a lot of cases through his advertising, but he wanted more. So he offered a $150 finder's fee to anyone in the office who brought in a new case that he accepted.

When I heard that I couldn't believe it. Why didn't somebody tell me about this? I mean, my average case is three hours, or thirty bucks. And here he's paying $150 for a single sign-up. It was too good to be true.

After that, I took extra retainer kits with me wherever I went, and I kept my eyes open. And sure enough, two days later there I was in the pediatrics ward in Lincoln Hospital in the Bronx signing up an eight-year-old boy who'd fallen off the swing in the school playground, and looking covetously at the boy in the next bed with his leg in traction whose mother had just come to see him, and wondering how I could make a move on them without appearing to be too seedy. The best plan I could think of was to talk very loud, hoping the mother would overhear and approach me.

It happened that the mother of the kid I was signing up was Hispanic and didn't speak any English and had brought along another woman to interpret. So I was relaying messages back and forth from the interpreter to the mother to the kid, who spoke some English, and occasionally answered directly back to me. At the same time I was keeping an eye on the other bed to see if the other mother was picking up on the conversation. So I almost missed it when the interpreter said to me, during a lull in the translation, "You know, my daughter was hit by a car last week." I did a double-take, and then looked at her to see if what I thought was happening was happening, and sure enough, what she was trying to find out was whether I could help her daughter too.

I certainly could.

The woman's name was Maria Alvarez. She was about 30, bright, and intelligent, and I would have loved to have talked to her about her daughter's case, but while we were still signing the papers for the kid in the hospital my beeper went off, and when I called in Richard had an "emergency" signup in Brooklyn and I had to run. I took her telephone number, called her that night, made an appointment, and drove out there first thing the next morning.

Maria Alvarez lived in the Melrose Houses, a huge project in the South Bronx running between Courtlandt and Morris Avenues from East 153rd to East 156th Street. It's one of those projects made up of a whole series of separate buildings, where the street address is a main gate that lets you into the complex and then you wander around a huge courtyard looking for your particular building.

When I found mine, there were a couple of six-foot-four teenagers hanging out in the lobby. Maria Alvarez lived in 6D but, to tell you the truth, I find teenagers even more scary than adults, and I wasn't too keen on having those guys in the elevator with me if they chose to come, so I took the stairs, and I was breathing a little hard when Maria Alvarez answered the door and let me in.

So now I'm sitting on a couch in the living room of her apartment, and Maria is sitting in a chair, and there's a four-year-old girl playing on the floor, and I'm filling out the fact sheet and dollar signs are flashing in my head. And Maria's just as intelligent as she'd seemed to be, and she has all the right information, and is giving me all the right answers: yes, it was a hit-and-run at the corner of Willis Avenue and East 140th Street; yes, the police came, from the 40th precinct; yes, they caught the driver; yes the ambulance came and took her to Lincoln Hospital. And Maria's smiling and talking, and the kid's playing on the floor, and I'm writing down the information, and everything's going great, and at the same time I can't help feeling that something is wrong. But I can't for the life of me figure out what it is. And I go on with the information about the hospital, and I get to, "What were her injuries?" and Maria points to the girl on the floor and says, "Well, there's a bruise on her leg, and there's a scratch on her cheek, it's faded now, but right there, you see it?" And I look at the kid on the floor and suddenly I realize what's been bothering me. No cast. No scars. Nothing. Just a happy kid playing on the floor. No injury!

And I'm furious. I don't let it show, but I'm furious. Here's a hundred and fifty bucks out the window. I mean, Richard's really gonna file suit for a bruise and a scratch. No injury, no case. And I won't even get paid for my time and mileage, 'cause I wasn't assigned it, I did it on my own. A whole morning wasted driving up to the Bronx, and for what? A bruise and a scratch! I mean, come on lady, you got me up here to listen to your goddamn case, there's got to be something more than this!

And suddenly I realize, Jesus Christ, here I am, sitting here, furious because a four-year-old girl *isn't* hurt. *Wanting* her to be hurt. *Wanting* her to have a broken arm or leg, or at least an ugly facial scar.

Wanting her to have gone through pain and suffering. *Wanting* her to have a serious, and perhaps permanent, debilitating injury. *Furious* to find out she's all right.

I felt as if the bottom had dropped out of my stomach. Again, I didn't let it show, which was harder this time. I just went on and, as calmly and as quickly as possible, filled out the rest of the fact sheet, had Maria sign all the papers, took pictures of the kid, and got out of there.

I turned in the case to Richard, knowing he'd reject it, and, of course, he did. And I never, ever, attempted to chase down an IB case again.

Until now.

See, the thing is, I was really strapped. What with paying off Rosa and renting the car and the bugging equipment, Albrect's grand was long gone, and I'd dipped heavily into the cash machine again. I was up against it, and I needed some fast cash to keep the operation going. And so, in desperation, I did what in the holy names of wife and family I had never been able to bring myself to do. I stooped to the lowest form of ambulance chasing—open solicitation.

I had an appointment with a patient in Harlem Hospital at nine in the morning. Visiting hours aren't till 2:00, but I can always get in by showing my I.D. and saying I'm from the lawyer's office. I got a pass at the desk, went in, and signed up George Grant.

And then I stayed. With the Visitor's Pass protruding prominently from my clipboard, the room number, of course, carefully obscured, I wandered the halls of the hospital, dodging orderlies and interns, playing hide and seek with doctors and nurses, poking my head into people's rooms, and looking for broken arms and legs.

The responses varied from "No shit? You a lawyer?" to "Get the fuck out of here." Like Babe Ruth, I struck out a lot, but also like the Babe, I hit a lot of home runs. Four hours later I left the hospital with six sign-ups under my belt.

I rushed them down to Richard's, bullied my way past Kathy into his office, and threw 'em on his desk.

Richard was surprised. He cocked his head at me, narrowed his eyes, and said, "It isn't like you to chase ambulance. Is everything all right?"

I had to suppress a smile. Richard isn't used to dealing with people on a personal level, at least he never has been with me, and I would assume that would apply to others as well. Richard is at his best when he's in an adversarial position, going for someone's throat, and he's perfectly at home in any business situation, but I have a feeling personal relationships make him uneasy, perhaps because there's no right or wrong answer and thus no real guideline to him as to how he should act. At any rate, he always comes off clumsy and forced when he tries it. Now it was as if I could see him thinking to himself, "How do I show benevolent concern?"

I waved away his inquiry. "Fine," I told him. "Just fine."

"You sure?"

"Yeah, sure. I just got a little behind on my bills."

Richard nodded, and clearly happy to be back on familiar ground, began looking over the cases. He wound up taking four of the six. Whatever Richard's other failings might be, he was certainly a man of his word. He wrote me a check on the spot—$600.

It was a quarter of three when I got out of there. I beat it down to the bank, got in just under the wire, and cashed the check. Stanley Hastings, detective, was back in business.

I got in my car, which I'd left at a meter on 14th Street, and drove out to Pluto's to check my tapes. I changed the tapes on both machines and got out of there fast. I beat it back to the office to listen to them. On the way back I stopped at one of the hole-in-the-wall appliance stores on 42nd Street and bought a reel-to-reel tape deck for $149, and a pair of stereo earphones for $30. Then I went back to the office to listen to Pluto's Top 40.

There were no interesting phone calls, but I had managed to get the tail-end of Pluto's meeting with Tony. I missed the part about Tony's fling with Marsha, but what I did get was great. Two separate pieces of information, each telling me I was making all the right moves.

The first came up when Tony asked Pluto if he had a hit of coke. Pluto came down on him, saying Tony ought to know he always kept his house clean, that when he made a deal he always brought the stuff in from where he had it stashed minutes before it was going out, and that the police could search his house any time and they'd find nothing. So my idea of framing Pluto with Albrect's kilo wasn't that farfetched, after all.

The second was that Tony had been unable to line up another courier, but by boosting the ante, he had managed to talk Forrester into going again.

So I'd been right to leave the tracking device in place. Red was making one more run.

24

I TRACKED RED AS HE CAME THROUGH NEW YORK HEADED FOR MIAMI. I picked him up just west of Patchogue, Long Island and tracked him till he went out of range, somewhere north of Camden, New Jersey.

I wasn't sure why I was tracking Red. It was just something to do. That and the fact that eventually I wanted to get my transmitter back. But as far as helping me along with my problem, it really didn't. I mean, I knew Red was on his way to buy drugs, and I'd know when he was coming back. If I wanted, I could pass the information on to the cops and get Pluto and the boys busted for drug trafficking. But I didn't want to get them for drugs. I wanted to get them for murder.

Red had gone down over the weekend, so I had some free time on my hands while I waited for him to get back. That should have been great, considering the double duty I had been pulling lately (the Albrect thing and Richard's cases had kept me going around the clock) but it wasn't. Just the opposite. At least while I was racing around like a madman, I was occupied, I was doing something. Now I had nothing to do but think, and that's never good.

Because the first thought that came to mind was, what the hell did I think I was doing? In the first place, I was neglecting my family. What I'd told Richard about being behind on the bills was absolutely true, and what was I doing about it? Nothing. If anything, I was avoiding work. And for what? Because somehow or other I'd gotten myself obsessed with some neurotic need to prove myself useful? Great. Good goal. The best way to accomplish it, I'm sure, is to let your wife and kid starve. And justify it all because you're caught up in some farfetched, glamorous, storybook crusade to avenge the death of dear old Martin Albrect. Which wouldn't be so bad if it weren't so futile. I mean, when you came right down to it, what was I really doing in the affair Albrect, besides withholding evidence, compounding a felony, and conspiring to conceal a crime? Instead of going to the police, I was attempting to solve the whole thing singlehanded. Great. Who the fuck did I think I was, Sam Spade? What did I expect to accomplish?

At least, if I went to the police, maybe they could do something about it. I couldn't give them any proof, but I could tell them who did it, and surely they could take it from there. And if they couldn't, wouldn't that mean that it couldn't be done, that it had been impossible to begin with, that I'd taken it as far as it could go and done everything I could?

The reason these thoughts taunted me so much was, basically, I *had* done everything I could. I'd managed to plant a transmitter on a car, tap some phones, and confiscate a kilo of contraband, but that was it. I'd shot my wad. I was tapped out, drained, fresh out of ideas. If something helpful came in on Pluto's phone tap, it might at least point me in the right direction, but barring that, my basic problem was I simply didn't know what the hell to do.

It was beautiful on Saturday, so I took Tommie to the Bronx Zoo. We're family members. I figure if you have to be a member of something, the Bronx Zoo is a good thing to be a member of. As members, we have a book of tickets to get into the parking lot free. We also have a membership card that gets us in the main gate, and tickets for the rides. The ride tickets are great at the Children's Zoo, which is always mobbed on weekends. We skip the long ticket line and go straight through the gate with our passes.

We did the Children's Zoo first. We sat in birds' nests. Then we crawled into tunnels and stuck our heads out of the plastic tops and pretended we were prairie dogs. Then Tommie climbed a giant spider web made of rope. I would have liked to climb it too, but I'm too big.

We pressed on to the slide, which is two stories high, and spirals around inside of what is made to look like the trunk of a large tree. I went down it once. Tommie went ten more times, while I waited at the bottom.

On our way to the petting area where you can feed the animals, we stopped at the men's room beside the path. I tricked Tommie into going by saying I had to go—a trick that usually works.

I had to lift him up to the urinal. The urinals at the main restroom go all the way to the ground, and Tommie can use them himself. The ones in this restroom were attached to the wall at a height just a bit more than he could reach. The man next to me was holding up his son, who must have been 3 or 4. Tommie and the other boy finished together, and I learned a universal truth. When you pee, you shake your penis to get the last drops off. When you hold up your son to pee, you shake the whole child.

The other man and I shook our sons together, and smiled at the common knowledge.

Tommie and I washed our hands, and went on to the petting area. We fed a goat and a sheep, at twenty-five cents a whack for a handful of food from the machine. I'm not sure, but I think when he was younger, it was only a dime. And he's only five.

After the Children's Zoo, Tommie wanted to ride the Skyfari. He loves the Skyfari, a tiny green cable car that carries you high over the top of the zoo. I am slightly less enthusiastic—I can never help checking the bolts and wondering what keeps the damn thing from falling down, but I ride it for his sake.

We waited in line for fifteen minutes. Then an attendant locked us in our own private car, and, after a minute and a half, during which the two cars in front of us took off, we lurched forward, and swayed up into the sky.

I checked the creaking nuts and bolts while Tommie peered happily out the windows saying things like, "We're higher than the trees!" which gladdened my heart.

We passed over the restaurant and the duck pond, and the reptile and ape houses. As we passed over the mountain goats, I looked out at the meadow in the distance where the giraffes stood among the trees.

A boy near the fence frightened a small giraffe, which shied away and ran on stilt-like legs. The other giraffes hadn't seen what had frightened him, but they saw him running, so they ran too.

I stared at the giraffes. A simple fact of nature. Scare the weakest one and they all run.

"Daddy, look at the giraffes!" Tommie cried.

"I see them," I told him.

"Aren't they funny?" he said. He had to ask me twice.

"Yes they are," I told him.

I knew what I had to do.

25

LEROY TWIRLED THE COGNAC AROUND IN HIS GLASS AND
PURSED HIS LIPS. I'm not certain that I understand you
correctly," he said. "You want a what?"

We were sitting in Leroy's living room in Queens. I
had declined his offer of champagne or cognac, and
was contenting myself with a Diet Pepsi Free.

I repeated my request.

Leroy frowned. "You will pardon me for asking,
but just what do you want with a gun?"

"You're better off not knowing," I told him.

Leroy nodded judiciously. "That bad," he said. He
cocked his head in my direction. "Do you think I'd be
stupid enough to engage in my chosen profession while
in possession of a gun?"

"Certainly not," I said. "I just thought you might
have picked up some rare curio somewhere in your
travels."

Leroy smiled. He got up, and went up the stairs to
his bedroom. He returned minutes later carrying a
nasty-looking piece of machinery.

"Now this," Leroy said, "is a genuine German Luger
from World War II. I cannot swear to the number of
G.I.'s it has punctured in its day, since I am not
familiar with its pedigree. But I can vouch for its
authenticity."

He held it out to me. I took it gingerly. I'm scared
shitless of guns.

"Is it loaded?" I asked him.

"It is not," Leroy said. "That is its only drawback. It has no ammunition."

I turned the gun over in my hands. It still scared me, even knowing it wasn't loaded. I took the grip in my hand, put my finger on the trigger. I aimed at what I assumed was a genuine Degas, or at least a genuine something. If Leroy were wrong, it was going to cost him, not me.

I pulled the trigger. The gun clicked. I lowered the gun and looked at Leroy.

"That's all right," I said. "I don't need any bullets."

Leroy looked at me curiously. "Might I inquire," he said, "what you intend to do with a gun and no ammunition?"

I shook my head. "Believe me, Leroy, you don't want to know."

26

RED HIT TOWN AT THREE IN THE MORNING, just as he'd done before. My wife didn't have to wake me up this time. I'd estimated his time of arrival, and I was in the living room waiting for him. I was dressed and ready to roll when the unit picked up his signal.

I'd rented another car, a big, black Chevy, and outfitted it the day before. I packed up my briefcase, went out, and got in the car.

I didn't make the mistake of heading downtown this time. Red was a creature of habit. He'd stick to the tried and true and come in over the bridge.

I got on the highway and headed uptown. When I reached the bridge ramp I kept going, got on the bridge, and went over to Jersey. I got off at the Fort Lee exit, turned left, crossed over the highway, and went down one of the access roads to the bridge. I stopped at the booth and paid my two dollars, and drove over the bridge again. Probably the nicest trip I've ever made to Jersey.

I came down the ramp off the bridge and got onto the highway heading south. I drove down a few hundred yards, found a breakdown alcove, pulled off and waited. All right, Red, I'm ready. Just don't fuck up and change anything on me.

Red didn't. The tracking unit showed he was heading straight for the bridge. Ten minutes later he came over, and the machine went crazy again as he went through the exit loop.

There were no cars on the highway. The lights coming up on me had to be him. The tracking unit confirmed the fact.

As he went by, I pulled out and gave chase. He had a lead, but I sped up to sixty-five and closed the gap. I rolled down my window, and slapped the red, flashing light which I had rented, onto the top of the car and switched it on. I gave a blast on my mock siren. It sounded pretty damn good.

Red heard it. I saw his head go up and see the flashing lights in his rear-view mirror.

I hoped he wouldn't panic and run; that would have spoiled everything, but somehow Red hadn't seemed the type for that. I figured he'd be more apt to feign innocence, talk fast, and hope for the best.

I figured right. Red's brake lights came on, and he pulled over to the side and stopped.

I stopped behind him. It might have been better procedure to cut him off from the front, but I didn't want him to see me or my license plate.

When I got out of the car I felt slightly unsteady on my feet, and for the first time I realized how scared I was. I had to tell myself, Red's the weak one, Red's the one who's gonna be scared. But what if I'm wrong? What if Red has a gun and decides to pull it? He's sitting on twenty kilos of coke. He can't afford to get caught; what if he's got a gun? Bullshit. Red's a pantywaist. He's the weak one. Scare the weak one and they all run. Just do it.

I walked up next to the driver's side door. I'd kept my face averted on the way. Now, with the top of his car blocking my head from view, I reached up and pulled a ski-mask over my head.

Red had rolled down his window and just begun his, "Gee officer, what did I do?" spiel, when I leaned down and stuck the Luger square in his face.

"All right, Asshole," I growled."Give me the car keys."

Whatever anxiety I might have had about Red pulling a gun vanished the moment I saw his reaction. I don't know if he peed in his pants, but if he didn't he must have just made a pit stop. I never saw a guy so terrified. I felt bad about frightening some poor respectable citizen out of his wits, but respectable citizens shouldn't be making drug runs for guys who go around cutting people's dicks off.

Red seemed incapable of complying with my request, so I reached over him and yanked the keys from the ignition.

"Get down on the floor," I told him. "And don't move."

He might not have heard me. I poked him with the gun and he got the picture. He hit the floor.

"Don't move or I'll kill you," I said.

I hurried to the back of the car, popped the trunk, and pulled out the suitcase. I bent down, grabbed the transmitter and wrenched it off the bottom of the gas tank. I slammed the trunk shut, ran and threw the suitcase and the transmitter in the back seat of my car. I hurried back to Red's car. Red hadn't moved.

"All right, Asshole," I said. "Just listen. I'm not going to kill you if you do as I say, so listen good. I'm driving off. I'll drop your car keys in the middle of the road about a hundred yards south. I could throw 'em in the river, but I'm just a nice guy. I don't want to see your head in that window, or I'll blow it off. You wait a full five minutes after I drive off. If you don't, I'll know, and I'll kill you. After that, you're free to get your keys and go. Got it, Asshole?"

There was no response.

"I said, got it, Asshole?"

A whimpered "yes" came from the floor.

I ran to my car, hopped in, pulled off the ski-mask, pulled the light off the car, and drove off. I dropped Red's keys out the window as I'd told him I would. I went on down the highway obeying the speed limit. I sure as hell didn't want to be stopped.

I pulled up in front of my office building, lugged the suitcase out of the back seat, and went in. At least the elevator was on the ground floor. I took it up, unlocked my office, threw the suitcase in, locked the door, and left. I didn't have to look in the suitcase. I knew what was in it. It would be pure, too. Red wouldn't have the knowledge or the guts to cut it, as Albrect had done.

Back outside, I went to a pay phone on the corner and called Tony Arroyo. He must have been letting the casino run itself, because he was home. The phone rang ten times, then his bleary voice answered.

"Hey, Shithead," I said. "I got news for you and it ain't good."

"What? Who is this?"

"Never mind, Shithead. Just listen. In about a half an hour your errand boy's gonna call you up with some bullshit story about how some guy in a ski-mask held him up and took his suitcase. Before you decide to stick his dick in his mouth, I just wanted to let you know that his bullshit story is true."

I hung up the phone, got in the car, and drove home. It was late, and I was tired. Let Tony wait up for developments.

27

I WOKE UP THE NEXT MORNING IN A COLD SWEAT. Jesus
Christ, what had I done? I'd just ripped off a half a
million dollars from a group of guys who went around
killing people. And I'd left two tape recorders there as
a calling card. Still, I'd covered my tracks pretty well,
rented the car using a fake driver's license supplied by
the same shop that made me the bank I.D. The machines couldn't be traced to me. I was still safe. Then
why the cold sweat?

"My god, what's the matter?" my wife asked.

"Nothing, I'm fine," I told her, but it was no go.
The sheets were drenched with sweat.

"You're burning up with fever," she said, and it was
only after taking my temperature and proving to her
that it was normal that I was able to persuade her that
I was well enough to go to work.

I drove out to Woodmere. I knew it was risky as
hell, but I had to get those tapes. I made three passes
by the place before I actually stopped. There seemed
to be an unusual amount of activity around Pluto's
place today, cars going in and out of the driveway,
people talking in the yard. But then I'm just a natural
coward. Still, I told myself, this time I'm in my own
car and my license plate could be traced.

Finally, I pulled in behind the parked car. I lifted
the trunk. Both tapes had been used, and the one on
the room was still going. I wasn't about to wait for it

to stop. I ripped both tapes from the machines, threaded
fresh tape in, reset the machines, closed the trunk,
and got the hell out of there. This time I took the
repairman costume.

I think my heart stopped pounding somewhere around
Shea Stadium. I beat it back to my office and played
the tapes.

This time the phone calls got interesting. There
were a few routine calls first, then this:

"Hello?" That was Pluto's man, Tall, Dark and Ugly.

"It's Tony. Get me Victor."

TDU: "You out of your fucking mind? You know
    what time it is?"

TONY: "It's important. Wake him up."

TDU: "Are you kidding?"

TONY: "Wake him up, damn it!"

There was a pause, then:

PLUTO: "Damn it, Tony, this better be important."

TONY: "It is. Forrester got ripped off."

PLUTO: "What?"

TONY: "Someone held Forrester up and took the
    suitcase."

PLUTO: "How do you know that?"

TONY: "I just got a phone call. Some guy, I don't
    know who. He said in about a half an hour I'd get
    a call from Forrester saying someone held him up
    and ripped him off. He just wanted to let me know
    that that was absolutely true."

PLUTO: "The guy said Forrester would be calling up
    to tell you this?"

TONY: "Yeah."

PLUTO: "Then get off the fucking phone so Forrester
    can call you and we can find out what the fuck is
    going on around here."

The next call was even better. Pluto answered it
himself, a good indication of his interest in the matter.

PLUTO: "Tony?"

TONY: "Yeah. He just called."

PLUTO: "And?"

TONY: "Same thing. Exactly what the guy said. Some guy forced him off thc West Side Highway and took the suitcase."

PLUTO: "What guy?"

TONY: "He doesn't know. He was wearing a ski-mask."

PLUTO: Well, what the fuck *does* he know?"

TONY: The guy was in a black car of some kind. He doesn't know thé make or year. He had a light on top and a siren. He pretended he was a policeman and pulled Forrester over. When he got out, he was wearing a ski-mask and holding a gun. He put Forrester on the floor and ripped him off."

PLUTO: "That's all he knows?"

TONY: "So he says."

PLUTO: "Would he recognize the guy's voice?"

TONY: "Probably not. He said the guy just grunted and growled."

PLUTO: "Sound like the guy who called you?"

TONY: "Yeah. It does."

A pause.

PLUTO: "Any chance Forrester is in on this?"

TONY: "Not a chance in the world. He wouldn't have the guts to rip his grandmother off. It was all I could do just to talk him into making the run."

PLUTO: "O.K. He's probably clean. Tell him to go home and forget it. Tell him to keep in touch."

TONY: "That's gonna scare the shit out of him."

PLUTO: "I can't help that. We got our own problems."

TONY: "Yeah."

PLUTO: "Is he where you can reach him?"

TONY: "Yeah. He's hanging out at a pay phone, shitting in his pants."

PLUTO: "O.K. Tell him to go home. Then get the hell over here."

They hung up. I figured the next important conversation would be on the room bug, but I ran the telephone tape ahead anyway. I was right. There were two phone calls from the next morning, rapidly terminated by Tall Dark and Ugly. Neither caller got through to Pluto.

I switched to the other tape. I had to wade through a lot of meaningless shit from the day before before I got what I wanted. It was Pluto ushering Tony into the room.

PLUTO: "So? Anything new?"

TONY: "Not yet."

PLUTO: "What about Forrester?"

TONY: "I sent him home."

PLUTO: "He give you any trouble?"

TONY: "No. He's scared to death."

PLUTO: "You tell him not to talk?"

TONY: "Sure. I read him the riot act. Don't worry. I told you he's scared to death."

PLUTO: "Yeah. O.K." (shouted) "Carlos!" (that would be Tall, Dark and Ugly) "Get in here!"

I heard the sound of Carlos entering the room.

PLUTO: "Sit down, Carlos. We gotta talk something over. I want you here."

TDU: "Sure, boss."

PLUTO: "Briefly, someone ripped off the shipment last night."

TDU: "So I gathered."

TONY: "How you know that?"

TDU: "Come on. That's my job."

PLUTO: "Yeah, fine, stop congratulating yourself and be some help to me. O.K. we gotta figure out who did this and we gotta figure it out fast. I'm gonna have to call Ospina on this. He's not gonna want to have any part of it. It was my messenger, my fuckup, so I'm gonna have to eat it. He's got his money, he's not gonna wanna split the loss.

But I'll have to call him. Now, before I do, I wanna know what the hell's been going on around here."

TONY: "What do you mean?"

PLUTO: "Am I not making myself clear? Our man got ripped off en route. Aside from us, who the fuck knew he was bringing in the stuff? Cause One way or another, there's been a fucking leak."

TONY: "That's right."

TDU: "Yeah."

PLUTO: "So who the fuck was it?"

TONY: "How about Forrester himself?"

PLUTO: "You think that?"

TONY: "No. I don't. I mean, I'd like to think that, it would be nice, but, realistically, not in a million years. He's just too scared."

PLUTO: "He might not brag a little? To someone he wouldn't think would know what he was talking about?"

TONY: "No. Someone else might, but not him."

PLUTO: "Not even to his wife?"

TONY: "Especially not to his wife. Believe me, I know his type."

PLUTO: "O.K. You're sure, you're sure. I gotta go with that."

TDU: "How about at the other end?"

PLUTO: "Well, that's the other thing, and that's why I gotta call Ospina and try to shift some of the burden down there, but it ain't gonna be easy. The guy got ripped off at our end. You wanna make Ospina believe someone followed him all the way from Miami to rip him off in New York, well that's a problem. It'd be a smart as hell move, by the way, but it's still hard to believe anyone'd do that."

TONY: "Some of Ospina's friends may be smart as hell."

PLUTO: "Sure they may. I gotta start him worrying about that, but that's another story. It doesn't concern us now. We gotta forget Miami and say, if it came from our end, where'd it come from?"

TONY: "I have no idea."

TDU: "Me neither, boss."

PLUTO: "Well, think, damn it. Is there anything that happened lately, anything out of the ordinary?"

I tensed up. I was afraid Tall, Dark and Ugly'd chime in, "What about the phone being out?" but he said, "Nothing, boss."

I let out a sigh of relief. Then Tony said something that stood my hair on end.

TONY: "Yeah. There was something, boss. About a week ago. Murphy brought some guy around the casino, some guy from Miami. Said he knew Albrect."

In the silence that followed my beeper went off and I almost jumped out of my socks.

28

I SHUT OFF MY BEEPER. Seconds later, I shut off the automatic safety check. I shut off the tape recorder. I knew I had to hear what came next, but not just yet.

Back when I was 25 or 26 and doing summer stock, I remember that after the show one night a bunch of us actors were sitting around drinking and shooting the shit, and one of the guys had a *Penthouse* magazine that everyone had been reading during rehearsal all day, and we got to talking about some of the more bizarre letters in the *Penthouse* Forum. One was from a guy who claimed he could perform fellatio on himself, and got off on having people watch him do it. We were laughing and joking about that, and one of the actresses in the company asked if such a thing were possible, and we all laughed and said, "No." Then one guy laughed and said, "And we all knew the answer," and we all laughed some more.

That, to the best of my recollection, is the only time in my life I ever consciously considered what it would be like to have my penis in my mouth.

Until now.

I took deep breaths, hyperventilating, trying to keep the nausea from overpowering me. I couldn't quite do it, but I managed to calm down somewhat. I forced myself to turn the machine back on.

Pluto was saying, "Good thinking. Good thinking, Tony. That's exactly what I mean. Something like that. Now when did you say this was?"

TONY: "A week or two ago. I don't remember exactly. Just that Murphy brought him around."

PLUTO: "Well, was it before or after Albrect was killed?"

TONY: "After."

PLUTO: "You sure?"

TONY: "Yeah, I'm sure. In fact, it was right after. I remember now. Cause I had to play cute with Murphy. You know, ask him if Albrect was coming. And he told me Albrect was dead."

PLUTO: "You sure about that?"

TONY: "Yeah. I remember now."

PLUTO: "Then it must have been the next night. I mean, Albrect must have been killed just the night before."

TONY: "That's right."

PLUTO: "And the very next night this guy shows up, says he knows Albrect, says he's from Miami?"

TONY: "Yeah. That stinks, don't it?"

PLUTO: "It sure does. What'd the guy look like?"

TONY: "I don't know. Dark hair. About 30. Six feet. 160 pounds."

Great. Younger, taller and thinner. My world is collapsing and they're trying to flatter me.

PLUTO: "You think Murphy had anything to do with this?"

TONY: "Naw. Murphy's a civilian. He don't know shit."

PLUTO: "He knows too damn much. Look, get him on the phone, find out what he knows about this guy."

TONY: "O.K. You want me to tell him what it's all about?"

PLUTO: "Fuck, no. The less he knows the better. Look, tell him we might want to cultivate this guy to take over Albrect's run. Don't let him know anything's wrong. Right? Just tell him you want some info on this guy and ask how you can get in touch with him."

TONY: "Right."

There was the sound of footsteps, of Tony walking to the phone. Something was wrong. I mean, aside from the obvious fact that everything had turned to shit, something didn't make sense. I didn't know what it was, I just knew that somehow, something I had just heard didn't fit in with my known facts.

Before I could figure out what it was, the sound of footsteps suddenly stopped and there was silence.

I turned the volume up on the machine. Dead air. There was nothing there.

Suddenly, I realized what had been bothering me. Tony's phone call to Murphy. It hadn't happened. It wasn't on the tape. I'd just listened to the last calls on the tape, and they were incoming calls immediately terminated by TDU. If Tony was about to call Murphy, the call should have been on the tape. But it wasn't. It wasn't on the phone tape, and it wasn't on the room tape. Somehow the tapes had fucked up.

My first thought was that they'd found the bug. That *would* be my first thought—always think the worst. Then it hit me. The tape hadn't fucked up. They hadn't found the bug. For whatever reason—it didn't really matter why—Tony hadn't gone straight to Pluto's that night. He'd gotten there that morning, and not too far ahead of me. The conversation I'd been listening to hadn't taken place in the early hours of the morning. It had taken place that very day, just as I'd been out there to change the tapes. The phone call wasn't on either tape, because I'd ripped the tapes out of the machines just before it happened.

Now it made sense that Tony could call Murphy. He couldn't have called him at home early in the morning and made it seem casual. But he sure as hell could have called him at the office that day. And that's just what he had done. Only I'd missed the goddamn call because I'd changed the tape just before he made it.

On the heels of that realization came another one. I had to go out there and get the tape and find out what was said. Now that they were on to me, now that they'd gotten a lead to me, now that they were focusing all of their efforts toward finding out who I was, I had to go out there virtually under their noses and get the tapes.

What if they'd found the bugs? What if they'd traced them and found the car? Ironically, there was no way of knowing without having the tapes.

My beeper went off again, and I almost welcomed it. Good. It must be important. It'll give me something to do. Give me something that's important enough that I have to do it and can put off, at least for a few hours, having to get those tapes.

I dialed the office.

"Agent Blue," I said.

"It's about time," Kathy snarled. "Don't you ever answer your beeper?"

"I had to get to a phone."

"Oh yeah? I'll bet you're in your office."

"Why would you think that?"

"I don't hear any traffic."

"Remind me to tape record some and play it back when I'm inside."

"Never mind that, this is important. It won't wait."

"Then you'd better tell me what it is."

She did. An old man in Queens had just gotten out of the hospital. It had been a medical malpractice case, so taking pictures in the hospital had been out of the question. The doctor in the hospital had been treating the patient's leg. Gangrene had set in. The old man had lost his foot. The kicker was, that was his good leg. His other leg had already been cut off at the hip.

Richard must have been salivating over this one: I mean, it's not as if the pictures wouldn't keep—the guy wouldn't have any legs tomorrow, either. But Richard was adamant. It had to be done today.

Fine, I thought. Anything, rather than the tapes. I

wrote down the address, and pulled out the Hagstrom map.

It was way the hell out in Rosedale, right on the way to Pluto's house.

29

ON MY WAY OUT TO ROSEDALE IT BEGAN TO RAIN REALLY HARD. I don't know how other detectives handle the rain. I suppose James Bond has an umbrella, but he's British, he could get away with it. I don't see Mike Hammer carrying one, somehow. I think it's always sunny when he's on a case.

I have a problem with rain. I've never liked umbrellas or raincoats. I guess it goes back to my childhood, when my mother always wanted me to wear a raincoat or take an umbrella, or both, and I never wanted to because they interfered with my play. I preferred always to sprint madly wherever I wanted to go.

I still do, but with the job, it's a problem. I started my detective work in February, so there wasn't any rain to contend with. Then the summer came. I still have no raincoat. Tommie and I got free CitiBank umbrellas by going to Yankee Stadium on umbrella day, so on rainy days I'll take that, since I have to protect my suit. But I always take it home again, and leave it there. So when a heavy shower starts up in the middle of the day, I'm always unprepared.

I was thinking this as I drove along in my car, and at about Shea Stadium I started giggling uncontrollably. Here I was on my way out to Rosedale in the hope of taking a picture of where someone's foot used to be, en route to picking up a tape recording that would tell me if a bunch of hoods were taking out a contract on me, and suddenly my biggest problem is that I'm caught in the rain.

I left my jacket and tie in the car, put the *New York Post* (god love it, the ink doesn't run like the *Time*'s) over my head, and sprinted for the house.

It only took ten rings before they let me in. I suppose I shouldn't have expected anything better from a man with no legs, but it was his wife who answered the door, and she had two of 'em.

I've taken some pretty gruesome injury pictures in my day: an eyeball hanging in a man's socket by a few stitches and a prayer; a scar that ran from the cheekbone to the hip; and a penis sliced open in a motorcycle accident and stitched back together again, to name a few, and I've become pretty inured to them. But there's something about an amputee, particularly a double leg amputee, that is disturbing. I mean, they just lie there helpless as you photograph the stumps, and you can't help feeling sick. And it's not because the stumps are gory—the wounds have usually completely healed before you get a camera on 'em. It's just somehow so moving.

Today, I felt nothing. The old man's plight was pitiful indeed, but I couldn't focus on it. As his wife pulled the sock covers off his stumps, all I could see was the assignment I had to shoot. I shot it, wished them well, and got the hell out of there.

It was pouring harder now, and suddenly I blessed the rain. Nobody would be out on a day like this. It was perfect.

I sped down to Pluto's. The rain was still coming down in buckets. I pulled up right behind the rented car, got out, and opened the trunk. The tapes had both been used, though neither was moving. I changed them quickly, got back in my car, and drove off. It was a piece of cake.

My beeper went off on my way back over the Triboro Bridge. I didn't want to answer it, but if I didn't, they'd start calling my wife again, and I was running out of excuses for why my beeper wasn't working.

I came off the bridge and went through the toll booths. I automatically asked for a receipt, as if the damn dollar seventy-five really meant anything to me at that moment.

On the right side of the toll plaza there was a bank of pay phones by the side of the road. I pulled up next to them. The rain had eased down to a slight drizzle. I got out and called the office.

Susan answered, and for once I was glad. I didn't feel up to dealing with Kathy. She had a new case for me. I didn't care. I wasn't going to do it anyway. I'd just called to stop them from bugging me. I planned to call the client and stall him off till tomorrow.

But I couldn't do it. Susan informed me in a cheery voice that drove me to the point of despair that the client had called from work, was now on his way home, and had no phone, and she had therefore made the appointment for me, and I was to be at his place at five.

I told her I was sorry, but I just couldn't do it. She told me to hang on, and put me on hold. I was debating whether or not to just simply hang up when there was a click on the line, and Richard's voice exploded in my ear.

"What do you mean you can't do it?" Richard cried. "Of course you can do it. You have to do it. You went out to Rosedale, didn't you? You're on your way back from there, aren't you? Well, this is right on the way. All you gotta do is swing by and see the guy."

"I can't, Richard, I—"

"Yes you *can*. This is a big case. The guy's got severed tendons, he may lose the use of his arm. The top of his window fell on him when he went to open it, it's defective, it smashed on the floor, for Christ's sake. Be sure you get the pictures before they fix the damn thing."

"But—"

"Look, I got nobody else who can do it, the guy doesn't have a phone, so you have to do it. You *want* this job, you gotta *do* this job. Stop bellyaching and sign the guy up."

There was a click and the line went dead.

I was hopelessly torn. The tapes that held my future were right there in the car, and I was desperate to hear them, but if I stood up the client, the repercussions would make my life so complicated, that in my present state of mind, I'd probably never be able to straighten everything out. I felt like a juggler trying to keep seventeen balls going at once. The line of least resistance was to keep the appointment.

It was in Manhattan, which helped. I went over the Third Avenue Bridge and took the FDR downtown.

I parked the car at a meter two blocks away from the address. I must have been really rattled by that time, because the implications of the address "Bowery" never dawned on me till I got there.

The hotel was a flop-house. The entrance was just a narrow stairway up to the second floor. I climbed it, and when I reached the top I felt as if my mind had given way.

I was in a '40's movie. The desk had a wire-mesh screen around it. The old man behind the desk wore a faded, wide-lapelled suit and a visor. A cigar butt was stuck in his mouth.

The desk was at the top of the stairs, and was in between the hallway and staircase that led to the rooms in the back, and a medium-sized common room at the front.

The common room was what blew my mind. It had a row of old wooden school desks along one wall, the kind that are a chair with a small oval top curving out from the right side, the kind I used to sit in in high school. On the opposite wall was a coffee and hot soup machine, and I knew it! The identical machine had been in the rec room of my old school. When I was twelve years old, I used to stick my hand up through the cup dispenser, and pull out packets of powdered chicken soup.

A half-dozen men were sitting in the school desks.

A few others were milling around, walking in and out. One young, black man with no shirt and his pants unbuttoned kept parading around for no discernible reason. But most of the men were old. Old, filthy bums, just like the ones who stopped you in the street. Or passed out in doorways. Or cleaned your windshield against your will, if you stopped at a red light.

On a table by the front window was an old color TV. It had twisted rabbit ears, but the reception was still pretty good, although the color was almost undiscernible. And the men in the room were all watching it. Devoutly. Quietly. Glued to the set. These ragged old men, so help me god, were all watching "The Newlywed Game."

My client wasn't home yet, so I sat down at one of the school desks, and watched with them.

The wives had already answered the questions, and now the husbands were trying to match their answers. The question was, "In your neighborhood, does the sun rise in the east or the west?"

One husband, a dumb, goofily handsome type, who had already gotten everything else wrong, said, "The east." His wife, a young blonde, cried, "No, stupid!" and held up her card which said, "west." "It said, in *your* neighborhood," she cried in exasperation, and everyone on the show laughed at him.

The bums watched all this without expression or comment. None of them volunteered any theories about the sunrise. They merely watched.

I sat there as if in a dream. Is this real or just fantasy? Are these bums real? Are the people on TV real? Am I really a detective? Is Pluto real? Or illusion? Is that the fantasy and this the reality?

I really didn't know.

30

UNTIL I PLAYED THE TAPES.

I sat in my office, shivering from the rain, or from fear, or probably both, and played the tapes.

They picked up right where the other had left off. Tony called Murphy, fed him the bullshit line Pluto had suggested, and got the name Nathan Armstrong and the phone number of the Whitney Corporation of Miami. Tony called the Whitney Corp. and, strangely enough, was told they had no such employee as Nathan Armstrong.

After that phone call, I switched back from the phone tape to the room tape. I sped past the repeats of the two phone conversations, and got to the part where Tony hung up.

TONY: "No such person."

PLUTO: "You're sure?"

TONY: "*They're* sure."

PLUTO: "Any chance Murphy was wrong about the company?"

TONY: "Not at all. He says he sat with the guy and went over the account. The guy knew all about it."

PLUTO: "You mean the guy learned all about it by stringing Murphy along. This is one slick customer."

Praise from Pluto was somehow the last thing I needed at the moment.

TONY: "So this is the guy."

PLUTO: "It's gotta be. It all fits. It's the night after Albrect got hit. He knows about Albrect. He shows up at the casino. He gave a phony name, he's got a phony background. What the fuck else could it be?"

TONY: "So what are we gonna do?"

PLUTO: "I want the fucker, and I want him bad. I want the coke back, but that's incidental right now. I just want the fucker hit."

TONY: "Agreed."

I'd known this was coming, but somehow hearing it made it worse. It was like hearing a judge sentence you to death.

PLUTO: "I want him hit, and I want him hit fast. That's one thing. There's another thing."

TONY: "What's that?"

PLUTO: "How the hell'd he get on to us in the first place?"

TONY: "I don't know."

PLUTO: "Yeah. Well, I do. Murphy fucked up."

TONY: "Murphy's a civilian."

PLUTO: "Yeah, well he fucked up."

TONY: "Yeah, but Murphy doesn't know enough to fuck up."

PLUTO: "Maybe not, but he did. This guy got in through Murphy. Now Murphy may be a civilian, but he knew Albrect was making the run. He may not have known why or what for, but he knew Albrect was doing something for us. And somehow, some way, Murphy let this guy in."

A pause.

TONY: "I'm not sure what you're saying."

PLUTO: "I'm saying Murphy may be a civilian, but he's become somewhat of a liability, you know what I mean?"

TONY: "Yeah."
PLUTO: "I gotta make a call. I gotta call Ospina."

I should have switched to the telephone tape, but I couldn't. I was hypnotized, transfixed by what I was hearing. I just sat there, unbelieving, as Pluto dialed the phone.

PLUTO: "Hello, let me talk to Angelo . . . Hello, Angie, Victor . . . I got a problem . . . With the last shipment . . . No, it's not your problem, it's my problem. At least, I don't think it's your problem. I think it's at my end. If it is, I take full responsibility. If it turns out it's at your end, we can make an adjustment later, O.K.? . . . Yeah. Good . . . Well, it's like the Albrect thing, only worse . . . We got ripped off . . . The whole shipment . . . I tell you, I take responsibility. Only the problem goes a little deeper than that. I mean, the whole operation could be in jeopardy . . . Yeah. So I could use a little help . . . Yeah, like with Albrect. So can you put Pedro on a plane . . . Yeah . . . One or two. At least one, right away, but there's a second, and the second is the important one . . . Tonight? . . . O.K. . . . Have him call with the flight number and Carlos will pick him up at the airport . . . great . . . I'll keep you posted."

There was the sound of Pluto replacing the receiver.

PLUTO: "All set. Pedro will fly in tonight. Carlos, you pick him up at the airport like before."
TDU: "Sure, boss."
PLUTO: "Tony, you'll have to coordinate this."
TONY: "Me?"
PLUTO: "Yeah. Murphy's your boy. You'll have to point him out. Take Pedro there in the morning, and point him out on his way to work."
TONY: "O.K."

PLUTO: "He can't do it then, though. This can't be a
quick hit and run. It's gotta be a message, like the
other two. We gotta give the fuck who ripped us
off something to think about. So after you finger
Murphy, bring Pedro back here. He can pick him
up when he leaves work. He can get him at home,
in a restaurant bathroom, or a parking lot, that's
no problem, we leave that to Pedro, he knows his
job."

TONY: "I know."

PLUTO: "Then we nail that other son of a bitch."

There was more, but it was all along the same lines.
I listened to it all, and shut the machine off.

Despite what I had just heard, I was remarkably
calm. I'd dreaded hearing the tape, but now that I'd
heard it it wasn't that bad. I mean it was that bad, but
the realization wasn't as bad as the anticipation had
been. At least I knew exactly what they were going to
do.

And, finally, I had a plan.

31

MURPHY WAS SMILING ALL OVER HIS FACE AS HE USH-
ERED ME INTO HIS INNER OFFICE.

"Mr. Armstrong, how nice to see you again."

"That's fine," I told him. "But the name's not Armstrong. I'm a private detective, and I'm investigating
the Albrect murder. Incidentally, your buddies weren't
too pleased about you bringing me around their little
establishment, so they've put out a contract on you.
Aside from that, how are you?"

Murphy turned white as a sheet, and sank down
onto his couch. I went over to the bar and poured him
a brandy, just as he'd done for me the time before. He
took it and drank it with trembling hands.

"What are you talking about?" Murphy said, when
he'd recovered his power of speech.

"Your friends want to kill you. Tony Arroyo and
the boys. They killed Albrect, in case you didn't know.
They think you can tie them to it. They also blame
you for bringing me to the casino. Corny as it sounds,
they've hired a hit man. They're going to kill you.
Unless you have no objection to being discovered in a
parking lot tomorrow morning with your dick in your
mouth, I suggest you listen carefully and do exactly
what I say."

32

AT FIVE THAT AFTERNOON I WAS SITTING IN MY CAR OUTSIDE FABRI-TEC INC. WITH A BULGE IN MY HIP POCKET. The bulge wasn't a gun—the only gun I had was the Luger, and with or without bullets, I didn't think it would be any match for Pedro, even if I could bring myself to fire it, which I knew I couldn't. The bulge was made by the sap, or cosh, or blackjack, or whatever-the-hell it is thugs use to knock each other out with when they're not using the butt of a gun. I'd picked it up at a pawnshop earlier that afternoon. I felt funny when I bought it, and I felt funny having it in my pocket, but I needed something. It felt strangely reassuring too, just to know it was there. Christ, am I getting macho? Not likely. Just stupid. Pedro had a gun and ate people like me for breakfast. So what the hell was I doing with a sap?

All this was running through my head when I spotted Murphy leaving work. He stepped straight out into the street and hailed a cab, just as I'd instructed him. As the cab pulled out, a dark sedan pulled out from between two trucks and fell in behind.

I'll say this for Pedro. He was good. I'd been looking for his stakeout and hadn't spotted him. I knew for sure he wasn't sitting in that car, because I'd driven by it checking out the block fifteen minutes earlier. And I hadn't seen him anywhere on the street. But somehow, between the time Murphy left the building and hailed the cab, he'd managed to get to his car.

I let two taxis go for insurance, then pulled out and fell in behind.

Murphy was following my instructions to the letter. He was scared not to. He headed for the East Side, and turned up Third Avenue.

I'm slow on the uptake, I must admit. In fact, at times I am more than a little bit dense. But it wasn't until we turned up Third Avenue, that I consciously realized that what I was doing was exactly what Albrect had asked me to do not two weeks ago, when I had turned him down, when I had told him in no uncertain terms how unqualified I was for the job.

I wasn't any more qualified now. And I wasn't any braver. If anything, I was twice as scared. But I sure as fuck had motivation.

Murphy's cab pulled up in front of a fairly posh restaurant, again following my suggestion. He paid off the cab and got out. I wondered how Pedro would handle the situation. There was no parking anywhere to be seen. But Pedro just pulled up and double-parked. I should have known. Hit men don't sweat parking violations. If he got towed, he'd take a cab home. Probably write the towing charges off as a business expense. Well, if you can, I can. I double-parked and got out in time to see Pedro follow Murphy into the restaurant. I got a good look at him as he went in the door. It was my old friend, Floridian #1.

I went in the front door. It was just after five and the place was just beginning to fill up. There was no line. A waitress had just shown Murphy to a table. Another waitress was guiding Pedro to a table on the other side of the room. A third waitress descended on me.

"One," I said.

The waitress frowned. I wondered if she were suspicious, but immediately dismissed the thought. A sudden influx of single diners just at rush hour meant lousy tips, that was all.

I saw Murphy order a drink, which I was sure he needed. Pedro did the same. I ordered a seltzer.

The drinks arrived and Murphy gulped his down. He was trying hard not to look at me, and even harder not to look at Pedro. He ordered shrimp scampi. I couldn't hear what Pedro said to the waitress, but I couldn't help wondering what one ordered before cutting someone's dick off. I ordered a tournedaux bernaise. If I'd been less petrified I might have had a tinge of regret knowing that I'd never get to eat it.

Murphy got up and headed for the john. He disappeared through a curtained hallway at the far end of the room. Pedro waited about thirty seconds, then followed. I followed right behind.

Pedro opened the door of the men's room and stepped in. I came in right behind him and brought the sap down hard on the back of his head.

Pedro went down as if he'd been shot. His legs buckled, and he sprawled, face down on the floor. His head twisted to one side, and I could see the flesh on his face begin to sag, as if his life were draining out of him.

As Pedro melted into the bathroom floor, my body suddenly felt limp and I had to grab the edge of the toilet stall to keep from falling. My head was spinning, and my vision was so fuzzy I could hardly see. I felt as if I'd been kicked in the stomach. That may seem an extreme reaction to such a simple act, but the truth is, I had never coshed anyone before. I can't even recall ever having punched anyone before, nor can I recall ever seeing anyone go down and out from a blow to the head except, of course, in a prize fight, and even that would have been on TV, never in person. So I was not taking it particularly well.

For all that, I was still doing better than Murphy, whom I found curled up in a fetal position next to the toilet. I don't know if he knew I was in there with him. I don't know if he was aware of anything at all. He might have been merely waiting for the bullet.

I put my hand on his back. "Stay there," I told him. I needn't have bothered. He wasn't going anyplace.

I stumbled back out of the toilet stall. Pedro lay face

down on the floor. He hadn't moved. I stepped over the body and locked the outer bathroom door, just as Pedro surely would have done if I hadn't snuck in right behind him. Then I bent over the body.

He was alive. I could tell that at once from the shallow and raspy breathing. He was definitely out, but I couldn't tell how long he'd be out. After all, as I said, I'd never coshed anyone before. I'd hit him hard, I knew that, and the sap was good and solid. I wondered if I'd fractured his skull. I was afraid he'd die, but I was even more afraid he'd come to.

I rolled the body over. It wasn't easy. He must have weighed about 220 pounds. But I got him onto his back.

His right hand was inside his jacket. I tugged it out, reached inside, and pulled out his gun.

I don't know much about guns, so I couldn't tell the make or the caliber, or anything like that. All I knew was that it was an automatic. And that it had a silencer.

I handled the gun, as they say, on long fingers. I pushed it across the floor, being careful to keep it pointed away from me. Slowly, gingerly, I picked it up. I knew I ought to stick it in my pants, but I also knew I'd be sure to shoot my balls off. I set it against the wall, as far away from Pedro as possible. Then I went back to the body.

I figured the gun wasn't the only weapon Pedro had on him. I was right. In his inside jacket pocket I found a straight razor, the kind that barbers use. I'd have been willing to bet you Pedro had never shaved with it. I slipped it into my jacket pocket.

Pedro was showing no signs of coming around, but neither was Murphy. I went inside the toilet stall and shook him, but I got no response. With an effort, I pulled him to his feet. He looked at me with uncomprehending eyes. I slapped him hard in the face. He blinked, staggered, said nothing.

"Murphy," I shouted. "Snap out of it. You're alive. Nothing happened. It's all right. We gotta get out of here."

Murphy looked around dazed. Then he saw Pedro lying on the floor. His knees sagged again, and I had to hold him up.

"Come on," I said. "We're getting out of here."

I got him to the door and leaned him against it. Then I bent down and picked up the gun. I hated to do it, but I had to. I stuck it in my left inside jacket pocket. It stuck way the hell out, what with the silencer and all, but by keeping my left arm rigid, I was able to hold it in place. I unlocked the bathroom door, grabbed Murphy, and steered him out of there.

"All right, Murphy," I hissed at him. "Here's the pitch. You're sick, and I'm helping you out of here. Just act sick."

The dramatic coaching was totally unnecessary. Murphy was already giving a hell of a good impression.

We were conspicuous as hell going through the dining room. The two waitresses who had taken our orders hovered solicitously, as they saw their potential tips heading for the door.

"This man is sick," I said. "I've got to get him to a doctor."

I pulled a hundred dollar bill out of my pants, and handed it to one of the waitresses. "Here," I said. "This should cover it."

I hoped the hundred dollar bill would do the trick, but it didn't. It was too much money. As with Rosa, it only made them suspicious. The maitre d' came rushing over.

"Is something the matter?" he said.

"This man is sick," I repeated. "I've got to get him to a doctor. I gave the waitress a hundred bucks to cover the charges. Hold my order. I hope to be back to eat it. I doubt if he'll be back for his."

The maitre d' didn't look convinced, but I kept moving toward the door. I had to get out of there fast, before someone used the john. Shit. I should have propped Pedro up on the toilet, the way he would have done with Murphy if he'd gotten to kill him. But

I'm an amateur, and then again, Murphy didn't weigh any 220 pounds.

I was about halfway across the room when I saw what I'd been dreading. A guy at a table against the wall was rubbernecking around the room, looking for something. I dug my elbow into Murphy's ribs, trying to get him to hurry. He moaned slightly, but didn't seem to pick up the pace. Shit. The guy I saw at the table was getting up. He was heading for the curtain at the back of the room.

I half lifted, half dragged Murphy through the front door. The car was still there, double-parked right outside, as was Pedro's. Christ, we hadn't even gotten tickets. How lucky can you get? I threw Murphy into the back seat of my car, jumped in, gunned the motor, and got the hell out of there. In the rearview mirror, I could see the maitre d' come running out onto the sidewalk. He looked excited.

I got on the FDR Drive and took it and the Harlem River Drive to the George Washington Bridge. I went over the bridge, got off at the Ft. Lee exit, and took 9W north till I found a motel. I left Murphy in the car, went in, and registered as Murray Cross from Buffalo. The clerk never batted an eye. I went back out, drove the car around to the unit, got Murphy out of the car and pushed him inside.

Murphy was a little more coherent now, perhaps having realized that he was still alive. I took out a written set of instructions I'd typed that afternoon and slapped them into his hand.

"All right," I told him. "You're out of danger, at least for now, but you gotta do exactly what I tell you. It's all in the instructions, you can read them after I go. Basically, it's this: you stay here, you don't go out, and you don't call anyone. Particularly, you don't call anyone. I don't care if there's some girl who's gonna think you're dead, better she *thinks* you're dead than you *are* dead, if you know what I mean. And don't go out, not even for meals. They got room service here, you have your meals sent in. You stay here, watch

TV, and wait for my call. If I call and you're not here, you're in trouble, cause if Tony Arroyo doesn't kill you I will. You got it?"

Murphy was staring at me bug-eyed. He managed to nod.

"You got any money?" I asked him.

He wet his lips. "Ah, yeah, I got some."

"Fine," I told him. "If you can sign for your meals, great. Your name's Murray Cross. If you can't and you run short, go hungry. Don't under any circumstances get cute and use one of your credit cards. Not unless your wanna wake up with your dick in your mouth."

I left him there, got in my car and drove home.

I'd never been so tired in my life.

33

MY WIFE KNEW AT ONCE SOMETHING WAS WRONG. She always does. I can never hide anything from her. I had to say something, so I told her about the double-amputee I'd photographed in Rosedale the day before. It hadn't touched me at all, things being how they were, but I had to tell her something, so I told her how badly it had upset me.

She was all sympathy. Don't get me wrong about my wife. She does drive me crazy with her constant exhortations to better myself, to "be all that I can be," as the army would put it (I can never see that commercial without conjuring up the mental picture of a private on K.P. duty sitting peeling a mountain of potatoes, with the sergeant standing over him saying, "*This* is *all* that you can be"), but basically she's a very good person and I love her very much.

After the amputee story, I told her about the flop house and the bums watching "The Newlywed Game." I told her about the husband who was ridiculed for saying the sun rose in the east in his neighborhood, and she'd seen the same show! Not then; it was a repeat, she'd seen it years ago. But she remembered it, particularly because of the question about the sun and the east.

Unfortunately, I couldn't tell her the kicker to the story, that when the client finally showed up it turned out he was the super in the building, and even though he had been injured in his own room on his own time and not while working on his job, that technically made it a workman's compensation case, which meant there was no money in it and Richard wouldn't take it anyway. I couldn't tell her that, because I couldn't tell her I had tried to get out of taking the case. But it didn't matter, because "The Newlywed Game" thing was so funny, and we laughed about it a lot, and the end result was we wound up in bed.

But tonight it wouldn't happen. I couldn't get it up. Which shows you what a state of mind I was in. That's not to say it had never happened to me before. When I was young it used to happen to me all the time. That's because, like everything else, I was always scared of women. Scared of sex. Scared I wouldn't be able to perform, which, of course, made me incapable of performing.

Oh, I got by. I'd get drunk and kill my inhibitions. But I still had trouble, particularly with one-night stands. And, forgive me for being a sexist pig again, but when you're young, most girls are one-night stands, or are meant to be. And there's always such a frantic hurry the first time. Once you get her pants off, you want to get it in there before she comes to her senses, realizes the enormity of what she's doing, and puts them back on again. So you're always in a rush, and you always defeat your own purpose. Or I always did. I'm sure other people aren't necessarily so neurotic.

But that, as I say, is in the past. With my wife, with whom I'm secure, it's different. Give me a look at her tits or ass and generally I'm a goddamn pogo stick.

Tonight was different. My wife was really nice about it. She thought I was upset about the amputee, having a transference, going through castration anxiety. She helped me along and we got the job done, but it was a struggle.

She fell asleep afterwards, as is her fashion.

I turned out the lights, but I couldn't sleep. I lay there beside her in the dark, feeling somewhat lower than shit.

34

IT WAS EIGHT THE NEXT MORNING WHEN I PULLED INTO A DESERTED JUNKYARD OUT IN QUEENS. I got out of the car and looked around, but there was no one there. I wouldn't have been there either, if I could have helped it. The sun wasn't high enough yet to really steam up the garbage, but nonetheless the place really stunk. Well, I never expected the job to be easy. I gritted my teeth, and wandered out among the junk.

I found a king-sized mattress right off the bat. I hauled it out and propped it up against the shell of what had once been a Chevy van. I paused to catch my breath, then plunged back into the rubble for another mattress.

This time I couldn't find one. I found cars, refrigerators, TVs, washer-dryers, but no damn mattress. What was going on? Was someone running a used mattress concession? Had I been one step ahead of him in bagging a mattress someone had just thrown out the day before? Christ, I hoped not. The one I'd found I wouldn't have wished on my worst enemy.

I found another mattress, queen-sized this time. Well, the queen should go with the king. It was a longer haul this time but I got it there, and propped it up against the first one.

Once more into the breech. An even longer journey this time, and a less rewarding catch. Another king, but in terrible condition, the bottom edge resting in mud and all but rotted away. Well, beggars can't be choosers. I pulled it out, making a mental note to be sure to wash thoroughly and hoping such a precaution would be effective, in light of the strong possibility the mattress might have passengers aboard. I lugged it over and leaned it against the other two, putting the queen in a two-king sandwich.

I went back to the car, popped the trunk, and took out Pedro's gun.

I think I've mentioned I don't like guns. In fact, months ago, when Fred Lazar first asked me if I wanted the job as a private detective, my first question was, "Will I have to carry a gun?" Of course, I didn't have to. If I had, I wouldn't have taken the job. But, as I discovered, most private detectives don't carry guns. Oh, sure, some of them do. I'll be talking to some of Richard's other operatives and see that they have a piece tucked in the front of their pants. I always think, "How can they do that? Why aren't they afraid they'll shoot themselves in the leg, assuming they don't blow their balls off?" But somehow they never do.

In all my months on the job, I only had a gun pulled on me once. It happened on just my second week on the job, and it probably would have ended my detective career if we hadn't needed the money so damn badly. It happened that I had to serve a divorce summons in upstate New York. Richard doesn't generally handle divorce cases, just accident cases, but this was a favor he was doing for a former client. She and her husband were divorcing, so Richard gave me the papers to serve. I was told it was an amicable divorce, so rather than drive 50 miles upstate and find out the guy wasn't home, I called him up to ask him about it.

Naive me. It turned out the guy was living with his mother. I got her on the phone, and she gave me a song and dance about her son not being there and not knowing when he would be in. So I reported back to Richard, who called the client, who provided the information that the guy was indeed living there, and what's more, he worked in Manhattan somewhere and left the house for work every morning at seven sharp.

So Richard gave me a description of the guy, and told me to get up at five in the morning, drive up there, stake out his house, and serve him when he left for work.

So I did it. As I said, it was my second week on the job. It was the first summons I'd ever served, so it was almost even fun. I got up there by 6:45, found the address, and discovered it was a private house on a corner lot, with cars parked on both sides. I picked a spot across the street from which I could see both sides of the house, and sat in my car to wait.

Sure enough, at 7:00 the side door opened and a young man with long hair and a beard came out the door, carrying a coat over his right arm. I'd been given the description of a man with a mustache, but I figured a mustache could become a beard, given a little time, so I got out of my car and started across the road.

"Charles Petralini," I called out.

He stopped and turned around. "Yeah."

I had him. I crossed the road and walked up to him. He shrugged the coat off his arm. In his right hand was a single-barreled shotgun with no stock, your basic, ugly, lethal, concealed weapon.

"Whaddya want?" he snarled.

What I wanted was to get back in my car, drive off, quit the detective business, and never serve another bloody fucking summons the rest of my life. But I couldn't do that.

"I have divorce papers from your wife," I said. I reached into my jacket pocket, very slowly so he could see that was what I was taking out. I held them out toward him. "I was told you were expecting them."

He snatched them from me and looked at them. Then he looked up at me. "Yeah," he said bitterly. "That's cool." He looked down at the papers again. Then he looked straight at me, his face hot with anger, and his hand clenched around his gun. "But I never want to see your face again, douche bag."

I didn't ask him how he knew my name. I just got

back in my car and drove off. It was a good twenty miles before I convinced myself the son of a bitch wasn't following me.

That was my first experience with what I presumed was a loaded gun. Picking up Pedro's in the bathroom was my second.

This was my third. It was also my first time firing one. I'm sure I did everything wrong. I gritted my teeth and winced as I pulled the trigger. There was no noise, because of the silencer, but the gun jerked like a son of a bitch, and I nearly fell on my ass.

I steadied myself, looked, and discovered that by some miracle I had managed to hit the broad side of a king-size mattress, a good six feet away. It had been close, though. The small round hole was near the top edge of the mattress. I had aimed dead center. No matter. It would only make the bullet that much easier to dig out.

I took out my pocket knife and began to look for the bullet. It had gone clean through the first mattress. I flopped it over. There was an exit wound in the back. The king is dead, long live the king. The queen was also dead. I flopped her over too. There was no exit wound in the other king, so the bullet was still in it. I was glad. I was running out of royalty.

I began cutting away the material around the hole. I didn't dig for the bullet itself, because I didn't want to mark it with the knife. I dug out around it. Eventually I was able to pull out a wad of cotton stuffing. I spread it apart with my fingers. The bullet lay inside. I took out one of my father-in-law's plastic bags, dropped the bullet in it, and put it in my jacket pocket.

35

ONE OF THE FIRST THINGS I LEARNED ABOUT COPS WAS THAT THEY DON'T LIKE PRIVATE DETECTIVES. At least, private detectives of my type. The reason is, a lot of the claims we investigate are against the city for which they work, and sometimes even involve negligence, or even liability, on the part of the police department itself. So I've never got along very well with cops.

The desk sergeant was no exception. "You want to see who?" he said.

I didn't point out that he should have said "whom." "I want to see the guy who's in charge of the case of the businessman who got murdered in the midtown parking lot. I think the paper said his name was Albrect. The dead guy. Not the cop in charge."

"Why you wanna see him?"

"I have something I think might be evidence."

"Oh yeah? What's that?"

I'd like to talk to the guy in charge."

"You're talking to me. What have you got?"

"I found something in the parking lot."

"What?"

"I'm not sure, but I think it might be a bullet."

Things happened fast. One thing that didn't happen was my being ushered into the presence of the officer in charge of the case. Instead, I was placed in a room by myself and told in no uncertain terms not to leave. There was actually no question of my leaving, because, when I looked out in the corridor, I discovered they'd stationed an officer at the door.

They also took my bullet. I surrendered it when asked, rather than making them frisk me for it. I wasn't looking for trouble.

I sat in the room for about two hours. No one came in. No one even peeked in the door.

Then the whole world came in. First was a beefy guy who appeared to be a sergeant, and was, because when he got close enough for me to read his name tag, I discovered I'd correctly interpreted his stripes. He was followed by two junior officers and a stenographer. The stenographer sat at the table. The two younger officers stationed themselves along the walls. The sergeant drew up a chair to where I was sitting, turned it around, and put his foot up on it. He leaned in to me.

"All right," he said. "Why don't you tell us about it?"

"Tell you about what?" I asked him.

"Don't get cute with me, kid," he said, flattering to a 40-year-old. "You know. About the bullet."

"Is it a bullet?" I asked him.

"You know damn well it's a bullet," he said. "Now why don't you tell us about it."

"What do you want to know?" I asked him.

The stenographer coughed significantly. The sergeant gave him a look, but took the hint.

"Name," he asked.

"Stanley Hastings."

"Occupation."

"Private detective."

That caught him up short. He looked at me. "What?"

"I'm a private detective. But that's got nothing to do with it."

"Is that so? Let's see your credentials."

I handed him my I.D. He opened it, looked it over, then read it aloud so the stenographer could take down the information. He handed it back to me.

"Let me see your gun permit," he said.

"I haven't got a gun permit," I told him.

"You haven't got a gun permit?"

"No."

"How come you haven't got a gun permit?"

"I haven't got a gun."

"Oh yeah? Well, what the hell kind of a private detective are you if you haven't got a gun?"

"I don't do criminal work. I chase ambulances."

"Oh," he snorted. "One of those."

"Yeah. One of those."

"Why don't you tell us about the gun?"

"What gun?"

"The gun the bullet came from."

"I don't know anything about any gun."

"I think you can do a little better than that."

"You think wrong. I don't know anything about any gun. I found that bullet, if it is a bullet, in a parking lot. I found it last night. I parked my car in the lot. When I came back to get in, I saw it lying on the ground. I picked it up. It looked like a bullet. I remembered reading in the paper that a guy had been shot in that lot. I thought the bullet might be evidence, so I brought it in. I figured maybe the lab could match it up with the fatal bullet and see if it came from the same gun."

The sergeant just stared at me. I must say, he was good at it. He had the most wonderfully ironic, mocking look. His face said it all. He didn't believe a word I was saying.

"Was the bullet from the same gun?" I asked. I already knew the answer. They wouldn't be talking to me if it wasn't. But I needed to be sure.

"We're asking the questions here," the sergeant snapped.

This was the part I wasn't looking forward to. You see, I've always been intimidated by cops. I'm one of those people who, when they're driving along and they see a cop car with the lights flashing, immediately think, "Shit! They got me!" even though they're not doing anything wrong. And if a cop should pull me over and ask me for my license and registration, I'd give it to 'em. It would never occur to me to say, "No," or even, "Why?" Because police are authority figures, and it's just natural to do what they say. At least it is for me.

However, the sergeant had said, "We're asking the questions here," and I was never gonna get a better cue line than that for my purpose, so it was up to me to pick up on it. So I gritted my teeth and I did.

"Oh yeah," I said. "Well, you're going about it all wrong."

The sergeant's head shot up. Apparently he wasn't used to having his authority questioned any more than I was to questioning it. "What?" he said ominously.

"You're going about it all wrong," I told him. "If you're accusing me of a crime, you haven't advised me of my rights."

"No one's accusing you of a crime," the sergeant said.

That was what I expected him to say. It was also my next cue, and it was the biggie. I was ready for it, but it still took all my nerve to carry it off.

"Fine," I said. "In that case, I'm leaving."

The sergeant's mouth fell open. "What?" he said incredulously.

"I'm walking out of here," I told him. "It's been nice talking to you."

"Hey, wait a minute," he said. "You're not going anywhere."

"That's what you think," I said. "If you're not charging me with a crime, you got no right to hold me. I'm getting out of here."

"That's what *you* think. You're not getting out of here until you account for that bullet."

"Sorry, Sergeant, I don't have to. You wanna hold me, you gotta charge me. I know my rights."

The sergeant looked as if he'd just eaten a bucket of nails. "All right," he said. "You're under arrest. The charge is accessory after the fact to murder. I hope that satisfies you. Now what about the bullet?"

"You haven't advised me of my rights."

"You said you *knew* your rights."

"That doesn't matter. You haven't advised me of them."

The sergeant sighed. "All right, Nelson, read him."

Nelson, one of the cops against the wall began the drone, "You're under arrest. You have the right to remain silent. If you give up the right to remain silent, anything you say may be taken down and used in evidence against you in a court of law. You have the right to an attorney. If you cannot afford an attorney—"

That was my last cue, and I jumped on it. "That's it," I said. "I have the right to an attorney. I want to call my lawyer."

36

ASIDE FROM MONEY, there is nothing Richard likes better than bopping cops around. I'd called him once before, when the King's County Hospital security staff had attempted to impound my film for taking a picture of one of the patients. I'd called Richard and he'd been there in 20 minutes.

He beat that record today, and I'm sure it was not because he thought I was the best person in the world, or because he could not bear my sorry plight, but just because he absolutely loves confrontations.

The first words out of his mouth as he strode into the room were, "Did they touch you?"

I shook my head.

"All right, gentlemen," he said, surveying the room. "Perhaps we can still avoid a lawsuit. Who's in charge here?"

"I am," said the sergeant.

"All right, Sergeant, what seems to be the trouble?"

"This man brought in a bullet. It's evidence in a murder case. He claims he found it in the parking lot where the man was killed."

Richard's eyebrows launched into orbit. "Wait a minute. Wait a minute," he said. "Let me be sure I understand this. A private citizen came to the police station of his own accord to deliver to you something he thought might be evidence. In return for his effort, you have taken this conscientious good citizen, sequestered him in a room, held him incommunicado for hours, and then attempted to violate his rights by interrogating him outside the presence of his attorney, and what's more, have gone so far as to charge this good samaritan with a crime?"

"Well—" the sergeant began.

"Well, gentleman," Richard said. "I'm not sure, but perhaps it is not too late to avoid a suit for harrassment and false arrest. Now, my client and I are walking out of here. If any one of you lay your hands on us or attempt to detain us, I promise you, on my word as an attorney, that I will be spending every penny you ever make in your lives, and that includes your pensions."

Richard and I walked out the door. No one made any effort to stop us.

Outside, he turned to me and said, "What the fuck is this all about?"

"I found a bullet in a parking lot where that guy got killed. I thought it might be important so I brought it in. You know the rest."

"Assholes," Richard said.

"Listen," I said. "Thanks a lot. And you can do me a favor. Another favor, really."

"What's that?"

"Listen, I know this is a great story to kid me about and all that, but if you happen to call me on the phone don't mention this to my wife."

"Oh?"

"Yeah." I kicked shit a little. "My car shouldn't have been in the parking lot that night. I was supposed to be somewhere else."

Richard gave me his knowing, man-of-the-world look. I tried not to laugh.

"One more thing," I said.

"What?"

"I don't know if you could do this, but if you could—"

"What?"

"Well, after all that trouble, I'm curious as hell to know if the bullet I found really came from the murder gun. Do you suppose there's any way you could find out?"

Richard grinned. "It will be my pleasure."

I grinned back. I probably could have liked Richard, if the little prick weren't only 30 years old, and already well on his way to becoming a millionaire.

37

I CHANGED THE TAPES AGAIN THAT AFTERNOON. Maybe it was just that my escapade with Pedro made it seem tame by comparison, but this time it didn't really bother me. I went back to my office and threaded them up.

Most of it was just more of the same. Grousing, bellyaching, empty threats against whoever was fucking them over. I enjoyed the part when Pedro got back and related his side of what happened to the Murphy rubout. To hear him talk, I was a real pro. I tried not to get a swelled head. It was hard when he suggested there must have been more than one guy.

Still, there was nothing particularly interesting until I got to the end of the tape. That was the phone call from Angelo Ospina, from Floridian #2. He wasn't at all pleased with the way things were going. He was flying up the next day. He wanted to meet everyone at Pluto's at three in the afternoon.

"YOU GOTTA GO BELLY UP, Murphy."

"What?"

I was calling long distance from my office to his motel room in Jersey. I'd used the M.C.I. number because it's cheaper, although the connection isn't always as good. This time the connection was just fine, Murphy had heard me all right. He just wasn't sure what I'd said.

I was using my best tough guy lingo, an image I felt it best to promote with Murphy. To be honest, I was really doing Al Pacino in "The Godfather" telling Carlo, "You have to answer for Santino." So I wasn't surprised that Murphy didn't get it.

"You gotta roll over for the cops," I said, "You gotta tell 'em everything."

"I can't do that," he said.

"Yes you can. You have to."

"I can't. They'll kill me."

"You don't understand, Murphy. They're *already* trying to kill you. They don't need any more motivation. Right now, it's come down to you or them."

"Yeah, but—"

"You're not a principal, Murphy. You're not even gonna do time. You tell your story, you'll do all right."

"I don't know."

"Hey, it's not like you had an option. Murphy. You stay where you are, you go broke. You run it's the same thing. Maybe you think you could get away and start over, but you can't. It doesn't matter where you go. You got no money, and you can't use your credit cards 'cause they'll trace you through them. You can't even get a job, 'cause you can't bank on your references, 'cause you can't use your right name. You run, you die. You come back here, they kill you. There's only one way out for you, and I'm it. So you listen careful, and you do what I say."

I MET MURPHY AT THE MOTEL THE NEXT MORNING. I'd typed out his confession for him the day before. I hadn't wanted to type it on my own typewriter, knowing from detective stories that typing can be traced, so I'd gone out to a typewriter store to do it on one of the floor models. That turned out to be one of those things that works really great in the movies, but sucks in real life. To be fair, I guess in the movies they're always typing some one-paragraph ransom note they whip in the machine and dash off, whereas I had a five-page confession, which I guess wasn't very bright. I kept attracting the attention of salesmen, and had to keep moving from one machine to another, and the end result was the damn confession had at least five different type styles, which was gonna confuse the hell out of the police department, but there wasn't much I could do about it, seeing as how I was lucky just to get out of there without buying a fucking typewriter.

I went over the confession with Murphy a few times just to get him through the rough spots. There was a lot of stuff in it he didn't even know. It didn't matter. It didn't have to stand up in court. It just had to be strong enough to justify the warrant.

After I'd prepared Murphy for what he was going to do, I drove him back to Manhattan and dropped him off at a dirty-movie house with instructions to sit and stare at the screen until it was time to make his move.

Under the circumstances I couldn't think of a better place for him.

I went back to the office to get myself ready. There was a message from Richard on the answering machine, confirming that the bullet I'd "discovered" had come from the gun that killed Albrect. I was glad to get the confirmation, but it didn't matter. I already knew the bullet came from the gun from the way the police acted, and had been proceeding on that assumption, and, whether the confirmation had come through or not, I was going ahead. But it was nice to have.

I got out Pedro's gun and razor and laid them out on the table. I got out Albrect's kilo and laid it out beside them. A nice little collection. Just the sort of thing Pluto should have.

I called the time recording and checked my watch. Timing was going to be crucial in this thing. I wanted to go in at the last moment, so there'd be no chance of Pluto's boys finding the plant. But I had to be damn sure to get out in time. I felt really silly checking my watch, though. I mean, I wasn't talking seconds here. I was going to leave myself a good half hour.

It was my one shot, and it had to work. If it didn't, I'd never get another. Murphy's confession would be blown. In all probability he'd wind up dead. In all probability I'd wind up dead, too. That was pretty scary, but not scary enough to stop me. Fear is relative. Not doing it was pretty scary, too.

What I was going to do was terrifying, but quick. One way or another, it would be over. If I didn't do it, the fear would be less intense, but perpetual. No one could live in constant fear. I know I couldn't. So when you came right down to it, my bold move was really the coward's way out.

I didn't care. Fuck the motivation. Fuck the reasons. I had to do it. It was something I simply had to do.

And I could do it. I would do it. The wheels had been set in motion. Everything was right on schedule.

Nothing could go wrong.

40

"WHAT DO YOU MEAN, you rented it?"

The man at the theatrical costume shop shrugged. "I rented it. What can I say, I rented it."

"Are you trying to tell me that's the only telephone repair outfit you have?"

"No. I got six of 'em."

"So give me another one."

"I rented them all."

"You what?"

"I rented them. Some off-Broadway revue. They gotta musical number with dancing repairmen."

"Jesus Christ!"

"Yeah, I know. Sounds like a turkey to me, too."

"Where's the nearest costume house?"

"Aw, come on, how about a Con-Ed uniform?"

"Damnit! Where's the nearest costume shop?"

"Up Broadway. Four blocks."

I started for the door.

"But you come back here," he yelled. "I value your business."

I ran the four blocks. Asshole! Dumb fucking asshole! Any moron would have rented the costume first. I'd been so concerned with Murphy not blowing it that I was blowing it myself.

The shop had no telephone repair outfit. Reluctantly, the proprietor directed me to a third costume shop.

They had one. But the guy wouldn't hurry. Jesus Christ! Weren't there ever emergencies where actors were trying to make the curtain? They'd have missed the whole first act in this shop.

Finally I had it. I tried it on in the shop. It was a little big, but I had no time to be fussy.

"I can take that in for you," the old guy said.

I nearly punched him in the face. I threw money at him, grabbed my street clothes, and ran out the door.

It was only 8 blocks to my car, but I hailed a cab. Seconds counted now. I'd lost my precious half hour and more, nearly 15 minutes more. Maybe I could make it up by not having to change.

I got in my car and went through the midtown tunnel. It was jammed. Another 15 minutes lost. On the other side of the tunnel I finally passed the jack-knifed tractor trailer truck that was causing all the fuss. How you jackknife coming out of a tunnel onto a toll plaza is beyond me, but the guy had managed. I gave him the finger as I went by, unnecessarily cruel, I know, but I was beginning to lose it by that point.

I drove like hell. I'm not used to driving fast. On the job I always drive slow. That's because a speeding ticket will wipe out the entire profit for a four hour sign-up, making the trip meaningless. A parking ticket will do it too, and I've had a few of those, usually when I pulled up to a phone to answer the fucking beeper. Jesus Christ, why am I thinking about that now? Just concentrate like hell and keep the car on the road.

I sped off the L.I.E. on to the Grand Central. I took the exit ramp at 65, nearly lost it on the last curve, then straightened out, ducked in front of a semi, and shot out into traffic. I sailed down the Van Wyck, hoping there wouldn't be a jam up at the airport. There wasn't. Miracle. I shot onto the Belt Parkway, headed east.

My car has a digital clock and the fucking thing is always accurate, so I knew when 3 o'clock came. I wasn't even on the Southern Parkway yet, and Murphy would already be starting to spill his guts. Maybe they wouldn't believe him at first. Maybe they'd take time. Yeah, maybe.

But Ospina would be arriving right now. The meeting would be starting. All in all, it was a fucking mess.

I raced down Sunrise Highway, turned south, skidded around a few turns. I almost hit a kid on a bicycle. Great. Vehicular homicide on top of everything else. Asshole.

I slowed down for the last few turns, and suddenly there was the car. I pulled in right behind it, shut off the motor, grabbed my repair kit, and got out.

I strode off down the road toward Pluto's house. My pants were too big and kept falling down. The least of my worries. I reached the telephone pole. I could see in the driveway. The cars were all there, so Pedro must have gotten back from the airport. So that was that. The meeting had started. They were all inside.

I slipped the belt on and shinnied up the pole. I was getting pretty good at it by now, and I might have made good time if it hadn't been for my pants, which kept trying to fall down. I reached the top. I pulled the clamps from my pocket, connected them to the wires on either side of the connection. I pulled the electrical tape off, and tugged at the splice. Luckily, my splice wasn't very good. It gave like that. Seconds later I was sliding down the pole.

I unhooked the belt and strode up the driveway to the front door. There was no time to be scared now, which was a blessing in itself. No time for reflection. No time for thought. Just do it.

I rang the bell. I rang five times before Tall, Dark and Ugly opened the door. He frowned as he recognized me.

"What the hell do you want?" he said.

"The phone's out again," I told him.

He stared at me. "What?"

"The phone's out. Is that so hard to understand? Your phones are out again."

"No they're not. I used the phone this morning. It's working fine."

"Well, it's out now," I told him.

He wasn't convinced. "I don't understand," he said. "We didn't report the phone's out."

"You don't have to," I said. "It doesn't matter. See, what happens is, someone tries to call you and keeps getting a busy signal. Then they call the verifying operator, and the operator checks the number and finds out the phone's out. She reports it to my department, and they send me out to fix it."

"Without calling first?"

I looked at him. "What, are you nuts?"

He thought a second. "Oh," he said. But he still wasn't convinced, and I had a good idea his last call hadn't been that long ago.

But he let me in. His attitude changed a little when he picked up the kitchen phone and found it dead. I didn't even bother with it.

"Let's try the living room," I told him.

The living room phone was dead too.

There was no time to ask him for a soda, even if there'd been a chance in hell he would have gotten me one. I simply unscrewed the mouthpiece under the guise of examining it, and palmed the bug off it right under his nose.

"Looks O.K.," I said. "Let's see the other one."

He didn't seem too keen on that. "The trouble was outside last time. Why don't you start there?"

I looked at him. "Hey, buddy," I told him. "Are you telling me my job?"

Tall, Dark and Ugly knew better than to argue with a menial in the practice of his profession. Reluctantly, he led me to the study door.

"Wait here," he said.

He opened the door and went in. I stood in the hallway and looked through the half-opened door. And there they were. All of 'em. Pluto and Bambi and Floridian #1 and #2. All of 'em but Dumbo, who by now should be ratting on the rest to the local fuzz.

I'd never seen Floridian #2 before, and it startled me. I'd expected another broad-shouldered Colombian thug. Angelo Opsino was a frail old man, 85 if he was a day. He was sitting on the couch, and he looked as if it were taking all his strength just to keep his head from falling into his lap. It really floored me. I have this thing, where somehow I expect everyone to be as old as I am. It had shocked the hell out of me to find out a big drug dealer like Pluto was a 22 year old kid and not even Hispanic to boot. Ospina was certainly Hispanic, but, Jesus Christ, this was a cold-blooded killer and drug czar? This is the infamous Floridian #2?

Through the door I could hear the murmur of voices.

". . . telephone repairman . . ."

". . . who the fuck . . ."

". . . phone's out again . . ."

". . . now? . . ."

". . . just be a minute . . ."

". . . fuck it, we have to have the phone . . ."

Tall, Dark and Ugly came back out. "O.K.," he said. "But make it fast, will you?"

"Word of honor," I said.

I meant it. I had just checked my watch, and if my calculations were correct, I had five, maybe ten minutes before the police would be all over this place. I had to be out of there before then.

O.K., kid, this is it. You gotta do it. If you ever had any guts in your life, you better have 'em now. You gotta go into that room.

It was terrifying. Coshing Pedro was nothing compared to it. That was a simple, quick, impulsive action, spurred on by a tremendous flow of adrenaline. This required calm, precise, deliberate action, in *spite* of a tremendous flow of adrenaline. This took nerves of steel.

I didn't have 'em. Jesus Christ, what the hell was I doing here? Was I nuts? Going into that room with all of them watching me, Tony Arroyo included. Maybe I should have worn a disguise after all. Maybe people *don't* notice a fake mustache or a wig. Couldn't I at least have worn a pair of dark glasses? No, idiot, not in the house, and not with a hardhat. It would look funny and people would stare. Or would they? Haven't you seen hardhats with shades before? What's the difference? What does it matter now? Oh, Jesus Christ, there's TDU going through the door, you can't just stand here, can you?

I followed him into the room. I tried not to look at the men. I tried not to let them get a good look at me. I tried to keep my pants from falling down. I tried to keep from pissing in them, too.

I made my way to the desk. I put my toolbox on the floor behind it, out of sight of the men. I bent over the phone. I tried to keep my head down, keep my helmet over my eyes.

I couldn't help sneaking a look at Tony. He was looking at me kinda funny, as if trying to figure something out. I hoped he wouldn't do it. My hands were shaking slightly, and I was having trouble with the phone.

I suddenly had a paranoic flash that everyone was looking at me. I stole a look. They were! Holy shit! Then I realized. Of course they were looking at me. They wouldn't keep talking while I was in the room. They were all just waiting for me to leave.

Somehow I got the phone apart. I got the mouthpiece off, palmed the bug. So far, so good. But there was the other one under the desk. Not to mention the stuff in my toolbox.

I heard the faint sound of tires on gravel from the driveway, the sound of a car pulling in. Oh Christ! Not the police. Not now. Not yet.

I heard another one. Pulling in, coming to a stop. Hadn't they heard it too? I risked a glance. No one seemed to have heard but me. Had I imagined it? No, I'd just been listening for it, expecting it.

The sound again. A third car pulling in. It's real all right. It's happening. Get on with it. Get it done.

I bent down behind the desk. And then I heard Tony's voice, clear as a bell. "Wait a fucking minute!" he murmured as if in awe.

I couldn't help it. I looked up. He was staring straight at me, wide-eyed. There was no mistaking that look. Total recall. I'd been made.

Tony's hand flashed toward the inside of his coat. I stood like a statue. I should have been diving for my toolbox, but for that split second I was frozen in time. I could see it happen. The gun coming out of his holster, first the butt appearing clutched in his hand, then the barrel clearing the fabric of his coat, swinging around and aiming at me. His finger tightening on the trigger, the sound, the flash, the bullet smashing into my chest.

It didn't happen. At that instant there came the unmistakable squeal of brakes from out front, and then, god help me, one lone siren. Thank god for the one asshole cop in the bunch.

That one siren did the trick. They drew their guns all right, but not at me. They drew them and rushed for the door. All of them. Even Tony. Revenge is a hell of a good motivation, but fear beats it every time. Thank god for man's instinct to survive.

I bent down and ripped the bug from the bottom of the desk. I opened my toolbox, took out Pedro's gun and razor, and Albrect's kilo of coke. I pulled the desk drawer open, popped them in, and pulled it closed. Good. Even the stupidest cop couldn't help finding them.

I heard gunfire coming from the front of the house. All in all, it seemed a great time to get the hell out of there.

I ran to the window. It opened easily. There was a screen, but it slid open too. I pushed my toolbox through, climbed through after it, and dropped to the ground.

I had just picked up my toolbox and started around the house, when I head someone bark, "Freeze!" Jesus Christ! You mean people say that in real life?

I froze. The cop walked up to me. He seemed young. At least he seemed younger than I was. Right then I felt about a hundred and five.

"What the hell are you doing?" he asked.

I looked at him as if he were an idiot. "Fixing the phone," I said. "The phones are out."

"Well, you're not fixing it now."

"Hey, that's my job."

There came fresh gunfire from the front of the house.

"You hear that?" the cop said. "You deaf? Now get the hell out of here."

God bless police psychology. If I'd tried to leave he'd have held me. He hurried back toward the front of the house. I cut into the next-door neighbor's yard and walked out to the road.

There were five police cars surrounding the place. Cops were stationed everywhere out front, and guns were blazing. It seemed like an awfully good time to get the hell out of there, but I didn't want to leave any trace. Anything that would give the cops the idea the phone had been wired. Anything that might start them thinking.

So I hooked on my belt and started up the pole again. No one noticed. Everyone's attention was quite well riveted on the ground. I reached the top, settled in, began to work on my splice.

I was still there when the news crews arrived. I have no idea how they get wind of these things—someone must tip them off—but they sure arrived fast. The shootout was still on when the first crews arrived, and the police had to keep pushing them back so they themselves wouldn't become the fatalities on which they were about to report.

By the time the last crew arrived it was over. Those poor slobs were still setting up as the police led the handcuffed prisoners out of the house. Tail, Dark and Ugly and Floridian #1 came first, along with Tony's driver. I hadn't even known he was there, and I still didn't know his name, but it didn't matter, they had him.

Pluto came next, looking just like a little kid who'd been caught with his hand in the cookie jar. Big, bold

Pluto, killer and dope dealer, who looked like he wanted to cry and run home to his mother.

Floridian #2 came next. He was so frail two cops had to help him. He looked as if he were being assisted into a retirement home, which, in a way, he was.

Tony came last, and he came on a stretcher. Two medics were desperately working on his chest, but even from my high perch I could see it was too late. Alas, poor Bambi, I knew him well.

I completed my splice and slid down the pole. No one bothered me. No one seemed to notice. I went back to my cars. I opened the trunk of the rental car, took out the tape recorders and all the equipment, and threw it in the back of my car. I got in my car and drove off. I'd come back for the rental car later, if I got a chance. It didn't matter if anyone found it, seeing as how I'd rented it with the phony driver's license made by the guy who made the bank I.D. Let the cops go nuts combing the Bronx looking for Julius T. Coosbaine.

41

I DROVE BACK TO MANHATTAN. All in all, I felt pretty good. After all, I'd done it, hadn't I? In my own, bumbling, ineffectual way, I'd done everything I'd set out to do. True, I hadn't done it heroically, dramatically, like some fucking TV detective. I hadn't shot anybody. I hadn't even confronted the enemy. As my wife so justly accuses me, I'd avoided all personal confrontation. Aside from briefly meeting Tony in the casino, and Tall, Dark and Ugly in my repairman guise, I hadn't even met any of 'em. My one assertive act, aside from frightening poor Red out of his wits, had been coshing Pedro on the head, and that had affected me almost as much as it had him.

But I'd had to play it that way. I am not Mike Hammer, nor was meant to be.

My actual personal involvement in the case was so limited that no one knew I was connected with it at all. And that's the way I wanted it. That's the way I intended to keep it. Oh yeah, I had the tapes, and I should have turned them over to the police for evidence, but they didn't need them. They had Murphy's confession, and it covered everything; I'd seen to that. It even covered things he couldn't know, but that didn't matter. The cops had the murder weapon. They had the guys dead to rights. With all of them in separate cells, all talking their heads off, trying to pin it on the others to save their own skins, the D.A. would have all he needed and more.

No one could connect me with the case at all. The only one who might have was Tony, and he was dead. Murphy knew me by sight, but he didn't know my name. And even if he found out, he wouldn't talk. I'd read him the riot act before I'd turned him loose on the cops. And he didn't know I was an ineffectual schmuck. He thought I was a tough son of a bitch, capable of carrying out my threats. Murphy was just as chicken shit as I. He'd keep quiet till doomsday.

The only thing that could have involved me was the bullet I brought to the cops, but that was no real worry. I'd made sure of that, by telling 'em I'd found it in the parking lot. The police theory of the case, and what I'm sure actually happened, was that Albrect was killed somewhere else and dumped in the lot. The bullet contradicted that theory. Therefore, the D.A. would never mention it. The defense attorney certainly would, if he knew of its existence, but I was sure that would never happen. The cops wouldn't let it. The bullet would just quietly disappear.

So I was home free. Uninvolved. Invisible. The man who wasn't there. And that's the way I wanted it. That's the way it had to be. I have a five-year-old kid. I couldn't live with the knowledge that somewhere, somehow, someone might strike back at me through him. Or through my wife. Or through me, for that matter. I'm a coward still.

Yeah, I'm still a coward, but all things are relative. I mean, after all this, I don't think I'd find the projects quite so scary anymore. Not that I was planning on visiting the projects any time in the near future.

I pulled up in front of my office, put the blinkers on, and took the recording equipment inside, screw the "NO PARKING-TOW ZONE" sign (see, I'm braver already).

I lugged Red's suitcase back down to the car. It hadn't seemed that heavy when I'd yanked it out of Red's trunk that night with all my adrenaline flowing, but it sure weighed a ton now. I flung it in the back of the car and drove off, heading for the West Side Highway and home.

Yeah, I think I've had it with the detective business. After all, it was never meant to be permanent. It was always a source of income, nothing more.

I know an actor named Phil who's a cokehead, who deals grams just so he'll have something around to snort. He's not big time, or anything, but he probably moves about an ounce a week. I don't know what he pays for his coke or how good it is, but I do know that if I offered him what I have at $1500 an ounce he'd probably come in his pants.

Let's see now, there's 16 ounces to a pound. A kilo's over two pounds; I'm not sure exactly what, it's never come up in my life before. So two pounds is 32 ounces; round it off to 30, say 30 ounces a key, times 20 keys, or 600 ounces. That'll bring me 1500 tax-free a week for at least the next ten years. Well, if I can't get any writing done with that much free time, I might as well hang it up. I'll worry about it when I'm 50. Jesus, do people really get to be 50? I guess they do. It surprised the hell out of me to discover they got to be 40.

Yeah, I know, all this talk about dealing dope makes me a bad person. But I've done the right thing all my life and been fucked over by everyone I've ever met. Over half the jobs I've ever had, I never got paid for, or at least never got paid for in full. I've been pushed around all my life by asshole producers, directors, agents, editors and bosses. I've never gotten anywhere. I'm 40 years old and I'm tired, and I've got a wife and kid to feed, so can you blame me for taking the free ride?

Look, a lot of people do coke, and they're gonna go on doing it whether I get my weekly skim or not. And it's not like I'm hanging out by the schoolyard trying to get the kids hooked. No one in the world is gonna do any more or any less of the stuff whether I get paid or not. So why not get paid?

Yeah, I know, it's a lousy moral justification. So I'm

a bad person. What can I say. I look at my assets after 40 years of struggling through life, and what do I see? Nothing. Zero. With the small exception of 20 kilos of coke.

All right, it's illegal. But my father-in-law cheats on his income tax, and Richard sues innocent people and bilks insurance companies out of millions of dollars, and Leroy's a thief, for Christ's sake. They think nothing of it, but they would all look down their noses at me as a dirty filthy dope peddler. Shit. If I'd just had the presence of mind to hit Red on his way *down* to Miami, and rip off the drug *money* instead of the drug, they'd think it was just great. Well, fuck 'em all. You gotta do what you gotta do.

I got on the West Side Highway and headed uptown. Ahead, in the distance, I could see the sign for the 79th Street Boat Basin.

Yeah. The coke was mine. I'd worked hard for it. I'd earned it. I had every right to keep it. I had every right to sell it.

Like Albrect.

Jesus.

Just like Albrect.

I pulled into the Boat Basin, stopped the car, and got out. I took the suitcase full of coke and threw it in the Hudson River.

Tough luck, Phil.

I threw my beeper in too.

Tough luck, Richard.

I got in the car and drove home.

Yeah, you gotta do what you gotta do.

42

DRIVING HOME ON THE WEST SIDE HIGHWAY, I got to thinking about the case again, and I had a revelation. I guess it's not surprising for a guy who just threw a half a million dollars in the river to experience a revelation, but actually, that had nothing to do with it. What set it off was the fact that I realized I was referring to the Albrect affair as "the case," just as if I were a real detective. Which of course struck me funny, seeing as how the whole time I'd been working on "the case," my big problem had been that I *wasn't* a real detective.

And then, for the first time, I started thinking about what a real detective was. Up to now, my only definition of a real detective had been one that wasn't me. I'd never really taken it any further than that. But why wasn't I a real detective? Because I hadn't kicked down any doors or shot anybody or had any high-speed car chases? Because I hadn't captured the bad guys single-handed and held them at bay until the police arrived? Just what was a real detective, anyway?

Well, Fred Lazar's a real detective. What would he have done in this case, assuming he took it at all, which I doubt? Well, he might have had some ex-cop who would have been willing to bodyguard Albrect. What would have happened then? One of two things. One, Albrect and the bodyguard would have got killed, in which case Fred would have reported what he knew to the police, end of case. Two, the bodyguard would have shot Pedro. What would have happened then?

249

Would Fred have covered it up, kept Albrect out of it, and gone after the cocaine ring? Not on your life. Fred has a license, and he's not dumb. He'd have made a full disclosure to the police, withholding only the specifics of Albrect's story, stating that Albrect had hired his agency to provide a bodyguard for reasons unknown, and this had been the result, end of case.

Yeah, that's what Fred would have done. He wouldn't have solved the Albrect murder. But if he'd gotten involved at all, he'd have made damn sure someone paid him a fee. He's a *real* detective.

So it dawned on me that the whole time I'd been upbraiding myself for not being a real detective, what I'd been thinking of as a real detective wasn't real at all. I'd been coming down on myself for not being a TV detective, a movie detective, a paperback hero that doesn't even exist. The macho fantasy figure I'd been disparaging all along—that was the guy I'd been unable to measure up to. That was the guy I'd felt useless for not being able to be. He wasn't real at all.

I got so wrapped up in thinking this I nearly missed the 96th Street exit, and I had to swerve in front of a car that was pulling onto the Highway from the entrance at Riverside Drive and 95th. The driver gave me the horn and the finger, and deservedly so. I didn't care. I coasted down the exit ramp under Riverside Drive, lost in a world of my own.

Schmuck. You total schmuck. Your real detective wasn't even real. *"And the princess and the prince discuss what's real and what is not."* Jesus Christ, Bob Dylan sang that song over twenty years ago. Think how old that makes you, and yet you still cling to your idiotic, romantic, childhood notions. Stanley Hastings, P.I. Stanley Hastings, coward, incompetent, bungler, fool. What's the difference? You did it, you son of a bitch.

I turned the corner onto my block. There was a parking space right in front of my building. Some days you get lucky. I parked the car, set the code alarm, and went in.

The Mets had won that day, and Jerry was insufferable in the elevator, but I didn't care. I barely heard. I got off at my floor, put my key in the lock, and opened the door.

Tommie was waiting for me with his Red Sox hat and glove on. He held out my glove to me. As I took it from him, my wife exploded from the kitchen, a letter clutched in her hand.

"There you are, finally," she cried. "Do you know what this is? The goddamn Master Charge people sent the bill here again. After all the times you've told them to switch it over, they sent it here again, and guess what? You know how much it's for? Nineteen hundred and seventy dollars! I called them up and said what the hell is going on, our limit is fifteen hundred, for Christ's sake, and they said they sent a letter raising it, but we never got it. So you know what's happened? Someone's stolen one of our cards and is charging stuff all over the place. Airline tickets. Hotel rooms. Well, I gave the people at Master Charge a piece of my mind, and you know what they said? We gotta pay it. I told them the card must have been stolen, but they say since we didn't report it stolen we gotta pay. Can you believe that? Nineteen hundred seventy dollars and they say we gotta pay! Do you know how much the damn interest is on all that? It's unbelievable. I was so mad I told 'em to cancel our card, but they said we couldn't cancel it until we pay the damn thing off, and I'm so mad I want to take 'em to court, if we could afford a goddamn lawyer. Do you think Richard would do it? No, he doesn't handle that kind of stuff, does he? So what the hell we gonna do now, huh?"

She paused for breath, looked at me. "You're very late. I hope you had a big day, 'cause we really need it. So tell, me, how many hours did you get today?"

I'd been trying to keep a straight face, but this was too much. I chuckled.

I put my glove on, banged it once with my fist. God, I felt good.

I smiled at her, and shook my head.

"Not a damn one."

About the Author

Parnell Hall has worked as a songwriter, actor, playwright, and screenwriter. His most recent screenplay was for the film *C.H.U.D.*, which was praised by the New York *Daily News* as "entertainment that makes us shudder and laugh at all the right times." He makes his home in New York City, where naturally he moonlights as a private detective. His second novel, *Murder*, also featuring Stanley Hastings, will be available from Onyx Books this winter.

MYSTERY PARLOR

**Buy them at your local
bookstore or use coupon
on next page for ordering.**